# DEATH OF A NEIGHBORHOOD WITCH

Center Point
Large Print

Also by Laura Levine and available from
Center Point Large Print:

A Jaine Austen Mystery
*Pampered to Death*

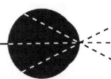

**This Large Print Book carries the
Seal of Approval of N.A.V.H.**

# DEATH OF A NEIGHBORHOOD WITCH

## A Jaine Austen Mystery

# LAURA LEVINE

CENTER POINT LARGE PRINT
THORNDIKE, MAINE

This Center Point Large Print edition
is published in the year 2013 by arrangement with
Kensington Publishing Corp.

The text of this Large Print edition is unabridged.
In other aspects, this book may vary
from the original edition.
Printed in the United States of America
on permanent paper.
Set in 16-point Times New Roman type.

ISBN: 978-1-61173-593-2

Library of Congress Cataloging-in-Publication Data

Levine, Laura, 1943–
  Death of a neighborhood witch : a Jaine Austen mystery / Laura Levine.
  — Center Point Large Print ed.
    p. cm. — (A Jaine Austen mystery)
  ISBN 978-1-61173-593-2 (lib. bdg. : alk. paper)
  1. Austen, Jaine (Fictitious character)—Fiction. 2. Halloween—Fiction.
    3. Large type books. I. Title.
PS3612.E924D43 2013
813′.6—dc23
                                                    2012036766

For the real Kevin Moore
and the wonderful folks at the
Anaheim Public Library Foundation

# Acknowledgments

As always, I am enormously grateful to my editor John Scognamiglio for his unwavering faith in Jaine (and for my treasured Count Chocula and Frankenberry Hot Wheels).

Heartfelt thanks to my agent, Evan Marshall, for his ongoing guidance and support. To Hiro Kimura for his frightfully fabulous cover art. To Lou Malcangi for his eye-catching dust jacket design. And to the rest of the gang at Kensington who keep Jaine and Prozac coming back for corpses and Chunky Monkey each year.

Special thanks to Frank Mula, man of a thousand jokes. And to Joanne Fluke, who takes time out from writing her own bestselling Hannah Swensen mysteries to grace me with her insights and her brownies—not to mention a blurb to die for.

A belated thanks to George and Gloria May, for all the funny health spa stories they told me for my last book.

Thanks to Mark Baker, who was there from the beginning. To John Fluke, product placement guru and all-around great guy. And to Jamie Wallace (aka Sidney's mom), the genial webmeister at LauraLevineMysteries.com.

A loving thanks to my friends and family for hanging in with me all these years. And a special shout out to all the readers who've taken the time to write me and/or show up at my book signings. You guys are the best!

And finally, to my most loyal fan and sounding board, my husband Mark. I couldn't do it without you.

# Chapter 1

I dashed into the market for a carton of orange juice. I swear, that's all. An innocent carton of orange juice.

But then I saw it. The giant display of Halloween candies, luring me with their shiny wrappers, a siren song of chocolate in a sea of nuts and caramel.

I tried to pretend they weren't there, but it was no use. I could practically hear the Mini Snickers calling my name:

*Jaine, sweetheart! We're only seventy-two luscious calories. Surely just one can't hurt, can it?*

Like the chocolate junkie I am, I fell for their come-on. Before I knew it, I was loading my cart with those sneaky Snickers, along with some Kit Kats and Reese's Pieces.

It's the same old story, I'm afraid. Every year I vow not to buy any Halloween candy. And every year, like the sniveling weakling I am, I break that vow.

The truth is, I have absolutely no need for Halloween candy. Here in the slums of Beverly Hills where I live, south of Wilshire Boulevard (so south it's practically in Mexico), there are very few children. People on my block are either singletons or retirees. The only trick-or-treaters who've ever shown up on my doorstep were a pair of surly teens with squinty eyes and multiple body piercings. And I'm guessing all they wound up with at the end of the night was a bagful of restraining orders.

By now I was at the checkout counter, my orange juice long forgotten.

"Just stocking up for the trick-or-treaters," I lied to the checker, a hardened blonde with thin lips and a concrete beehive. "Can't disappoint the kiddies."

The checker snapped her gum, oozing skepticism. She knew darn well the only one who'd be chomping down on those candies was me.

At the last minute, I threw in a miniature pumpkin, painted with a happy face, hoping to convince her of my Halloween spirit, but she still wasn't buying my "for the kiddies" act.

I heard her whisper to the bag boy as I walked away, "Ten to one she'll be breaking into those Snickers at the first stoplight."

How utterly ridiculous.

I didn't break into them until the third stoplight.

Back home, I found my cat, Prozac, doing battle with a pair of my brand-new panty hose. How she manages to raid my underwear drawer I'll never know. But there she was, tearing into my Control Top Donna Karans with all the gusto of a Jersey Housewife on estrogen.

"Prozac! What are you doing?!"

She shot me an impatient stare.

*Vanquishing the enemy, of course!*

Then back to my Donna Karans.

*Die, spandex infidel! Die!*

After wrestling what was left of my panty hose from her claws, I started unloading my groceries. When I took out the miniature painted pumpkin and put it on the counter, Prozac's eyes widened in alarm.

*Omigod! An evil vegetable from the Planet Carotene!*

One look at the goofy painted face with the crossed eyes and missing front teeth, and she forgot all about her war with my panty hose. Before I could stop her, she leaped onto the counter, digging her claws into Pumpkin Face.

"Cut that out," I said, whipping it away from her. "This is a perfectly harmless pumpkin, and I'll thank you to keep your paws to yourself."

With that, I trotted over to the door and put the pumpkin outside on my front step.

"You'll be safe here," I said, giving it a little pat.

Not really.

Like a furry missile, Prozac whizzed out from behind me and, snapping up the pumpkin's stem in her jaws, took off like a shot. I chased her up the street and groaned to see her bounding up the path to a once elegant but now dilapidated old house.

Of all the houses on the block, why did she have to choose this one?

The crumbling Spanish hacienda belonged to the neighborhood witch, a grouch royale named Cryptessa Muldoon. That wasn't her real name, of course. That was the name of the character she played, decades ago, on a third-rate sitcom—a sorry cross between *Bewitched* and *The Munsters*—called *I Married a Zombie*. Cryptessa was the zombie in question, delivering her lines in a long black wig and slinky dress cut so tight it was practically a tourniquet. After one laugh-free season, the show had been canceled, and Cryptessa, as everyone on the block still called her, never worked again. Which over time had turned her into a bitter, whackadoodle dame.

She'd been living on the block ever since I could remember, growling at me whenever I'd had the temerity to park my car in front of her house.

I'd tried my best to stay under her radar, and up until that moment, I'd pretty much succeeded.

But all that was about to change.

Now as I raced past her DO NOT TRESPASS sign, desperately trying to catch up with Prozac, Cryptessa came bursting out of her front door, eyeing me with wild-eyed paranoia. No longer the least bit slinky, she wore ketchup-stained sweats, her stringy hair dyed a most startling shade of shoe-polish black.

"Hi there!" I said, hoping to disarm her with a friendly wave.

Alas, it did not work.

"Get off my property," she shrieked, "or I'll call the police!"

"Absolutely," I assured her, "just as soon as I get Prozac."

"What do you think I am, a pharmacist? I don't have any Prozac."

"No, my cat, Prozac."

I dashed around the side of the house, where I found Prozac staring transfixed into Cryptessa's window, Pumpkin Face lying abandoned in the grass.

Following her gaze into the open window, I saw a dull green parakeet perched on wobbly legs in a cage, feathers mottled with age.

The poor thing had been minding his own business, no doubt dreaming fond dreams of juicy worms, when he looked down and saw Prozac staring up at him. I guess he must have seen the bloodlust in her eyes. Because without any further ado, he let out a strangled peep and proceeded to keel over.

"Omigod!" cried Cryptessa, who'd raced up to the window. "You've killed Van Helsing! You've killed Van Helsing!"

And indeed, the poor little critter had kicked the bucket.

"I'm so very sorry," I said. "But really, I didn't do a thing. I was just standing here."

"You've killed Van Helsing!" Cryptessa wailed again, unable to let go of the thought.

"I know it's small consolation for the loss of your beloved pet, but I hope you'll accept this colorful Halloween pumpkin as a token of my apology."

I held out Pumpkin Face.

"Get the hell out of here!" she shrieked.

Only too happy to oblige, I grabbed Prozac and scooted off to freedom, leaving the pumpkin behind, just in case Cryptessa changed her mind.

Back home, I read Prozac the riot act.

"Bad kitty! Very bad kitty! You ran away from home and scared a poor little parakeet to death! Whatever am I going to do with you?"

She looked up at me from where I'd plopped her on the sofa.

*I'd suggest a nice long belly rub, with some bonus scratching behind my ears.*

I'm ashamed to confess that, after a calming Mini Snickers or three, I was actually in the middle of giving her that belly rub when I heard a loud banging at my front door.

I opened it to find Cryptessa standing there, eyes blazing, her shoe-polish hair standing out in angry spikes.

"You killed him. Now you have to help me bury him."

"Pardon me?"

"I need you to dig a hole for Van Helsing's grave. I can't do it. Not with my bad back."

"Of course, of course. I'd be more than happy to."

I wouldn't have been so damn happy if I'd known what was in store for me.

I followed Cryptessa to her backyard, a landscaping nightmare with ancient patio furniture, spider-infested bushes, and a ragged patch of dying weeds posing as a lawn.

"Watch out for the oil slicks," she warned, too late, as I stepped in a puddle of black goo. "Gardener's damn lawn mower keeps leaking."

I looked down in dismay at the new pair of Reeboks I'd just taken out of the box that morning. They'd never be white again.

Cryptessa had chosen a shady spot under a hulking magnolia tree for Van Helsing's final resting place.

"Start digging," she said, handing me a rusty shovel.

The soil, clearly not having been watered in the last two decades, was like cement, and before long I was gushing sweat. Not happy with a shallow grave, Cryptessa made me dig at least three feet below the surface. When at last the grave had been dug to her satisfaction, she barked, "Wait here!"

And then she disappeared into the house.

I stood leaning on my shovel for a good fifteen minutes before she finally came sailing back out again in a long, black, moth-eaten dress, with matching veil—stolen no doubt from the wardrobe department of *I Married a Zombie*. In her hand she carried the "coffin"—a Payless shoe box, lined in pink Kleenex, Van Helsing's stiff little body nestled in the folds.

Then, gazing into his beady eye with all the pathos of a failed sitcom actress, she began singing:

> *The way you held your beak*
> *The way you sang off key*
> *The way you used to shriek*
> *No, no, they can't take that away from me*
>
> *The way your wings just flopped*
> *The way you chirped "twee twee"*
> *The way your poops just popped*
> *No, no, they can't take that away from me*

Wiping a tear from her eye, she put the lid on Van Helsing's coffin and slowly lowered him into the grave. I had no doubt that somewhere out there the Gershwin brothers were rolling over in theirs. Then, as Cryptessa hummed "Taps," I filled in the earth.

At last, my ordeal was over. Or so I thought.

"As long as you're here," Cryptessa said, "would you mind planting these for me?"

She pointed to a bed of bright pink petunias by her fence.

"I'd do it myself," she said with a long-suffering smile, "but my back is killing me."

*So is mine, lady,* was what I felt like saying.

But, still feeling guilty about Van Helsing, I picked up the shovel and started digging.

I spent the next half hour on my hands and knees, jamming petunias and potting mix into the concrete soil. Cryptessa stood over me, much as I imagine Simon Legree must have done down on the plantation, barking orders and hollering at me not to bruise the leaves.

Finally, when every petunia had been planted, she released me from captivity. My fingernails cracked and filled with dirt, my Reeboks stained black, I trudged back to my apartment, cursing Cryptessa every step of the way.

My mood took a slight turn for the cheerier, however, when I got to my duplex and found an absolute cutie pie of a guy ringing my doorbell.

"Oh, hello," he said when he saw me coming up the path. "I'm Peter Connor. I just moved in up the street and dropped by to say hi."

"Nice to meet you," I said.

Indeed it was. There was something about this guy's smile that radiated kindness. And I badly needed a dose of the stuff. I was still licking my wounds from yet another failed relationship with a guy named Darryl who I'd met up in central California. He'd been driving down to see me on weekends, bunking with an old college buddy of his. Before long, love blossomed, and Darryl proposed marriage. Not to me, I'm afraid. But to

17

his old college buddy, a pert redhead named Tatiana.

So when I saw Peter standing there that day, smiling that sweet smile and looking like the kind of guy who would never fall in love with his old college buddy, my heart melted just a tad.

Now he held out his hand to shake mine, and I suddenly remembered my filthy fingernails. And sweaty armpits. And heaven only knew what my hair must have looked like. I'm guessing Early Bride of Frankenstein.

"You'll have to excuse me," I said. "I've just been gardening and I'm afraid I'm a mess."

"You look fine to me."

And I have to say, the feeling was mutual.

As noted before, Peter was one primo cutie pie: slim yet muscular, with a shock of thick sandy hair, soft brown eyes, and—just beneath that sweet smile—the most amazing cleft in his chin.

I happen to find chin clefts immensely attractive. It was all I could do not to run my finger along his. But of course I didn't. I knew the rules. I knew how to play it cool.

"Anyhow," he said, shooting me a winning grin, "I'm throwing a little housewarming party, and I was hoping you could stop by."

"I'd love it. Absolutely. I'll be there! For sure!"

So much for playing it cool.

"Sunday at about three o'clock?"

"Can't wait!" I gushed.

"See you then," he said, heading down the path.

I sailed into my apartment on cloud nine. True, the whole Van Helsing funeral thing had been a bit of a downer. But on the upside, it looked like I had just met a potential soul mate.

Ah, yes, I thought as I trotted off to the shower. Things were definitely looking up.

How wrong I was.

Dead wrong.

# Chapter 2

After a good twenty minutes in the shower, scrubbing away the dirt from my grave-digging duties, I was about to reach for a towel when I heard a disembodied voice call out:

"Hurry up and get dressed, Jaine."

No, I do not have a haunted bathroom.

I do, however, have a neighbor with X-ray hearing. His name is Lance Venable, and the man can hear toilets flushing in Pomona. Lance is a great guy, but for some reason he considers the paper-thin walls that separate our apartments a mere formality, never hesitating to barge in on my life when the spirit moves him.

"Get a move on, lazybones," he now instructed me. "I'll be over in five minutes."

And indeed five minutes later he came bursting through my front door, clad in the designer togs he wears for his job as a shoe salesman at Neiman Marcus.

"Fabulous news!" he gushed, his blond curls quivering with excitement. "I've met the man of my dreams!"

I stifled a yawn. You should know that Lance meets the man of his dreams about as often as he gets his roots done.

But I wasn't about to burst his bubble. I was in

a most benevolent mood, having just met the man of my dreams myself.

"What a coincidence," I started to say. "Why, just a little while ago—"

"You won't believe how wonderful he is," Lance said, plopping down on my sofa and grabbing a Snickers from the bag on the coffee table. "So warm and friendly. The minute I met him, I felt like we'd known each other in a former life. There was something about him, a certain aura . . ."

I nodded, on autopilot, still fighting that yawn. These paeans of his could go on forever. I watched as he unwrapped his Snickers, marveling at his ability to chow down on chocolate and still maintain his sylphlike figure. I'm guessing his secret is the ninety-seven hours a week he spends at the gym.

"And he's so good-looking," Lance was blathering. "Tall and lanky, with a fabulous smile and the most amazing cleft in his chin."

*Whoa, Nelly!*

"Cleft in his chin?" I piped up.

"Yes. Isn't that heavenly?"

"Yeah, swell. Look, your dreamboat doesn't happen to be Peter Connor, does it? The guy who just moved in up the street?"

"My God, Jaine. You're positively psychic! Isn't it fabulous? The man of my dreams—just five houses away! What's wrong? You look like you just swallowed a lemon."

"For your information," I said, the merest hint of frost in my voice, "Peter Connor happens to be *my* dream man."

"Oh, please," Lance said with a dismissive wave. "Peter couldn't possibly be interested in you."

"Why on earth not?"

"Aside from all the obvious reasons," he said, shooting a none-too-subtle glance at my thighs, "Peter happens to be gay."

"Oh, really? How can you be so sure?"

"My gaydar," he boasted, his perfectly toned pecs swelling with pride, "is infallible."

In Lance's world, any guy who isn't surgically attached to a woman is gay. Really. According to Lance, notable gays of history have included Napoleon, Trotsky, and Homer Simpson.

"Peter didn't seem the least bit gay when I was talking to him a little while ago," I said. "On the contrary, I got the distinct impression he was flirting with me."

"Flirting? With you?" This accompanied by a most annoying chorus of giggles. "Jaine, sweetheart," he said, taking my hands in his, "you know I adore you, but I have to be honest. Peter was probably just being kind. No doubt he took one look at your elastic-waist pants, imagined your lonely Saturday nights with just a cat and a pizza for company, and decided to brighten your day with a little ego boost. It was obviously a charity flirt."

"A charity flirt?"

Of all the nerve!

I sprang from the sofa, grabbing the bag of Snickers.

"For your information, I do not need charity flirts! That flirt was for real, and I say Peter Connor is straight."

"Well, I say he's gay," Lance snapped.

"I say you're wrong," I snapped right back.

"Wanna bet on it?" he asked, a malicious glint in his eye.

"Absolutely. Game's on."

"Whoever loses has to buy the winner dinner at the restaurant of his choice."

"Of *her* choice, you mean."

"We'll see who Peter goes out with first," Lance said.

"Yes, I'll let you know how it went. Now if you'll excuse me, I have some important work to attend to."

"Yeah, right," Lance said, eyeing my bag of Snickers. "Just don't eat them all in one sitting."

I was an idiot to make that bet with Lance. For all I knew, Peter Connor marched in the gay pride parade with a tattoo of Judy Garland on his chest. But Lance's "charity flirt" crack got my dander up.

Now, however, I was having second thoughts. Maybe Lance's gaydar was right. Maybe Peter was just being friendly with me and I'd misinterpreted it as flirty. He probably flashed his cleft chin to everybody he met, an equal-opportunity cleft flasher.

These were the thoughts flitting through my mind that night as I drove over to meet my friend Kandi for dinner. Kandi Tobolowski and I met years ago at a UCLA screenwriting course, where we bonded over bad vending machine coffee and our mutual dislike for the pompous jerk teaching our class.

Kandi had gone on to a high-paying job as a staff writer on *Beanie & The Cockroach*, a Saturday morning cartoon popular with insect-loving toddlers, while I made my way in the far less lucrative field of freelance advertising, writing copy for clients like Toiletmasters Plumbers (*In a Rush to Flush? Call Toiletmasters!*), Ackerman's Awnings (*Just a Shade Better*), and Fiedler on the Roof Roofers.

Kandi was already seated when I showed up at Paco's Tacos, our favorite Mexican restaurant, where the margaritas are to die for and the burritos are the size of cruise missiles. Heading into the dining room, I saw her sitting by the restaurant's tropical fish tank. I could tell she was upset by the mopey way she was nibbling on a corn chip.

True, Kandi always nibbles at her food—one of the reasons she's an enviable size six, while I, who have been known to swallow Oreos in a single gulp, am a size none-of-your-business.

But I could tell something was bothering her.

"Hi, honey!" I said, sliding into the seat across from her.

She smiled vaguely in my direction and then turned her attention back to the fish tank.

"Have you ever wished you were a fish?" she asked, staring at the guppies zipping by.

"Not particularly," I said, grabbing a handful of chips.

"What a life," she sighed. "Swim a few laps, eat some fish food, watch people get drunk on Jose Cuervo. No heartaches. No aggravations. No disappointments."

Yes, there was something on her mind, all right.

"Okay, Kandi. What's the matter? Tell Auntie Jaine."

"The most depressing news ever. I went out on a blind date last night."

"So what else is new?"

Kandi happens to be a kamikaze dater, leaving no frog unkissed in her search for her Prince Charming. The woman has Speed Dated, Match-DotCommed, E-Harmonied, and gone on enough blind dates to qualify for honorary membership in the Braille Institute. So I couldn't understand why she was so upset.

"He didn't attack you or anything?" I asked, beginning to get alarmed.

"Oh, no. Leonard was a perfectly pleasant if somewhat boring accountant from Pasadena."

25

"Then what was so depressing?"

"From the minute we met," she said, nibbling another millimeter off her chip, "there was something familiar about him. He said the same about me. And then, when he ordered us blueberry pie for dessert, I remembered how we knew each other. He was my very first blind date when I first moved to L.A. ten years ago. That's what he ordered ten years ago."

"Wow, what a coincidence."

"A coincidence? It's a tragic commentary on my life. Don't you see? Leonard's been married and divorced twice since our date. And I still haven't been anywhere near an altar. I've made absolutely no progress in ten whole years of dating. I'm back to square one."

"Yes, but on the plus side," I reminded her, "you had blueberry pie for dessert."

"Jaine, please!" she said, shooting me a wounded look.

"Oh, honey," I said, reluctantly abandoning the chips to take her hand, "you mustn't let it get to you."

"Easy for you to say," she sulked. "At least you've been married."

"To The Blob? That hardly counts. The man— and I use the term loosely—showed up at our wedding in flip-flops and watched ESPN during sex—with himself."

Our waiter, a skinny guy with enormous brown

eyes, who had sidled up to take our orders, tsked in sympathy.

I get that a lot when people hear about The Blob.

"What'll it be, señoritas?" he asked.

We ordered our usual: tostada salad for Kandi, chicken chimichangas with refried beans and rice for *moi*.

"Look, Kandi," I said as the waiter walked off. "You try harder than anyone I know to get out there and make things happen. I'm certain that someday you're going to meet your special somebody."

"That's exactly what Madame Vruska said."

For the first time since I'd walked into the restaurant, I saw a glimmer of hope in her eyes.

"Madame Vruska?"

"The most amazing new psychic I went to. I drove past her place on my way home from my date with Leonard. There was her sign, right next to the place where I get my nails done. *Madame Vruska, Palm Reader*. Like a beacon shining in the wasteland of my dating life. The very next day, I went in for a consultation."

"What did she say?"

"First, how much she loved my nails. And then she read my palm and told me I'd soon be meeting the love of my life. Someone in the arts. Oh, Jaine!" she said, licking a grain of salt from the rim of her margarita glass. "Doesn't that sound exciting? A painter or a musician. Or maybe a tango dancer. I've always wanted to date a tango dancer."

And just like that, she sloughed off her depression and took a whole bite of her chip.

That's what makes Kandi a kamikaze dater. No matter how many knocks she takes, she's constantly rising from the ashes of her bad dates, ready once again to meet Mr. Right.

The woman can go from storm clouds to silver linings in the time it takes me to polish off a bowl of chips. Which by now I had pretty much done.

"So what's new with you, hon?" she asked.

I told her about Peter Connor and my bet with Lance.

"I thought Peter was flirting with me, but Lance is probably right. Chances are, Peter's gay."

"Don't be silly. Lance thinks everyone's gay. Didn't he once say Karl Marx was gay?"

"No, Groucho."

"Whatever. Lance has no idea what he's talking about. I'll bet Peter *was* flirting with you. Now you just have to be cute and flirty right back at him."

Sad to say, Cute and Flirty are subjects I flunked long ago in adolescence. (Although I did get outstanding grades in Awkward and Tongue Tied.)

"Next time you see him," Kandi said, "you're going to be a lean, mean flirting machine."

"Right." I nodded absently, my eyes riveted on the two golden chimichangas, smothered with guacamole and sour cream, that our waiter had just set down before me.

Kandi eyed them with alarm.

"Take back those chimichangas!" she cried. "She'll have a salad instead."

"Touch that plate," I told him, "and you're a dead man."

Sensing I meant business, he skittered off in a flash.

"Jaine!" Kandi tsked. "How can you possibly eat those fattening chimichangas at a time like this?"

"Like I always do," I said, reaching for my fork. "With extra sour cream."

And without any further ado, I dug right in.

# YOU'VE GOT MAIL!

**To: Jausten**
**From: Shoptillyoudrop**
**Subject: Halloween Happenings**

Hi, sweetheart,

Just got the cutest sweatshirt to wear to the annual Tampa Vistas Halloween party! Bright orange, with a sequined ghost that says, "Got Candy?" Leave it to the Shopping Channel to come up with such a clever idea for only $32.44 plus shipping and handling!

Meanwhile, Daddy's been glued to the television, watching all those godawful horror movies they show at this time of the year. I swear, if I hear one more person being hacked to death with a chainsaw, I'm going to throw away the remote.

And you're not going to believe this, but Daddy's entering the Halloween Lawn Decorating Contest. Again. You'd think after five consecutive years of losing, he'd give up. But no, Daddy is convinced this year he's going to win first prize with some lawn ornament he ordered from an infomercial. I just pray it's not as bad as those dreadful remote-controlled rats he ordered last year. He had the ghastly creatures running up and down our front path for weeks. Practically gave poor Edna Lindstrom next door a heart attack.

Gotta go, honey. The UPS man is here with Daddy's lawn ornament.

Keep your fingers crossed it's not too awful.
XOX
Mom

**To: Jausten**
**From: Shoptillyoudrop**
**Subject: The Worst Ever!**

I just saw the lawn ornament. It's Daddy's worst ever!

Your miserable,
Mom

**To: Jausten**
**From: DaddyO**
**Subject: The Best Ever!**

Exciting news, Lambchop! My Halloween lawn ornament just showed up and it's my best ever! An animated Count Dracula, complete with his own private crypt! Who says you can't get quality products from Ulan Bator?

I can't wait to assemble it!
Love 'n' hugs from,
Daddy

**To: Jausten**
**From: Shoptillyoudrop**
**Subject: Keep Your Fingers Crossed**

I do not exaggerate when I say that this year's Halloween lawn ornament is a new low in bad taste. Not just for Daddy. But possibly for all mankind.

It's a hideous vampire with fangs like chopsticks and a cheesy black cape that looks like it's made from Hefty bags. To top it off, it sits up and down in its own life-sized coffin. Oh, dear. Can you imagine? A coffin on our front lawn! Here in a retirement community? What will the neighbors say?

Just keep your fingers crossed that—like nine out of ten idiotic contraptions Daddy orders—he won't be able to put it together.

Your slightly frantic,
Mom


**To: Jausten**
**From: DaddyO**
**Subject: Fang-Tastic!**

You'll be happy to know I assembled Count Dracula without any problems, Lambchop. Easysneezy. He's out on the lawn right now, and all I can say is, he's fang-tastic!

Never has Tampa Vistas seen such a display of

Halloween artistry. I'm a shoo-in for first prize at the Tampa Vistas Halloween Lawn Decorating Contest.

Love 'n' hugs from
Your proud,
Daddy

# Chapter 3

Nine out of ten nutritionists say the worst way to start the day is to skip breakfast.

Nine out of ten nutritionists are wrong.

The worst way to start the day is to open an e-mail from my parents.

Although sweetie pies of the highest order, they are inevitably the bearers of distressing news. That is because they are bona fide disaster magnets. No matter where they go or what they do, catastrophe is never far behind.

Daddy is the main culprit. He can take an ordinary day and turn it into a headline on the evening news. And Mom is not without her quirks. She's the one who insisted they move three thousand miles across the country to Tampa Vistas, Florida, to be close to the Home Shopping Channel, in the mistaken notion that she'd get her packages faster that way.

In the words of the late great Henny Youngman: They don't have ulcers. They're just carriers.

So when I opened my e-mails the next morning and read about Daddy's "fang-tastic" Dracula, I smelled trouble ahead. What kind of trouble remained to be seen, but something told me I had not heard the last of the animated vampire on their front lawn.

Just as I was deleting a far less stressful e-mail offering to increase the size of my penis by several inches, the phone rang.

"Jaine, cookie!" A voice boomed over the line.

It was one of my clients, Marvin Cooper, aka Marvelous Marv of Mattress King Mattresses. For years, Marvin had been starring in his own commercials, sitting on a throne in a paper mache crown and ermine robe, yakking about his mattresses and closing with his tag line: "If you can find a cheaper mattress anywhere, I'll eat my crown."

"I've got a job for you, cookie."

Always music to my ears.

"I've decided to dump *Eat My Crown* and go in a whole different direction."

Not a moment too soon, in my humble op.

"I want to run some spots about how Mattress King mattresses are good for your back."

At last. A sensible approach.

"And I've got a great idea on how to go!"

Uh-oh. Sound the Bad Idea Alarm. Marvin's ideas, to put it as gently as possible, suck. After all, this is a man who's been offering to eat a paper mache crown for the past twenty years.

"I'm thinking we should have a character named Larry. Larry Lumbar. A guy with a bad back who goes around searching for a good night's rest. Sorta like Goldilocks. Only hip and edgy."

A hip and edgy Goldilocks with a bad back?

Suddenly that paper mache crown didn't seem so bad.

"How's that sound, cookie?"

Somehow I managed to croak, "Marvelous, Marv."

"Call me when you've got something."

"Will do."

I hung up and, after fortifying myself with coffee and a bagel, spent the next several hours working on the adventures of Larry Lumbar. After I'd roughed out a few spots, I decided to take a break with a nice, invigorating run.

Okay, so it wasn't a run. If you must know, it was a walk. A half a block down the street to the corner Starbucks for a giant chocolate chip muffin.

Scarfing down my muffin on the way back home, I glanced up and saw Cryptessa's house, her DO NOT TRESPASS sign hulking on her lawn. Still feeling guilty about the demise of her beloved parakeet—and not exactly eager to get back to Larry Lumbar—I decided to pay her a condolence call.

Licking muffin crumbs from my fingers, I trotted up the crumbling flagstone path to her front door—a once glorious hunk of wood with Spanish carvings, now pitted with wood rot. I rang the bell but heard no chimes inside.

I was about to give the heavy metal knocker a clang when someone called out behind me, "Hello, Jaine!"

The voice was pleasant, so I knew it couldn't be Cryptessa.

I turned to see Cryptessa's neighbor, Emmeline Owens, a white-haired wisp of a gal, heading up her front path with her fluffball pooch, Lana Turner.

"Oh, hi, Emmeline. How's Lana today?"

It was well known on the block that Emmeline doted on her bichon frise; rumor had it the dog had her own closet.

Today Lana sported a pink bow in her hair, along with a matching pink cashmere sweater.

"Lana's just fine," she said, swooping the dog up in her arms, "no thanks to that witch Cryptessa. Did you know she tried to kill my little angel?"

"Really?" I asked. "What happened?"

But I was not about to find out because just then Lana began yapping impatiently. "Oops." Emmeline said. "Must run. It's time for *The View*, and Lana never misses that show. Lana just loves Barbara Walters! Well, nice talking to you, Jaine."

And with that, she scooted into her house.

Musing over Emmeline's accusation of attempted doggiecide, I gathered my courage and knocked on Cryptessa's door.

"Hold your horses," came Cryptessa's unmistakable snarl. "I'm coming.

"Oh, it's you," she said, when she saw me.

She wore the same ketchup-stained sweats she was wearing the day before, her stringy hair having been nowhere near a shower—or a brush—in the last twenty-four hours.

Hanging in the foyer behind her was a full-length portrait of Cryptessa from her glory days—her hair thick and lustrous, her eyes shining, her pale complexion luminescent against the deep black of her boob-baring dress.

What a contrast to the crone she had become, I thought, looking at her now-gaunt face, cross-hatched with wrinkles, a road map of disappointment.

For a minute I figured she was going to slam the door in my face; after all, I had disobeyed the Do Not Trespass rule. But to my surprise, she flung open the door and said, "Don't just stand there. C'mon in."

She led me past her portrait into a spacious but dimly lit living room, furnished in very Early Munster, with a hectic jumble of Victorian settees, fringed lamps, and ornately carved chairs and end tables.

Sticking out like a sore thumb amid all this Victorian kitsch was a nubby oatmeal recliner into which she plopped down with a sigh, leaving me to park my fanny on a stiff chair that felt like it had been upholstered in sandpaper.

"Rosita!" she shrieked.

Seconds later a slim Hispanic woman, holding a dust rag, came hurrying into the room. "Yes, Miss Eleanor?"

After all these years thinking of my nasty neighbor as Cryptessa, I'd almost forgotten her real name was Eleanor Jenkins.

"Bring me a Coke." Then she turned to me. "You want one? I'm afraid I'm on a bit of a budget, so I'm gonna have to charge you for it."

Yes, you read that right. She actually wanted to charge me for a Coke.

"That's okay. I'm good."

Cryptessa watched as Rosita skittered off, then, not even bothering to lower her voice, declared, "The woman's robbing me blind. If it's not nailed down, she steals it."

Oh, please. Not for one minute did I believe that shy little woman was a thief.

"So whaddaya want?" Cryptessa asked, cutting to the chase with breathless speed.

"I just stopped by to see how you're coping with the loss of Van Helsing."

"It's been hell," Cryptessa said with a dramatic sweep of her arm. "Sheer hell. Bela and I are positively beside ourselves with grief."

"Bela?"

"My beloved bat." With that, she pointed to a hideous stuffed bat I'd failed to notice, who was perched on the mantel. I vaguely recognized it as a prop from her old sitcom.

"They gave me Bela when my show was canceled. You remember my show, don't you? *I Married a Zombie*."

"Of course," I nodded, smiling as if I'd actually watched it.

"I was the fourth most popular monster mom in sitcom history."

"How wonderful for you."

"Anyhow, they gave me Bela as a parting gift. Along with my wardrobe and several items of furniture. Well, to be honest, they didn't exactly give me the furniture. I sneaked it out of the studio in a U-Haul in the middle of the night. But I deserved it, after all the hard work I put in on that damn show. Right, Bela?"

She looked to the bat, as if for affirmation.

Then, turning to me, she whispered, "We're very close."

Uh-oh. Somebody call Rod Serling. Looked like I had just entered the *Twilight Zone.*

Rosita now returned with Cryptessa's Coke. She handed it to her quickly, eager to be out of firing range, then shot me a shy smile as she skittered away.

"Don't even think of taking a Coke for yourself!" Cryptessa shouted after her. "I count them, you know."

I'm sure she did.

"Yes," Cryptessa sighed, resuming her role as the grieving parakeet widow, "Bela and I would simply be lost if we didn't have *The Devil's Poodle.*"

I looked around, expecting to see a stuffed

poodle lurking in the shadows. But no, it turned out that *The Devil's Poodle* was the title of a book Cryptessa was writing.

"I've been working on it for years. Wait here," she said, hauling herself out of the recliner. "I'll show you."

Then she disappeared down the hall, leaving me to chew the fat with Bela. Which, I have to admit, was a pretty one-sided conversation.

Minutes later, Cryptessa came back to the room with a massive tome and plopped it on my lap. Sure enough, the title page read:

*The Devil's Poodle*
*By Eleanor Jenkins*

I could tell from the ragged typeface, the *o*'s flying higher than the other letters, that it had been typed on an old-fashioned manual typewriter.

"You should be honored," she said. "You're the only person I've ever shown it to. I keep it under lock and key so no one can steal it."

Paranoid much?

"It's about a poodle from hell who comes to earth and wreaks death and destruction wherever it goes."

"Sounds fascinating," I managed to lie.

"Oh, it is. I'm going to be the next Stephen King. Isn't that so, Bela?"

Once again, she looked to the bat for confirmation.

"Bela's so very supportive," she confided.

Okay, no doubt about it. This was Looney Tunes Central. Time to make my exit.

"I guess I should be getting back to work," I said.

"Not yet!" Her eyes widened in disappointment. "Not before you've had a chance to see my scrapbook."

And before I knew it, she'd whipped away her future best seller and replaced it with a slim ribbon-bound scrapbook filled with faded clippings from her short-lived TV career.

"That's me," she said, pointing out one of the pictures, "in my showbiz debut. As a corpse on *Hawaii Five-0*. The director said I was one of the most believable corpses he'd ever worked with. Here I am as Shopper #2 in a paper towel commercial. And here's the *Los Angeles Times* review for *I Married a Zombie*. With my name in the headline!" She beamed with pride. "*Eleanor Jenkins Adequate as Cryptessa Muldoon.*"

And as Cryptessa sat there, reliving her past, talking eagerly about how *The Devil's Poodle* was going to be her ticket back to the limelight, I couldn't help but feel sorry for her—a lonely old dame, living with nothing but her memories and a stuffed bat for company.

No wonder she was so damn cranky.

At last our stroll down memory lane came to an end and I managed to make my escape.

"I'm so sorry about Van Helsing," I said as she escorted me to the door. "I only wish there were some way I could make it up to you."

"Oh, I'll think of something," she said.

And indeed she would.

# Chapter 4

Cryptessa was pretty much forgotten in the next few days, during what I would soon come to think of as the Peter Wars.

Lance shaped up for combat by spending every available hour at the gym. I, on the other hand, took a somewhat more casual approach, spending several highly productive hours soaking in the tub, daydreaming of my honeymoon as Mrs. Peter Connor.

The Sunday of Peter's housewarming dawned bright and sunny, and after a hectic morning exfoliating, buffing, moussing, and moisturizing, I got spiffed up in my best elastic-waist jeans and an Eileen Fisher top I'd bought (on sale, of course) especially for the occasion—a charcoal gray scoop neck tunic that gently draped over the dreaded hip/tush zone.

"So what do you think?" I asked Prozac, whirling around for her approval.

Unfortunately she was in the middle of a very important genital exam and could not be bothered to look up.

Leaving her to spend some quality time with her privates, I headed for the kitchen. I'd come up with a brilliant plan to impress Peter, and now was the time to put it in action.

Earlier that morning, I'd zipped over to Mrs. Fields and bought a dozen fudge brownies. Now I nuked the brownies till they had that warm, fresh-from-the-oven smell, and arranged all eleven of them (okay, so I ate one) on a plate with a doily underneath.

Voilà! Home-baked brownies.

I must say, I was quite pleased with myself as I covered the plate with plastic wrap and then headed up the street to Peter's house.

Our block is a mix of single-family homes and duplexes, the humbler duplexes scattered at the southern end of the street where I live. Peter's house was one of the upscale single-family residences, an English country Tudor with rustic wood beams adorning the facade.

As I made my way up the path to his front door, I wondered how many people would show up for the housewarming. I wasn't expecting much of a turnout. When it comes to neighborly spirit, our street is not exactly Wisteria Lane. We do not have block parties or backyard barbeques. Nobody runs next door to borrow a cup of sugar or a dose of Lipitor.

And so I wasn't surprised when I walked in the open front door and saw just a handful of people sitting in Peter's living room (a tasteful Techno-Deco affair featuring lots of chrome and black leather, set off in sharp relief against a white flokati rug).

I recognized Helen and Harold Hurlbutt, a middle-aged couple who lived across the street from me and whose high-decibel fights I'd been hearing for years. It was Mrs. Hurlbutt who did most of the yelling, Mr. H. jumping in with only an occasional "For cripe's sake, Helen. Put a sock in it!"

Now they sat on one of two matching leather sofas that flanked a gorgeous brick fireplace, Mr. Hurlbutt loading up on cashews from a bowl of nuts on the coffee table in front of them.

Sitting across from them on the other sofa was an upscale thirtysomething couple from here on the pricier end of the street, whom I'd occasionally seen zooming off to work in their matching His 'n' Hers BMWs.

Posed primly in an armchair next to them was Cryptessa's white-haired neighbor, Emmeline Owens.

And rounding out the crew was Lila Wood. Everybody on the block knew Lila, the neighborhood activist, always knocking on our doors with some petition or other to sign.

"I think it's imperative," Lila was saying as I stepped into the room, "that we band together to keep our street safe from the hands of rapacious developers."

The others were nodding in that stupor people tend to fall into when Lila starts yapping.

"Which is why," she said, "I'm proud to

announce I'm running for president of the neighborhood council. And I'm hoping I can count on all your votes."

The others murmured in tepid assent.

"Jaine!" Peter jumped up at the sight of me, clearly grateful for the interruption, and motioned me over to join the others.

"You know everybody here, don't you?"

"Not everyone," I confessed, eyeing the yuppie couple.

"We're the Moores," Mr. Yuppie said.

He was a slim, slick guy with designer-cut hair; his wife, a perfect piece of arm candy—cool and blond and packaged to size 2 perfection.

"I'm Matt, and this is my wife, Kevin."

"Kevin?" I said, gazing at the blond beauty. "What an unusual name for a woman."

"My mom was expecting a boy," she explained, "and she wasn't about to take no for an answer."

"Like mother, like daughter," Matt said, putting a proud arm around his wife's shoulder. "That's what makes her such a fierce realtor."

And indeed, in Kevin's otherwise lovely gray eyes, I could see the icy determination of a street fighter.

"What's this?" Peter asked, looking down at the plate in my hands.

"I baked you some fudge brownies," I announced with pride.

"How very thoughtful!" He shot me a smile

47

warm enough to melt the fudge clear off the plate. "They look delicious."

And so did he, with that amazing cleft in his chin.

Slipping off the plastic wrap, Peter set the brownies down on the coffee table.

"You made these?" Mr. Hurlbutt asked, eyeing them suspiciously.

"Um. Yes," I said, beginning to sweat just a tad.

"Looks like Mrs. Fields to me," he said, chomping down on one with gusto.

For a minute I was tempted to confess all and admit that the closest I ever come to baking is heating my undies in the oven when my dryer is busted.

But I decided to hang tough.

"Well, I made them," I insisted, with as much bravado as I could muster.

"Sit down, won't you, Jaine?" Peter patted the empty chair next to him, and I slid down into it gratefully.

Still stinging from Mr. Hurlbutt's accusation, I was relieved to see Matt Moore beaming me a broad smile.

"If you're looking to buy or sell," he said, reaching over from the sofa and handing me a business card, "give us a call."

I glanced down at the card, a glossy affair with the Moores smiling up at me, their whiter-than-white smiles assuring me that they were two of Beverly Hills' top-selling realtors.

"Actually, I just rent."

"Oh," Matt said, his smile fading. "You must live in one of those duplexes down at the end of the street."

"Yes," I confessed, "I'm in the renter's gulag."

And I couldn't even afford to live there, if it weren't for the fact that my duplex has not been updated since the Coolidge administration. My landlord's helpful motto has always been, "When trouble strikes, any time, day or night—don't come whining to me."

It's funny, I thought as I looked around the room, how Los Angeles real estate made strange bedfellows. People like Emmeline and the Hurlbutts, who'd bought their houses decades ago, could probably never afford to buy them now. And there they were, living side by side with upward strivers like the Moores. And, apparently, Peter. Buying or renting a place like this couldn't have been cheap.

"These sure taste like Mrs. Fields's brownies," Mr. Hurlbutt piped up again.

Jeez, couldn't he just let it go?

"So, Peter," I said, eager to get away from the blasted brownies, "what sort of work do you do?"

"Actually, I'm a book editor. Just moved out here from New York."

"How exciting!" Emmeline's eyes lit up, impressed. "You're going to have to meet my granddaughter, Becca. She majored in English in college! You'll have so much in common. And she's beautiful, too. She put herself through Stanford by working as a swimsuit model."

"Hey, can the granddaughter pitch, willya, Emmy? I saw him first."

Okay, so I didn't really say that. But I was thinking it as I shoved a brownie in my mouth.

And it was at that moment, just as I was chowing down on Mrs. Fields's finest, that Lance made his grand entrance.

He told me he'd be coming straight from work, having arranged to get off early from his shift at Neiman's. But clearly he'd made a pit stop at a tanning parlor. The guy was bronzed to within an inch of his life. Clad in immaculate khakis and a lime-green polo, he looked like he'd just stepped out of a Ralph Lauren photo shoot. In his hand he held the most elaborate white orchid I'd seen this side of a state funeral.

"Hey, Petey," he said with a tad too much familiarity, "I picked up a little something for your place."

"It's beautiful!" Peter said, taking it from Lance.

And indeed, everyone oohed and aahed in agreement as Peter set it on the mantel above his fireplace.

"Have a seat," he said to Lance, gesturing to one of the sofas.

But Lance ignored his seating suggestion and,

eyeing my prized position next to Peter, had the nerve to turn to me and say, "Jaine, hon, why don't you scoot over to the sofa so you can be closer to the brownies?"

"No thanks," I replied stonily. "I'm fine here."

Shooting me a filthy look, he nudged Mrs. Hurlbutt aside so he could take the seat on the sofa closest to Peter's chair.

"So sorry I'm late," he said. "Crazy busy at Neiman's."

"You work at Neiman Marcus?" Kevin Moore asked, a flicker of interest lighting up her eyes.

"Yes, I'm head shoe buyer," Lance said, giving himself a hefty promotion.

"Is that so?" Mr. Hurlbutt looked up from the nut bowl where he had been diligently rummaging for cashews. "I always thought you were a shoe salesman."

Oh, darling Mr. Hurlbutt! I felt like throwing my arms around him and kissing the dear man.

"Not anymore," Lance lied with the ease of a campaigning congressman. "I was promoted ages ago."

"Peter," Emmeline informed Lance, still agog at the news, "is a book editor!"

"So I've heard." Lance turned to Peter, waxing euphoric. "I just love to read! I mean, when I'm not working or volunteering with the homeless, I'm always reading. If there's one thing I love, it's literature!"

Oh, please. The only thing Lance ever read were his own tweets.

"How interesting you're a book editor, Peter," I horned in, determined to score a point for Team Jaine. "Actually, I'm a writer."

"Yes," Lance quickly interjected, "Jaine writes the quaintest toilet bowl ads. You can see them on bus stops all over town."

By now I was ready to strangle the bronzed monster. I tuned out as he hogged the conversation, yammering on about his love of literature.

At last his monologue was interrupted when another neighbor showed up, a cute young gal in her twenties who lived in the duplex next to the Hurlbutts'. I didn't know her name, but according to Lance, she was a graduate student at UCLA. Like Kevin Moore, she was a wispy size 2.

Most distressing.

"Welcome!" Peter said, jumping up to greet her and beaming her a smile just a little too friendly for my liking.

"I'm Amy Chang," she said, smiling up at him from under a thick fringe of bangs. "Just dropped by to welcome you to the block."

"Come in, come in!" he said, ushering her inside.

"Oh, don't they make a cute couple," Lila gushed.

Lance shot her an evil glare while I took the high road and merely pictured myself gagging her with her support hose.

Oh, well. At least Amy's arrival put an end to Lance's "I Love Literature" chat.

The Moores started telling Peter about the trendy new restaurants in the neighborhood, Mr. Hurlbutt told him where to get the best price on gas, and Emmeline once again offered to fix him up with her granddaughter.

"It's great to have such nice neighbors," he said as we pelted him with advice. "But I've got to ask. What about the lady across the street? The one with the DO NOT TRESPASS sign on her front lawn?"

"Oh, Cryptessa." Mrs. Hurlbutt rolled her eyes. "She's impossible."

A chorus of amens filled the air.

"Cryptessa?" Peter asked.

"Cryptessa Muldoon. From the old sitcom *I Married a Zombie.*"

"Really?" Peter's eyes were wide with surprise. "Cryptessa Muldoon lives on our block?"

"Much to everyone's regret," Matt said.

"The last time I rang her doorbell to have her sign a petition," Lila said, "the old hag had the nerve to slam the door in my face."

"That's nothing," said Mrs. Hurlbutt. "I'm convinced Cryptessa was the one who dug up our tulips last year."

"It could've been a squirrel," said Mr. Hurlbutt.

"Oh, please, Harold. It wasn't a squirrel. It was that godawful witch. She's always been jealous of

53

our front yard. The only things that ever take root in her garden are stinkweeds. Cryptessa killed our tulips. No doubt about it."

"She's a killer, all right," Emmy chimed in. "Last month, she tried to kill my darling Lana Turner."

"Lana Turner's her dog," Lance explained to Peter, taking advantage of the opportunity to shoot him a sickeningly gooey smile.

"Poor Lana was out on the back deck, barking at a bird," Emmy said, "and the next thing I knew, a big fat lemon came sailing over the fence from Cryptessa's yard. It missed Lana by just inches. I swear, if it had hit her, she'd have been dead as a doornail."

So that's the story Emmeline had started to tell me when I ran into her the other day.

"That's awful!" Amy gasped.

"Did you report her to the authorities?" Lila asked.

"Yes, I did, and she denied everything, of course. The woman is totally without scruples. What a curse it's been," she sighed, "having Cryptessa as a next door neighbor."

"You're telling us," said Kevin. "One weekend when we were away on vacation, she had our hedges hacked off."

"Said they were blocking her view of the sunset," Matt explained.

"The nerve!" huffed Mrs. Hurlbutt.

"We were going to call the police," Matt said, "but in the end we didn't. She's so pathetic, I guess we felt sorry for her."

"I know the feeling," I said. And then I told them about Van Helsing's untimely demise and how pitiful Cryptessa had seemed when I'd paid my condolence call.

"Your cat killed her bird?" Mrs. Hurlbutt asked, aghast.

"No, of course not. Van Helsing just happened to drop dead as my cat was looking in the window."

"Maybe it wasn't Cryptessa who dug up our tulips," I heard her whisper to Mr. Hurlbutt. "Maybe it was her cat."

"It was sweet of you to pay that condolence call," Peter said to me, a look of admiration in his soft brown eyes.

Score one for Team Jaine.

"It's so important to be a caring person," Lance piped up, not to be outdone by my act of kindness. "That's why I work with the homeless at the Downtown Mission."

Oh, for crying out loud. The closest Lance ever got to the Downtown Mission was on his way to the Ahmanson to see a revival of *Gypsy*.

"Yes," I said, grabbing back the reins of the conversation, "when all was said and done, I just couldn't help but feel sorry for Cryptessa."

"I wouldn't feel too sorry for her," Kevin said. "Yesterday she told me she was going to sue you in small claims court for the wrongful death of her parakeet."

"Why, that old crone!" I cried.

And at that very moment, the crone in question came storming into Peter's living room.

# Chapter 5

Y ou must be Peter Connor," Cryptessa said, marching up to him in her ketchup-stained sweats. (Did she never take them off?)

"That's me," Peter said with a warm smile. "Welcome to my housewarming."

"Hope you don't my tagging along." We all turned to see a short bald guy trailing behind Cryptessa. "I'm Eleanor's nephew. Warren Jenkins."

"I'm so glad you both could make it," Peter replied, ever the gracious host.

But Cryptessa was in no mood for idle chit-chat.

"I heard you're a book editor."

In her arms, she lugged a tattered manuscript box, tied shut with dirty twine.

"I've written a masterpiece," she said, thrusting it into Peter's hands.

I remembered the hernia-inducing novel she'd shown me on my condolence call. Some claptrap about a poodle from hell.

"I won't take anything less than a million dollars for it," she informed him. "I'm going to be the next Stephen King, you know."

"I'm sorry," he said, thrusting her masterpiece right back at her, "but for legal reasons, I'm not allowed to read unsolicited manuscripts."

"You're not going to read it?" she asked, blinking in disbelief.

"Afraid not. But I wish you the very best of luck with it."

"In that case," she sniffed, "all I can say is, you'd better not throw any loud parties in this joint, because at the first hint of noise, I'm calling the police."

"As a matter of fact," Peter said with an unruffled smile, "I happen to be throwing a Halloween party next week, and you're all invited."

"Cryptessa can come as a witch," I heard Emmeline mutter. "No costume required."

"A party! Isn't that nice, Aunt Eleanor?" said her nephew with a nervous smile.

"No, it is not nice, Warren. If you think I'm going to mix and mingle with a known bird killer"—this accompanied by a nasty glare at yours truly—"you are sadly mistaken."

What a schizo! Just the other day she was practically weeping in my arms and today she was accusing me of parakeet-o-cide.

"I did not kill your ancient bird, who was on death's doorstep anyway," I cried, jumping up from the sofa.

"No, you had your demon cat do your dirty work for you."

"And I can't believe you've got the nerve to sue me after I planted all those petunias for you in the blazing sun."

"Oh, boo hoo on you. So you planted a few petunias. It's the least you could do. Besides, you were just being nice to me so I wouldn't press charges. Bela told me that after you left the other day."

"Your stuffed bat told you that?"

"Bela didn't like you. Not one bit."

Oh, boy. Somebody sure needed to switch her meds.

"Come, Warren," Cryptessa said, her ketchup-stained chest puffed in indignation. "We're leaving."

But she did not leave, as promised. Not right away. After tossing her manuscript to her nephew, she made a detour to the coffee table to reach for one of my brownies.

"Not so fast," I said, grabbing the plate. "I baked these brownies for Peter's guests. Not for nervy ingrates who are suing me in small claims court."

"Oh, please," she sneered. "You didn't bake these brownies. Anyone can see they're from Mrs. Fields."

"That's what I thought," Mr. Hurlbutt chimed in.

Then, in a surprise move, Cryptessa snatched the plate from my hands and started for the door.

My God. The woman had just hijacked my brownies!

"Aunt Eleanor!" her nephew cried, hurrying after her. "That isn't very nice."

But I was faster than Warren and got to the door before Cryptessa, blocking her exit.

"Give me those brownies," I said in my best tough gal voice. "Or else."

"Or else what? You'll sic your cat on me? Step aside, thunder thighs!"

Did you hear that? She'd called me thunder thighs. In front of Peter. The blood was pounding in my ears, I was so mortified.

"Something's got to be done about you, Cryptessa," I hissed. "And I just might be the one to do it."

And then, in a burst of fury, I yanked the plate from her hands.

A major mistake. Because, to my horror, the brownies went flying off the plate, landing— frosted side down, naturally—all over Peter's lovely white flokati rug.

"Now look what you've done!" Cryptessa crowed before grabbing a handful of cashews and storming out the door, followed by her flustered nephew.

"I'm so sorry, Peter," I said, now on my hands and knees, picking the chocolate goo from the rug.

"Jaine does stuff like this all the time," Lance helpfully pointed out. "She once totally destroyed a guest bathroom in Beverly Hills." (And it's true, I'm afraid. You can read all about that humiliating escapade in *Death of a Trophy Wife*, now available in all the usual places.)

"Don't worry about it," Peter said, getting down

on the rug with me. "I was going to have it cleaned anyway."

I'd often pictured the two of us together on a rug, but alas, never like this.

After the brownies had been picked up, my cheeks burning with shame, I made my excuses and left—fairly certain I'd taken Cryptessa's place as the hot topic of conversation.

Back home, I collapsed on my sofa.

"What a nightmare," I wailed to Prozac, who was sprawled out next to me. "I dropped a whole plate of fudge brownies on Peter's white rug."

Ever the empathetic kitty, Prozac graced me with a cavernous yawn.

*Yeah, right. Whatever. Did you bring back leftovers?*

"Don't you understand? It was one of the most embarrassing moments of my life. I lost my temper with Cryptessa, ruined Peter's carpet, and made an all-around fool of myself."

*Not only that, you've got a hunk of chocolate stuck between your teeth.*

She didn't really say that, of course.

But it was true. When I went to brush my teeth that night, there it was: A big hunk of brownie crammed between my two front teeth.

Way to go, Jaine.

# YOU'VE GOT MAIL!

**To: Jausten**
**From: Shoptillyoudrop**
**Subject: That Darn Dracula!**

Daddy managed to assemble that darn Dracula and the cursed thing will be the death of me yet. It's out on our front lawn, rising from its coffin, making the most godawful noises—moaning and groaning and singing, "Fangs for the Memories."

I've gotten at least three phone calls from the neighbors, asking us to please turn down the volume. But Daddy refuses. Keeps yammering about Dracula's inalienable right to Free Speech!

If Daddy thinks he's got a snowball's chance in hell of winning the decorating contest with that eyesore, he's got another think coming. You should see what Lydia Pinkus has done with her front lawn. You remember Lydia, don't you, darling? President of the Tampa Vistas Home-owners Association? Such a lovely woman. And so talented! She made the cutest ghosts, hand embroidered with smiley faces, and she's got them lined up along a ditch her gardener dug for some new sprinkler pipes. She's calling the whole thing a "Ghost Moat."

How clever is that?

Next to the Ghost Moat, Daddy's Dracula doesn't stand a chance.

Oops. Must run. Someone's at the door.

XOXO

Mom

**To: Jausten**
**From: DaddyO**
**Subject: Insufferable Battle-axe**

You'll never guess who had the nerve to come knocking on our door just now. That insufferable battle-axe, Lydia "Stinky" Pinkus.

"As president of the Tampa Vistas Home-owners Association," she said, standing on our doorstep like a one-woman execution squad, "I've come to request that you turn down the volume on that creature out there."

Can you believe her nerve? Asking me to turn down the volume on my Dracula??? That's like asking Leonardo da Vinci to wipe the smile off the *Mona Lisa*. I told her in no uncertain terms that I was not about to compromise my artistic integrity.

"I don't have time to stand here arguing with you, Hank," she sniffed in that snooty way of hers. "An old childhood friend is flying in from Minnesota to stay with me, and I've got to pick her up at the airport. So if you're not going to cooperate, you leave me no other alternative than to call the police."

Never in my life have I been so outraged!

The only reason "Stinky" Pinkus wants me to turn down the volume on my Dracula is to sabotage my chances of winning the contest. She knows her silly "Ghost Moat" doesn't stand a chance against my Fang-tastic vampire and will stop at nothing to shut me down.

But I'll go to my own grave before I let them tamper with The Count! There is nothing, I tell you, nothing that will make me change my mind!

Hugs 'n' cuddles from

Your outraged,

Daddy

**To: Jausten**
**From: Shoptillyoudrop**
**Subject: No Meatloaf!**

Lydia Pinkus just stopped by and asked Daddy in the nicest possible way to turn down his Dracula. You would've thought she'd asked him to drown a litter of kittens, the fuss that man made.

Honestly, I wanted to wring his neck. The minute Lydia left, I told Daddy if he didn't turn the sound down, there'd be no meatloaf and mashed potatoes on his dinner plate tonight.

Your disgusted,

Mom

PS. He's out front right now, adjusting the volume.

**To: Jausten**
**From: DaddyO**
**Subject: Fascist Machinations**

Dearest Lambchop,

Due to the fascist machinations of your mother, I have reluctantly agreed to lower Dracula's volume. I'm wounded to the core that my own wife would side with Stinky Pinkus against me, but such is life.

Yet even with his volume muted, I'm happy to report that my fang-tastic Dracula is by far the most creative lawn ornament in Tampa Vistas. I've checked out the competition, and it's safe to say no one has anything remotely like it.

I can practically feel the winner's trophy in my hands!

Love 'n' hugs from
Daddy

# Chapter 6

I woke up the next morning, Prozac snoring on my stomach, an ice cream spoon clutched in my fist. An empty carton of Chunky Monkey, scraped clean of all contents, lay abandoned on its side on my night table—a souvenir of the torrid encounter I'd had last night with the two most important men in my life—Ben and Jerry.

Licking the dried remains of ice cream from my spoon, I shuddered at the memory of Peter's housewarming.

Like clips from my own personal horror movie, I replayed my fight with Cryptessa. I saw the sneer on her face when she called me "thunder thighs." I saw my brownies land frosting-side down on Peter's beautiful white rug. I saw everyone looking at me, aghast.

Worst of all, I saw my chances with Peter flying out the window.

But I couldn't let it get me down. We Austens are made of sterner stuff. When poop hits our fan, we get out our pooper scoopers and start shoveling.

So what if I'd lost Peter? There were still roses to be smelled, books to be read, pizzas to be ordered. Life went on and I intended to go along with it. Today was a clean slate, a whole new beginning, the first day of the rest of my life—

My cavalcade of clichés was interrupted just then by a loud knocking at my front door.

Dislodging Prozac from her perch on my tummy, I threw on my robe and hurried to the door, where I found a guy in a shiny brown suit standing on my doorstep.

Oh, dear. I just hoped he wasn't from some wacko religious sect hoping to make me a convert.

"Are you Jaine Austen?" he asked.

"Yes," I replied warily, looking to see if he had any pamphlets up his sleeve.

He had no pamphlets. But he did have something worse. Far worse.

"You're being served."

I got the distinct impression he wasn't talking about breakfast.

"Summons to appear in small claims court," he said, slapping some official-looking papers in my hand.

Uh-oh. Looked like the first day of the rest of my life was getting off to a less-than-spectacular start.

"Have a good one," my friendly process server said, before trotting off to bring misery into some other poor sap's life.

By now Prozac was up and about, howling for her breakfast. Tossing the summons onto a pile of junk mail on my dining room table, I shuffled off to the kitchen to open a can of Hearty Halibut Guts.

"Dammit, Pro," I moaned. "Mommy has to go to small claims court."

She swished an impatient tail.

*You're not my mommy, and hurry up with those halibut guts.*

I fed my demanding princess her halibut glop and had just finished nuking myself a cup of Folgers' finest when there was another knock on my door.

This time, it was Lance, looking annoyingly chipper in cutoffs and a tank top.

"Morning there, sleepy head!"

"I'm not talking to you," I snarled.

"I come bearing jelly donuts!" He held up a big paper bag, dotted with grease and faint red spots where the jelly was oozing through.

"If you think you can worm your way into my apartment with a measly bag of jelly donuts—you know me only too well," I said, snatching the bag from his hand. "But I'm still mad at you."

"Why?" All wide-eyed and innocent.

"As if you didn't know." I began mimicking his simpering patter from the housewarming. "Jaine writes the cutest toilet bowl ads." "Why doesn't chubby Jaine sit on the sofa so she can be closer to the brownies?" "Jaine makes a fool of herself at parties all the time."

"I'm sorry, hon. I admit I played dirty. But all's fair in love and *Celebrity Apprentice*."

"Oh, well," I sighed. "After yesterday's brownie

fiasco, I don't stand a chance with Peter anyway."

"Honey, you never did. I'm telling you. My gaydar is infallible."

Conceding defeat, I nuked Lance a cup of coffee, and we sat on my sofa, scarfing down the jelly donuts. Okay, I did most of the scarfing. Lance ate a calorie-conscious half a donut and spent the rest of the time commiserating with me over my upcoming lawsuit.

"Don't worry, sweetheart," he assured me. "The judge will take one look at that psycho gleam in Cryptessa's eyes and dismiss the case before you know it."

That's the thing about Lance. One day he sabotages you over the man of your dreams. And the next day he's offering comfort and jelly donuts in your hour of need. It's why I can never stay mad at him for very long.

"Thanks for the donuts," I said, as he got up to leave.

"All is forgiven?"

"All is forgiven."

"Good. Because I have a wee little favor to ask."

Uh-oh. I should have known there was a string attached to those donuts.

"What do you want?"

"Your books," he said, pointing to my floor-to-ceiling bookshelf. "I invited Peter over to see my library, and now I need a library. So how about it, hon? Can I borrow your books?"

"No, you may not borrow my books! You want to impress Peter? Buy your own darn books!"

"I understand," he said, patting my hand in a most patronizing manner. "You're feeling hurt and depressed by your public humiliation and that hunk of brownie that was stuck between your teeth all afternoon. And you're taking your anger out on me." Then, with a smile worthy of Stella Dallas in one of her braver moments, he added, "Not to worry. I have a friend who's a set decorator at one of the studios. He can loan me the books."

"Goodie for you."

"But how about your bookcase? Can I borrow that?"

"No, you may not borrow my bookcase!"

"Okay, okay. Don't get your panties in an uproar."

Then, as he scooted out the door, he called out over his shoulder, "Talk to you later, hon. And don't forget. As soon as I land my date with Peter, you owe me dinner at the restaurant of my choice."

I slammed the door behind him so hard I'm surprised it didn't come off the hinges.

Can you believe the nerve of that guy? Inviting Peter over to see his library and expecting *me* to provide the library?

I stomped around in a snit for a while, muttering curses and rinsing out the coffee mugs.

And I was just about to head off to the shower when there was yet another knock on my door.

Oh, hell. Probably Lance again. What did he want now? My kidneys?

"What?" I snapped, hurling the front door open.

But it wasn't Lance.

It was Peter, the cleft in his chin looking more kissable than ever.

"You forgot this," he said, holding out my brownie plate.

He was dressed for work, looking marvelously spiffy in a navy suit and celadon silk tie that brought out a hint of hazel in his eyes.

I, on the other hand, looked like Cryptessa's younger sister in my coffee-stained chenille robe, my hair a mop of untamed curls. For all I knew, I had a big hunk of jelly stuck between my teeth.

What did it matter, anyway? The Peter Wars were over and done with. I'd already lost to Lance.

"Thanks for bringing it by," I said with a feeble smile.

"No problem."

"I want you to know that I feel terrible about that scene at your housewarming."

"Please don't feel bad. Nothing livens up a party like a good fight." He shot me a mischievous smile. "To tell the truth, the housewarming was a bit of a snore till you showed up."

"Really? You're not just saying that?"

"I swear on a stack of brownies."

"But I ruined your carpet."

"You didn't ruin it. I got most of the stains out

with club soda. And I was going to send it out to the cleaners anyway."

"Well, I insist on paying the bill."

"There's no need for that. But there is one thing you can do for me."

"Anything," I said.

"You can come to my Halloween party."

And with that, he flashed me a smile with enough wattage to light up the Hollywood Bowl.

I didn't care what Lance's gaydar said. Peter was flirting with me. I may be packing a few extra pounds in the hip-thigh area, but I know when I'm being flirted with. And I was definitely the designated flirtee in this little tête-à-tête.

"I'd be happy to come," I said, melting in the warmth of his smile.

We bid each other a fond adieu, and I floated off to the shower on cloud nine.

It looked like The Peter Wars weren't over yet.

Not by a long shot.


Having showered and dressed, I tootled over to my office (otherwise known as my dining room table) to read my e-mails. Poor Mom. Daddy would drive her and the neighbors nuts before Halloween was over. But I couldn't worry about the Curse of the Fang-Tastic Dracula. Lest you forget, I still owed Marvin Cooper a bunch of commercials. I reached for my Mattress King file, fully intending to get some work done on Larry

Lumbar, when I noticed my summons to appear in small claims court.

In the excitement of Peter's visit, I'd forgotten all about it. But now I saw it staring up at me from where I'd tossed it on top of a Chinese takeout menu.

With a shudder, I saw that I was scheduled to be tried in a court of law for the wrongful death of Eleanor Jenkins's beloved parakeet, Van Helsing.

And I almost fainted when I read that Cryptessa was suing me for five thousand dollars!

No way could I afford to fork over five grand to that nutcase. Or any other nutcase for that matter. In fact, five grand exceeded my "disposable income" limit by about four thousand nine hundred and eighty-nine dollars.

Surely there had to be some way to make amends with Cryptessa and get her to drop the case.

Popping an Altoid and plastering a smile on my face, I headed up the street to do some serious groveling.

I'd simply tell Cryptessa how dreadfully sorry I was for everything that had gone down between us, that I'd be more than happy to "bake" her some more brownies or plant some more petunias, that there had to be some way we could mend our fences without involving the courts.

I was in the middle of rehearsing my humble apologies when suddenly I heard voices being raised.

"Get off my property!" I recognized Cryptessa's shriek right away.

"Not until you pay me for my chocolates!" That sounded like Emmeline.

And indeed, as I walked up the path to Zombieland, I saw Cryptessa standing out on her front steps, yelling at Emmeline, who was yelling right back, her fluffball dog yapping at her ankles.

"If you and your dog aren't off my property in three minutes," Cryptessa cried, shaking her fist, "I'm calling the police."

"Good!" said Emmeline. "I'll tell them how you ate my chocolates!

"Look, Jaine!" she cried, spotting me. "Look what this miserable woman did."

She held out a Godiva candy box, and when I looked inside, I saw that there was a bite missing from every single piece.

"My son sent these to me for my birthday, and the UPS man left them at Cryptessa's house by mistake. She had the nerve to return them to me this morning. Like this!"

Once again, she thrust the half-eaten candy in my face.

"Can you believe it?"

I was outraged, of course, as any true chocoholic would be. I was also tempted to try one of the remaining morsels, a goody with a pecan stuck in its center.

"Have you ever seen anything so outrageous?" Emmeline sputtered.

As much as I would have liked to chime in with a few harsh words of disapproval, I was there to make peace with Cryptessa. I could not afford to pass judgment.

So instead I merely smiled weakly and said, "Happy belated birthday, Emmeline."

Not exactly thrilled with my reply, she turned back to Cryptessa. "I've had it up to here with you. And so has Lana Turner!"

An angry bark from the fluffball.

"I didn't eat your stupid chocolates," Cryptessa insisted.

"Liar!" cried Emmeline. "I can see the chocolate on your chin."

And indeed there was a faint swath of chocolate across Cryptessa's chin.

"Oh, go fly a kite," Cryptessa snapped, swiping at her chin with the back of her hand.

Okay, that's not what she really said, but this is a family novel so I'll spare you the real four letter words involved. "How do you know it wasn't a possum who ate the chocolates? How do you know it wasn't your dog?" She pointed at me and added, "How do you know it wasn't *her?* I wouldn't put anything past her. She killed my bird, you know."

I was *this close* to hurling a few colorful four-letter words of my own in her direction when

Cryptessa's balding nephew came hurrying up the front path.

"Aunt Eleanor! What's going on?"

"Look, Warren!" Emmeline wailed, showing him the chocolate box. "She ate my chocolates!"

"Oh, no," he said, shaking his head. "Not again."

"She's done this before?" I whispered.

"Don't ask." Warren shook his head, exasperated. "Last time it was a Junior's cheesecake."

Excited to see a new face in the crowd, Lana let out a welcoming yip.

"If that mongrel barks at me one more time," Cryptessa snarled, "I'm calling animal control."

"Go ahead," Emmeline said, sweeping Lana up in her arms. "Call them. And I'll call the FBI. For your information, eating somebody's mail happens to be a federal offense!"

"I'm so sorry," Warren said to Emmeline. "We'll buy you another box."

"Oh, we will, will we?" Cryptessa whirled on her nephew with fire in her eyes. "The last time I checked, buster, you were dead broke. I'm the one with the bucks around here, not you. And if you think I'm giving you money to buy that falafel franchise you wanted, forget about it. Not when you keep siding with my enemies."

With that, she turned on her heels and stomped into the house.

"Aunt Eleanor!" Warren cried, running after her,

tiny beads of sweat sprouting on his brow. "Let's not be hasty!"

The door slammed behind them, leaving me alone with Emmeline. I watched as she led her dog over to the DO NOT TRESPASS sign.

"Go ahead, darling," she prompted.

Eager to please, Lana squatted down and left her calling card.

"Good girl!" Emmeline said, her eyes beaming pure malice.

Nope, there was just no making peace with a woman like Cryptessa.

# Chapter 7

Omigod!" Lance said, surveying the backseat of my Corolla. "So this is where old fast-food wrappers come to die."

Lance and I were headed over to Hollywood to rent costumes for Peter's Halloween party. I'd offered to drive, and already I was beginning to regret it.

"My car's not so bad," I said.

"Are you kidding? I think I see a ketchup packet from King Tut's Tomb."

"Okay, so it's been a while since I've cleaned. I've been very distracted. I've had a lot of things on my plate."

"Most of them with fries," he said, holding up an empty McDonald's bag.

"Hardy-har-har," I said, my voice dripping icicles.

"Lucky for me, I never travel without moist towelette sanitizers."

I reined in my annoyance as Lance ripped open a towelette and made a big show of sanitizing his hands.

"So how'd Peter like your 'library'?" I asked, determined to get off his car cleanliness kick.

"Slight snafu," he sighed. "Unfortunately, the only books my set decorator friend could get a hold of were a bunch of medical texts. In German. So if Peter ever asks, remember: I went to medical school in Heidelberg and dropped out to pursue my love of fashion."

Oh, man, this guy deserved the Pulitzer Prize in Whoppers.

"It was a magical evening," Lance gushed. "I looked divine, if I do say so myself. And I was the perfect host. I served Brie and crackers, washed down with a 1989 Châteauneuf-du-Pape."

"Châteauneuf-du-Pape? Doesn't that stuff cost an arm and a leg?"

"Technically, it was Two Buck Chuck, but I put it in a Châteauneuf-du-Pape bottle I bought at a thrift shop years ago. That bottle's come in so handy. I don't think Peter knew the difference."

"So how did this magical evening end? Did Peter ask you out?"

"Not exactly, but I can tell he's on the brink. There was something in his eyes that told me he was interested in me." Lance patted my arm in that maddeningly patronizing way of his. "I'm so glad you listened to reason and gave up your foolish dreams of dating the guy."

"Actually, I'm back in the dating game. Peter stopped by to return my brownie plate the other day, and there was something in his eyes that told me he was interested in *me*."

"You mustn't confuse interest with pity, hon."

"I'll keep that in mind," I said, barely restraining

79

myself from bopping him over the head with a stray Slurpee cup.

The rest of the trip passed in an icy silence. Well, I was the icy one. I doubt Lance even noticed. He was too busy sanitizing my dashboard with his moist towelettes.

At last we arrived at the costume rental place Lance had picked out.

"It's where all the Hollywood costume designers go!" he gushed.

"Estelle's Costumes and Beauty Supplies?" I said, eyeing the tiny storefront whose window was jammed with an eclectic mix of costumes and cosmetics.

"It's much bigger than it looks," Lance assured me.

And indeed it was. A long narrow space, it boasted endless racks of costumes, not to mention a back wall crammed with beauty supplies.

I stood there, breathing in the heady aroma of old clothes and hairspray, while Lance sprang into action, in full-tilt kamikaze shopper mode, flipping past costumes with lightning speed.

"Omigosh, hon!" he called out, holding up a huge puke green outfit. "This one's perfect for you."

"Forget it, Lance. I'm not going as Mrs. Shrek."

"How about this?" he asked, holding up a pink monstrosity.

"Or the Michelin Man."

"Spoilsport," he pouted.

"Why don't you just concentrate on getting your own costume, okay?"

Lance reluctantly agreed to go our separate ways, and before long he'd picked out a svelte werewolf-in-a-tux ensemble for himself.

"It's you, Lance," I said, nodding in approval. "Armani with hairy knuckles."

Meanwhile, I made my way down the racks, flipping past a white, plunging "Marilyn" dress, a Marie Antoinette extravaganza, and a Madonna outfit with bra cups pointy enough to drill holes in a two-by-four.

Then I spotted it: a saucy lace flapper dress, complete with a feather headband. I tried it on in Estelle's cramped dressing room. The outfit reeked of cleaning fluid, but it looked adorable, and I was thrilled to see it camouflaged the dreaded hip-tush zone quite nicely. (True, it was a little clingy around my tummy, but if I sucked in my gut and didn't eat a thing the night of the party, I'd be fine.)

Costumes in hand, we headed over to the counter where Estelle, a fiftysomething woman with neon-green hair and enough rings to stock a display case at Nordstrom, took our deposits.

"I'll be back on Halloween," Lance told our green-haired friend, "to pick them up."

"I still don't understand why we can't rent the costumes the day of the party," I said.

"Are you nuts? We have to reserve them now. All the good ones will be gone by Halloween."

My flapper ensemble was $49.99 more than I could afford to spend, but I kept my eye on the prize (Peter) and figured it was worth it.

"Beautiful choice," Estelle assured me with a nicotine-stained smile.

"What's this?" Lance asked, picking up a large plastic skeleton's skull from a display on the counter.

"It's a bumper decoration for your car," Estelle enthused. "Only nine ninety-nine. And the skeleton's eyes light up." She flipped a switch on the back of the skull, and indeed, its eye sockets lit up in bright red.

"I love it!" Lance exclaimed. "I'll take two."

"Two?" I asked. "Why do you need two?"

"One for me and one for you."

"I don't want a skeleton's skull."

"Of course you do, Jaine. If any car was screaming out for a skull, it's your Corolla. It's practically haunted by the ghosts of dearly departed Quarter Pounders."

And before I could stop him, he was buying the darn things.

"C'mon," he said when we got out to the parking lot. "Let's put one on your car."

"I am not putting a skeleton skull on my car."

"What's wrong with you, Jaine?" He tsked in disapproval. "Where's your Halloween spirit?"

"Oh, all right," I caved.

Maybe it would be fun to get into the Halloween spirit for a change. And besides, it was actually sort of sweet of Lance to buy it for me.

He clamped the skull onto my front bumper and turned on its blinking red eye sockets. It was beyond tacky, but what the heck? When it comes to gifts, it's the thought that counts.

I got in the car in a much better mood than when we started out.

"Thanks for the ride, hon," Lance said as we pulled out of the parking lot.

"And thanks for the skeleton skull."

"Oh, it was nothing. That's what friends are for. You can pay me back when we get home."

"Pay you back??"

"Omigod!" he gasped. "Is that a pizza crust in your glove compartment?"

And out came the moist towelette.

I squeezed the steering wheel as hard as I could, pretending it was Lance's neck.


Still fuming over my "gift" from Lance, I stomped into my apartment.

Talk about no good deed going unpunished. Here I'd been kind enough to drive him across town in L.A. traffic and what did I get for it? A tacky skeleton skull, hurtful slurs about my trusty Corolla, and a massive dose of moist towelettes.

Of course, he had a point about the Corolla.

Maybe my car did need a bit of a pick-me-up. So as much as I hated to admit he might be right, after a calming dose of Reese's Pieces, I headed back outside to clean up the litter.

I'd parked my car in front of the Hurlbutts' house, and as I walked across the street, I saw Mrs. Hurlbutt out on her front lawn, hacking away at her flower bed with a hoe.

"Damn that Harold," she was muttering. "He never turns the soil right. Does a lick and a promise and then it's back to the Weather Channel."

"Hi, Mrs. Hurlbutt," I called out.

"Oh, hello, Jaine." She eyed my trash bag. "Come to clean out your car? It's about time, if you don't mind my saying so."

Of course, I did mind her saying so, but I just slapped on a phony smile and restrained myself from telling her that her rusty old Camry with the Garfield bobblehead in the backseat was not exactly a painting in the Louvre.

"So are you going to Peter's Halloween party?" she asked, her eyes lighting up with excitement.

"Yes, I'm going as—"

"That Peter!" she gushed, clearly not interested in my choice of costume. "What a looker! If I were twenty years younger . . ." She sighed with longing.

Oh, for heaven's sake. Was there no one on the block who *didn't* have a crush on the guy?

But then Mrs. Hurlbutt forgot all about Peter.

"Goddamn slugs!" she shouted, glaring down at the upturned earth at her feet. "Stop eating my impatiens!"

And with that, she took her hoe and began stabbing at the critters with a vengeance.

Leaving her to her killing spree, I returned to the chore at hand and began cleaning out my car.

I must say I was quite surprised to see how quickly my few measly wrappers managed to fill up a rather large trash bag.

On the plus side, I found an earring I thought I'd lost two years ago.

I had just finished tossing the trash into the garbage can when my cell phone rang. It was Kandi.

"Meet me for lunch at Century City," she said without preamble. "I've got the most amazing news."

No way could I meet Kandi for lunch. I'd already wasted the morning at the costume shop, and I really had to finish those Larry Lumbar spots.

"Sorry, honey. No can do. I'm swamped with work."

"I'm thinking a Fuddruckers burger," she said. "With extra cheese."

"See you in a half hour," I said, reaching for my car keys.

What can I say? Apparently I've got tapioca where my spine should be.

A half hour later, I was parking my Corolla in the Century City Mall parking lot. As I got out of the car, I noticed a teenaged boy gazing at me in unabashed admiration.

*Whaddaya know,* I thought, with a carefree toss of my curls. *I've still got it.*

"It's neat," the kid said, "the way the eyes blink."

Oh, for heaven's sake. He was talking about the stupid skeleton skull.

"Thanks," I replied with a weak smile, and headed up to the food court.

It was a beautiful California day. The early morning fog had burned off and the sun was shining its little heart out. The food court was filled with the usual weekday assortment of retirees, shopaholics, and bizpeople from the nearby Century City law firms.

Kandi had nabbed a table on the outdoor terrace.

"Over here!" she called out, waving to me.

She was dressed in her "work" clothes, which in Hollywood means designer jeans, T-shirt, and blazer.

"Hi, sweetie!" She got up to give me a hug. "I ordered your lunch!"

I looked down at the table, expecting to see a Fuddruckers burger bursting with extra cheese. Instead, all I saw was a depressing plate of chopped vegetables.

"What happened to my burger with extra cheese?"

"You don't really want a fattening burger, do you, hon?"

"Yes, I do want a fattening burger."

"Well, too bad. I got you a lovely chopped vegetable salad. Now eat it. It's good for you."

Sometimes Kandi labors under the illusion that she is my mother.

I picked away at the shards of lettuce, trolling for croutons, while Kandi told me her amazing news.

"Remember Madame Vruska, my psychic?" she asked.

"Indelibly," I assured her.

"The woman is a genius! One of the things she predicted was that I would come into unexpected riches. And I did!"

"Really?"

"Yes, I was in Bloomie's just now, trying on a blazer, and guess what I found in the pocket?"

"What?"

"A dollar!"

She whipped out a dollar bill from her purse and waved it in triumph.

"Kandi, hon," I pointed out, "a dollar isn't exactly 'riches.'"

She graced me with an exaggerated roll of her eyes. "Must you be so literal? It's the principle of the thing."

"Did you buy the blazer?" I asked, eyeing a shopping bag at her feet.

"Yes," she admitted.

"How much was it?"

"A hundred and eighty dollars."

Thanks to her job dashing off quips for animated insects, Kandi can afford to drop one hundred and eighty clams on a blazer without blinking.

"So let's get this straight. You found a dollar. And spent a hundred eighty. And you came into riches how?"

"Oh, don't be such a spoilsport," she said, shoving the dollar back in her purse. "Madame Vruska said I'd come into money, and I did. And she said I'd meet my true love in the arts. And I will. I just know it!"

She had so much hope in her eyes I couldn't bear to disillusion her.

"Of course you will," I murmured, patting her hand soothingly while nabbing one of her croutons.

"So how're things going with the new guy on your block?" she asked.

"Peter? He invited me to his Halloween costume party." Eagerly I told her about the flapper outfit I'd just rented.

"Sounds adorable!" she enthused.

"It will be, if I remember to suck in my stomach all night. It's a little tight around the tummy area."

"Tight around the tummy?" She perked up in that way she gets when she's about to wax euphoric. "Then you must, absolutely *must,* get a Tummy Tamer."

"A Tummy Tamer?"

"A spandex miracle worker that takes inches off your tummy instantly," she said, morphing into an infomercial spokeswoman before my eyes. "I simply adore mine."

"Why on earth are you wearing a Tummy Tamer? You don't even have a tummy."

"That's because I'm wearing my Tummy Tamer. You wouldn't believe how fat I am without it."

Don't you just hate it when skinny women talk about how "fat" they are? Don't you want to just choke them with a celery stick?

"Honestly, Jaine," she said with a missionary gleam in her eye. "You have to promise you'll get one for Peter's party."

I could see there'd be no living with her unless I promised.

"Okay, okay. I'll get a Tummy Tamer."

Of course, I had no intention whatsoever of buying one of the silly things. Girdles are just too darn uncomfortable.

But after Kandi and I had hugged good-bye and I'd sneaked back to the food court for a giant salted pretzel, I happened to be walking through a department store I shall, for legal reasons, call Floomingdale's, when I ran smack into a display of the very Tummy Tamers Kandi had been raving about.

There they were, stacked high on a table, with the most amazing Before and After pictures propped up in the middle of the display. I gaped in amazement at a woman, who in her Before picture looked a lot like me after a rendezvous with Messrs. Ben and Jerry, and in her After picture resembled a runway model in Milan. Like magic, her tummy had disappeared.

"It's a miracle, isn't it?" a seductive voice whispered in my ear.

I turned to see a stick-thin saleswoman at my side.

"I'm wearing one now," she confided, running her hands down her size 0 body.

And for one crazy minute, I actually imagined I could look like a Milan fashion model with the help of a piece of spandex.

As if in a trance, I reached for a box.

"Is it very uncomfortable?" I asked, wondering what price I'd have to pay for such a fabulous body.

"Not at all," Ms. Stick assured me. "You'll hardly even know you have it on."

And like a fool, I believed her.

# Chapter 8

There's got to be a special place in hell for the guy (it can't possibly have been a woman) who invented the Tummy Tamer. A place of honor right next to the guys who invented bikini waxes and rice cakes.

It was the night of Peter's Halloween party, and I'd waited till the last minute to try it on.

Freshly showered, my hair blow-dried to perfection, I was standing in my bra and panties, admiring my newly sleek tresses, thinking how cute they'd look with the feather headband that came with my flapper costume. Prozac was stretched out on my bed, watching me get dressed, taking an occasional time-out to claw my comforter.

Up until that moment, everything had been humming along smoothly.

And then I reached for the Tummy Tamer.

When I took it out of the box, I groaned to see it was the size of a Barbie headband. Surely there had to be some mistake. Obviously someone had put a toddler's Tummy Tamer in the wrong box.

But no. When I checked the label on the Tummy Tamer, I saw it was the right size.

Gingerly I stepped into it, wondering if I would be able to get it up past my ankles.

You'll be happy to know my ankles were a breeze. The rest of the journey, however, was a struggle of monumental proportions. I tried valiantly to tug the diabolical band of elastic past my thighs and up around my hips, grunting and groaning every step of the way. All the while, I swear I could see Prozac snickering from her perch on my bed.

At last the battle of the bulge was over. Gasping from the exertion, I checked myself out in the mirror and was pleasantly surprised to see that the Tummy Tamer had lived up to its name. It had, indeed, whittled inches off my tummy.

True, it felt like my internal organs had been sucked into a space bag, but on the plus side, I couldn't help thinking how wonderful I was going to look in my flapper outfit.

Suddenly all the effort seemed worth it.

I was busy admiring my almost-washboard tummy in the mirror, imagining myself as a Keira Knightley-esque waif in an Upstairs, Down-stairs/English countryside/*Masterpiece Theater* production when there was a knock on my door.

"Hey, Jaine, it's me," Lance called out.

He'd graciously offered to pick up our costumes on his way home from work, and now I slipped into my robe to let him in.

He stood there with a garment bag in one hand and a large plastic shopping sack in the other.

"Hand it over," I said, reaching out for my adorable flapper costume.

"Tiny problemo, honey," he said, an undeniably shifty look in his eyes.

"What tiny problemo?"

I didn't like the sound of this.

"Estelle accidentally rented your flapper outfit to someone else."

"What??!"

"But don't worry. I got you something even better!"

He unzipped the garment bag, and to my horror took out a large hunk of matted black fur, reeking of mothballs.

"What on earth is that?" I asked, in shock.

"An ape suit!" he said, whipping a repulsive ape head out of the plastic sack. "Isn't it a hoot? And the best part is, you won't have to worry about wearing makeup!"

"You did this on purpose!" I said, advancing on him with fire in my eyes. "You switched my outfit so I'd look awful in front of Peter."

"Why, Jaine," he said lamely. "I don't know what you're talking about."

"Oh, come off it, Lance. If you looked any more guilty, you'd be in a mug shot."

"Okay, okay, I did it," he said, sinking down onto my sofa with a heavy sigh, John Barrymore at his absolute hammiest. "I don't know what came over me. I'm a terrible friend. I wouldn't blame you if you never spoke to me again."

He blinked his eyes furiously, in an unsuccessful attempt to work up some tears. "Can you ever forgive me?"

"No. Never."

"I'll make it up to you somehow, sweetie. I promise. I know! Want me to help you pick mothballs out of the ape's fur?"

"No!" I shrieked. "Just go!"

I shoved him out the door, wondering how the hell I was going to get out of this mess. Maybe it wasn't too late to drive over to the costume shop. But when I called the store, all I got was their answering machine. It was almost eight, and they were closed.

I considered going to the party in street clothes, but I didn't want to be the only one there without a costume and have Peter think I was a poor sport. I also considered wrapping myself in a sheet and going as a ghost, but unfortunately all my sheets have Martha Stewart daisies on them, and that didn't seem terribly ghostlike.

Oh, what the heck. I'd wear the damn ape suit. With any luck, Peter would think it was funny.

Wearily I tossed on jeans and a T-shirt. Then, taking a deep breath, I stepped into my costume. The stench of mothballs was overwhelming. I'm guessing the last time that ape suit had been worn was at the premiere of *King Kong*.

But I had to look on the bright side, to think positive thoughts.

If Peter really liked me, surely an ape suit couldn't come between us. Somehow I'd dazzle him with my witty repartee. Peter would see beyond my moth-eaten exterior to the charming, intelligent woman in the CUCKOO FOR COCOA PUFFS T-shirt beneath. And Lance, the traitor, in his werewolf togs, would watch me, wringing his hairy hands in jealousy.

Yes, I could make this thing work if I really tried.

And so it was with a spring in my step, hope in my heart, and an ape head under my arm that I headed up the street to Peter's party.

The party was in full swing when I showed up, with lots of people milling about, drinks in hand, the "Monster Mash" playing in the background. Most of the guests seemed to be Peter's friends and work colleagues, but sprinkled among them were a few of the neighbors.

Mr. and Mrs. Hurlbutt were there, decked out as Frankenstein and—in a perfect example of art imitating reality—the Bride of Frankenstein.

"Don't come whining to me when your dentures come loose," I heard Mrs. Hurlbutt tsk as Mr. H. scarfed down some candy corn.

Next I spotted Kevin and Matt Moore, the His 'n' Hers realtors, dressed as a pair of pirates, handing out their business card to a guy in a Tarzan loincloth.

As I glanced around, I was dismayed to see that half the people weren't even in costume. Indeed, there was little Amy Chang, the grad student, looking way too fetching in Capri jeans and a ruffled tee. If I'd known people were going to show up in street clothes, I never would've worn my ghastly ape suit.

Which, after only two minutes at the party, was beginning to get awfully warm.

And I couldn't help noticing that as I made my way through the crowd, people were giving me a wide berth.

"P.U.!" I heard Kevin say as I walked by, wrinkling her nose. "Something smells like mothballs."

Why did I get the feeling I wasn't about to be the life of the party?

Lance had Peter cornered over by the fireplace, and as I approached, I could hear him yakking about Thomas Mann and Marcel Proust as if he'd actually read a syllable more than their reviews on Amazon.

I lifted my ape head to wave at Peter, who was decked out in tight jeans and a T-shirt, a sign around his neck reading NUDIST ON STRIKE.

What a clever way of wearing a costume without wearing a costume. Why the heck didn't I think of something like that?

"Hey, Jaine!" he said, spotting me. "So glad you could make it. Great costume!"

"I picked it out!" Lance had the nerve to say.

I hoped he choked on his martini olive.

"But getting back to Proust," Lance went on, blocking me from Peter's view, "I just love the way he wrote about Madeleine. She was such an interesting character."

*A madeleine is a lemon cookie, you twit,* I felt like saying.

But of course, I did not help him out with that useful tidbit of info.

Instead I put on my ape head and wandered aimlessly for a while, reeking of mothballs, the designated party pariah.

I stopped to look at some of Peter's photos on an end table, hoping to get a clue about his sexuality. My heart sank when I saw him grinning into the camera, his arm slung around the shoulders of another guy. Then it soared when I saw another picture of him with a woman. Then it sank again when I realized she was an amazingly attractive woman.

Oh, well. Time to lift my spirits with some chow. And some spirits.

I headed for the buffet table in Peter's dining room, where Cryptessa's maid Rosita was busy replenishing a platter of cold cuts.

"Hi, there," I said, lifting up my ape head. "I didn't realize you worked for Mr. Connor."

"He just hired me for tonight. Please don't tell Cryptessa," she said, her eyes darting about in fear, as if she expected Cryptessa to pop up from behind Peter's china cabinet. "She'd have a hissy fit if she found out."

"It doesn't take much to get her hissy, does it?" I asked.

"No." She shook her head ruefully. "I'm afraid not." Then, remembering her duties, she added, "Have some cold cuts. They're delicious."

She didn't have to ask me twice.

I rustled up a corned beef and Swiss on rye, a wee bit o' chardonnay, and a Bloodshot Eyeball Cookie for dessert.

If I couldn't have fun with Peter, I might as well have fun with some corned beef.

I found a secluded seat in the corner, and with my ape head nestled on the floor beside me, I was just about to chow down when I heard—

"Jaine, honey!" It was Lila Wood, the neighborhood politico. "How wonderful to see you!"

At last. Someone who didn't mind the smell of mothballs.

It was not my company Lila sought, however, when she plopped down on the seat next to me, but rather the opportunity to go over her campaign platform. In excruciating detail. Before I knew it, she was rambling on about what a fantastic job she'd do as president of the Neighborhood Council, reminding me how hard she'd fought for the sanctity of our neighborhood and what a fearless leader she'd been in the battle to keep a rapacious real estate developer named Ralph Mancuso from putting up a mini-mall at the end of our block.

"Mancuso must be stopped!" she cried, thrusting some flyers into my hand.

Which wasn't easy to do, considering I was holding a corned beef sandwich at the time. But somehow she managed.

"If he had his way, there'd be a yogurt parlor on every corner of Los Angeles."

Frankly, a yogurt parlor on every corner seemed like a pretty good idea to me, but I kept on nodding as if I agreed with her.

She continued blathering away about Evil Ralph Mancuso as I polished off my sandwich and Bloodshot Eyeball Cookie.

Through it all, the woman showed no signs of shutting up.

There's only so much a person can hear about corruption in the Beverly Hills Planning Commission before she goes stark raving bananas.

"Oh, look," I said in an effort to save my sanity. "The Hurlbutts! They told me earlier they wanted to talk to you."

"They did?" she said, perking up.

I bet my bottom Pop-Tart she didn't hear *that* very often.

"Well, if you'll excuse me—"

*God, yes!*

"—I'll just run over and have a chat with them."

I breathed a sigh of relief as she bore down on the unsuspecting Hurlbutts.

At the last minute, they saw her coming and tried to make a run for it, but with the skill of a seasoned politico, Lila backed them into a corner and launched into her campaign speech.

I was free at last. And to celebrate, I went back to the buffet table for just one more Bloodshot Eyeball Cookie.

(Okay, two more.)

By now the interior of my ape suit had reached sauna-like proportions.

I could stand it no longer. I decided to do what I should have done the moment I walked in the party and take the damn thing off.

So I slipped out of the dining room and down a hallway to Peter's bedroom. At least, I assumed it was his bedroom from the row of Brooks Brothers suits I was nosy enough to peek at in his closet.

Wasting no time, I peeled out of my ape suit and tossed it onto Peter's bed, where several coats had been slung. How wonderful it was to feel the clean, fresh, room-temperature air!

And yet, although I was thrilled to be released from King Kong's captivity, I was not a totally happy camper. Lest you forget, I was still wearing my Tummy Tamer, which by now had pretty much cut off all circulation from my belly button down.

There was no doubt about it. That had to go, too.

But I couldn't risk getting undressed here in the bedroom. What if someone showed up to drop off a coat?

So I headed back out into the hallway in search of a bathroom. I soon found one, across from a room that looked like Peter's office.

I slipped inside and, locking the door behind me, took off my jeans.

Remembering my epic battle getting the Tummy Tamer over my hips, this time I decided to pull it up over my head.

Major mistake.

Because no sooner did I try to hoist the Tummy Tamer upward than the damn thing clamped around my chest like the jaws of death, pinning my arms to my sides.

I twisted and turned, but to no avail.

I was trapped in a spandex straightjacket, naked below the waist except for a pair of *Bottoms Up!* panties (a Shopping Channel gift from my mom).

I considered yelling for help, but I couldn't bear the thought of anyone—especially Peter—finding me like this.

My only ray of hope was that my right hand was free. If I could just find a pair of scissors, maybe I could cut my way out.

Frantically I searched Peter's cabinets for something sharp, but all I found was an electric razor.

Then I remembered the office across the hall. Maybe I'd find scissors there.

So what if I was practically naked from the waist down? I had to make a break for it.

With my free hand, I opened the bathroom door and peeked out.

Damn. There was the guy in the Tarzan loincloth, waiting to use the john.

"What's going on in there?" he asked, tapping his feet impatiently.

"Um. Plumbing emergency."

"I'll go tell Peter."

"No!" I practically shrieked. "He already knows. You'll have to use the other bathroom."

"What other bathroom?"

I had no idea if there was another bathroom in the house. But I wasn't about to let that stop me.

"Down there." I pointed vaguely at the other end of the hall.

And as Tarzan stomped away, I grabbed my jeans and sprinted out into the hallway, praying he wouldn't turn around and see me.

Thank heavens, he didn't.

I scooted into Peter's office, which, like his living room, was a sleek, black leather-and-chrome affair. If I hadn't been trapped in my Tummy Tamer, I'd have been sorely tempted to snoop around for more pictures of would-be lovers, but I had no time for that. Shoving the door shut with my shoulder, I began my search.

And for the first time all night, lady luck seemed to be on my side. Inside the very first desk drawer

I pulled open was a bright shiny pair of scissors.

Unfortunately they were the teeny tiny manicure kind. But they were all I could find.

So slowly, agonizingly, I began snipping my way to freedom. The minutes ticked by like decades as I hacked through the ironlike spandex.

By now I looked back fondly on the good old days of Lila's campaign speech.

At last I had snipped my way to the topmost, tightest band of elastic. A few more hacks, and then finally there was just a smidgeon of Tummy Tamer left.

This was it. Freedom was just a snip away!

My fingers stiff from the effort, I snipped my last snip—and sprong! The Tummy Tamer sprang free.

But to my horror, it sprang clear across the room to Peter's bookcase.

My heart sank as I heard the sound of glass breaking.

Oh, hell.

I dashed over to the bookcase, where I discovered that the Tummy Tamer had decapitated a porcelain figurine of Buddha. Poor Buddha's belly was sitting on the shelf, while his head smiled serenely up at me from the carpet.

When I checked the base of the figurine, I saw it was a Limoges. Holy Moses. It must have cost a fortune.

Carefully I balanced Buddha's head back on his belly and shoved the figurine behind a thesaurus, praying Peter wouldn't discover it until I'd had a chance to replace it.

And replace it I would. No way was I going to tell Peter about this unfortunate mishap.

Shuddering at the thought of how much a replacement Buddha would cost, I quickly donned my jeans and went back out into the hallway, where I promptly bumped into Mr. Tarzan.

"There's no other bathroom at the end of the hall," he informed me, loincloth aquiver.

"Really?" I replied, all wide-eyed innocence. "I could've sworn there was. Anyhow, the plumbing problem's all fixed."

Ignoring his dagger gaze, I strolled back into the living room, whistling casually, affecting an air of "What, me, worry?" nonchalance.

But I needn't have bothered. No one was paying the least bit of attention to me.

All eyes were riveted across the street, where police sirens were wailing.

I hurried to the window to see what the commotion was all about when Mrs. Hurlbutt came bursting in the front door.

"Omigod!" she announced with breathless excitement. "Cryptessa Muldoon's just been murdered!"

"No!" Mr. Hurlbutt gasped.

"Yes!" Mrs. Hurlbutt assured him. "Stabbed in the heart with her own DO NOT TRESPASS sign!"

# Chapter 9

Mrs. Hurlbutt's news triggered a minor stampede out the front door, and I raced across the street with the others to get a glimpse of the crime scene. Sure enough, if I peered over the heads of the rapidly swelling crowd, I could see Cryptessa's body sprawled in her doorway, the stake from her DO NOT TRESPASS sign protruding from her heart. A pool of blood was already beginning to clot on her sweat suit.

Emmeline Owens stood nearby in her bathrobe and slippers, her hair in sponge rollers, Lana Turner in her arms.

"I saw the whole thing, Officer," she was telling one of the cops on duty, a handsome black dude with muscles the size of small boulders.

"Someone was banging on Cryptessa's door, making a perfect racket, and woke Lana from her nap. Isn't that right, Lana, honey?" She gave the dog a peck on the nose, then held her out to the cop. "You can pet her if you like; she doesn't mind strangers."

"So someone was banging on Ms. Jenkins's door," he replied, ignoring her invitation to bond with Lana.

"I looked out the window and just assumed it was a trick-or-treater. I felt like telling whoever it was they were wasting their time. Cryptessa wouldn't hand out so much as an apple with a razor blade inside. Would you believe she was the only person on the block who didn't give a dime when I was collecting for the Heart Association?"

"Very upsetting, I'm sure. Now getting back to the murder, ma'am?"

"There's not much to tell. Cryptessa finally came to the door. But before she could open her mouth to say anything, the killer stabbed her. That part was really awful to watch, wasn't it, Lana, honey?"

Lana yawned, clearly not all that traumatized by recent events.

"Can you tell me anything about what the perpetrator looked like, ma'am?"

"Not really. All I know is, it was someone in an ape suit."

At which point several heads swiveled in my direction.

Oh, gulp.


I knew it was only a matter of time before I heard from the police. And sure enough, not an hour after I'd tiptoed home, they came knocking at my door.

The muscle-bound cop who'd questioned Emmeline showed up with his partner to tell me that the detective in charge of the case was at Cryptessa's house and wanted to see me.

As they led me up the street, I saw Mrs. Hurlbutt

practically hanging out her front window to catch all the action.

"They've got her in custody!" I heard her shout to Mr. Hurlbutt.

Oh, well. At least I wasn't wearing handcuffs.

Inside Cryptessa's house, I was ushered into the living room, where a burly redheaded detective was talking on his cell phone.

I just hoped he wasn't ordering a warrant for my arrest.

"It has to be in DVD mode, honey," he was saying. "Just press the button that says DVD. The little green one. Then press PLAY, the big red one. Got it? . . . Great."

He hung up with a sigh.

"We've had the damn machine for seven years, and my wife still can't figure out how to play a DVD."

Hallelujah! No arrest warrant. I was still a free woman.

"Come in, come in," he said, motioning me over to the same seat I sat in when I visited Cryptessa on my condolence call. He sat across from me on a stiff Victorian sofa, while Bela the bat stared down balefully at both of us from his perch on the mantel.

"Detective Casey," my interrogator said, showing me his badge with a genial smile.

I suddenly felt foolish for being so afraid. He seemed like a perfectly pleasant fellow, a chunkier version of the Lucky Charms leprechaun, his pug nose splattered with freckles, his burly bod stuffed into his suit like a freshly packed sausage.

"I suppose you've heard about Ms. Jenkins's murder," he said, breaking the interrogational ice.

"Yes, I have."

"Tragedy," he sighed.

"A tragedy," I echoed, trying to look suitably innocent.

"Such a talented woman," he tsked.

Well, I wouldn't go that far, but I nodded as if I agreed with him.

"I was a real fan of her show when I was a kid," he said, his eyes growing soft at the memory. "Never missed an episode."

So he was the one.

"In fact, I had quite a crush on Cryptessa Muldoon. Helped get me through my adolescence."

Oh, great. The one person in the world who actually liked Cryptessa had the power to arrest me for her murder.

"I intend to track down her killer," he said, a nostalgic fervor burning in his eyes, "if it's the last thing I do. Which brings me to you."

Uh-oh. I didn't like the way this conversation was going. Not one bit.

"Apparently the killer was wearing an ape suit."

"Oh?" I said, as if I hadn't heard Emmeline blab that bit of info to the world.

"And from what several witnesses have told us,

you were the only one at Mr. Connor's party in an ape suit."

"Yes, that's true. But I swear I didn't kill Cryptessa."

"You mean some stranger in an ape suit came along and did her in?"

"That's possible. But more likely it was someone from the party."

"How's that?" he asked, oozing skepticism.

"I was so hot in my costume, I took it off and left it on Peter's bed. Anyone at the party could've seen it there and put it on."

"What time did you take off the ape suit?"

"At about 8:30."

"Ms. Jenkins was killed at a little before nine. Your neighbor, Emmeline Owens, saw the whole thing."

Damn that Emmeline. If she hadn't been such a nosy parker, I wouldn't be sitting here right now.

"So between 8:30 and nine, I'm assuming plenty of people saw you at the party, chatting in your street clothes."

"Well, not exactly."

"Why not?"

"I was, um, otherwise detained."

"What's that supposed to mean?"

The last thing I wanted to do was share the saga of the Tummy Tamer from Hell, but I had no choice.

"I was trapped in my Tummy Tamer."

"Your Tummy Tamer?"

"It's a spandex girdle. When I tried to take it off, my arms got jammed inside and I needed to get out, but all I could find in the bathroom was an electric razor so I had to run to Peter's office in my *Bottoms Up!* panties and cut myself free with tiny manicure scissors, which took forever."

I tend to babble when I'm nervous.

When I was finished, Detective Casey shook his head, boggled.

Even Bela the bat seemed to be giving me the fish eye.

"So let me get this straight. While someone was killing Cryptessa, you were cutting yourself out of a girdle."

"Yes," I nodded, red-faced with embarrassment.

"Got any proof of that?"

"As a matter of fact, I do," I said, pulling out the remains of the Tummy Tamer from where I'd jammed it into my jeans pocket.

"Wait a minute," he said. "That little thing was supposed to fit around your hips?"

"It's ridiculous, isn't it? I plan on reporting these people to the Better Business Bureau for faulty sizing. If I don't get arrested for murder, that is. Haha."

But Detective Casey wasn't laughing.

"So nobody saw you during all that time? No one who can corroborate that you were at the party and not across the street killing your neighbor?"

"Yes!" I cried, remembering Mr. Tarzan. "Someone saw me. One of the other guests at the party. He was waiting to use the bathroom when I first got trapped inside the Tummy Tamer."

Thank heavens! I had an eyewitness who could back up my story. I'd be exonerated in two shakes of a lamb's tail.

"Was this someone," he asked, consulting his notes, "a Mr. Tim Rogers?"

"Tim Rogers?"

"A man in a loincloth. Dressed as Tarzan."

"Yes, Tarzan! That's him."

"According to Mr. Rogers, when he knocked on the bathroom door, you were behaving most suspiciously. And then when he ran into you some twenty minutes later, you seemed equally uneasy. Twenty minutes during which you could have been across the street murdering your neighbor. The same neighbor who was suing you in small claims court for killing her bird, Van Helsing."

No, this conversation was not going well at all.

"Several witnesses," he said, flipping through some more pages, "have confirmed that you and Cryptessa had quite a nasty run-in at Mr. Connor's housewarming party. Involving fudge brownies."

"Okay, so we weren't on the best of terms."

"You were quoted as saying, *Something's got to be done about you, Cryptessa. And I just might be the one to do it.*"

"I may have said something along those lines. But I swear I didn't kill her."

He grunted a most unpleasant grunt.

How on earth could I have ever thought he looked like a leprechaun? The more I looked at him, the more he looked like the sadistic prison warden in *Cool Hand Luke*.

"Just don't leave town," he warned.

I got up to go, and as I walked out of the room, I could practically hear a jail cell door slamming shut behind me.

I was heading up the path to my apartment when Lance came racing out from his apartment.

"Omigosh!" he cried. "You're free. Mrs. Hurlbutt told me they carted you off to jail."

"That'll come any day now, I'm sure. But for tonight, all they did was question me."

"Oh, Jaine! Why did you do it?" he tsked. "You should have come to me. I would've talked you through your anger management issues."

"But, Lance—"

"Fear not, sweetheart. I've got everything under control. I've already lined up one of the finest lawyers in L.A. to defend you."

"But you don't understand—"

"We'll plead insanity—diminished capacity due to your pernicious addiction to Chunky Monkey. It'll go down in legal history as the Chunky Monkey Defense!"

"But—"

"I'll handle everything!" he said, his eyes shining with anticipatory zeal.

Ten to one he was planning what to wear to his first press conference.

"I hate to rain on your parade, Lance," I finally managed to break in, "but I didn't kill Cryptessa."

"You didn't?"

Did I detect a scintilla of disappointment in his voice?

"But Mrs. Hurlbutt told me the killer was wearing an ape suit."

Wearily I told him how I'd taken off the cursed costume and left it on Peter's bed.

"So someone else put it on and killed Cryptessa?" he asked.

"That's the plot as I see it."

"Do you have any idea who could have done it?"

"I figure it's got to be one of our neighbors. None of Peter's friends even knew Cryptessa. Did you notice anyone leaving the party after 8:30?"

"Sorry, hon," he shrugged. "The only one I know who left the party was me."

"You?"

"Peter ran out of ice and I drove over to the supermarket to get some. By the time I got back, Cryptessa was already dead. I'm furious I missed all the action. But on the plus side, Peter was really grateful to me for getting the ice. You should've seen the smile he gave me when he thanked me.

Did you ever notice how white his teeth are? And did he or did he not look hot in those jeans?"

"Lance!" I snapped my fingers. "Let's focus, shall we? The topic under discussion is me and the murder charge looming over my head."

"Not to worry, sweetie," he said, reluctantly tearing himself away from his Prince Charming. "Like I said, I've already lined up an attorney for you. Raoul Duvernois is a legal mastermind. Why, he once got me two grand when I slipped on an anchovy at the California Pizza Kitchen!"

"I don't need a personal injury lawyer, Lance. I need someone who handles murder charges."

"Oh, Raoul does everything. Personal injury, traffic tickets, murder. It says so on all his bus posters."

"Oh, what's the use? I can't afford an attorney anyway."

"No problem, honey. Raoul said he'd take your case pro bono."

For free? The price was sure right.

"Now let Uncle Lance make you a nice cup of hot chocolate," he said, leading me into his apartment, "and I'll tell you about all the fun I had helping Peter clean up after the party."

"Why on earth would I want to sit around and listen to you blather about Peter?"

"I'll throw in some extra marshmallows."

"Okay," I sighed. "Start blathering."

# YOU'VE GOT MAIL!

**To: Jausten**
**From: DaddyO**
**Subject: Travesty of Justice!**

Dearest Lambchop,

Can you believe those idiots on the judging committee gave the Halloween Decoration Trophy to Stinky Pinkus and her idiotic "Ghost Moat"? What a travesty of justice!

I can only conclude that the contest was rigged. Lydia seemed awfully chummy with those judges.

Needless to say, I maintained my composure and conceded defeat graciously, but inside, Lambchop, I was steaming.

Your outraged,

Daddy

PS. I'm not the only one who suspected something fishy was going on. The gal who's staying with Lydia, her old pal from Minnesota, seemed very upset. I saw the two of them exchanging words over by the punch bowl. It can't be pleasant to discover that your old childhood chum is a decorating cheat.

**To: Jausten**
**From: Shoptillyoudrop**
**Subject: Poor Sport**

After all Daddy's fussing and strutting over his silly vampire, guess who won the Halloween decorating contest? Lydia Pinkus. Just like I said she would. The judges thought her "Ghost Moat" was adorable.

Daddy was a dreadful sport about it, grumbling to anyone who'd listen that the contest had been "fixed." The way he was carrying on, you'd think he'd just lost an Oscar.

I pretended I didn't know him and mixed and mingled. I got to meet Lydia's old childhood friend from Minnesota who's staying with her for the week. Irma Decker. Such a lovely woman. She baked the most wonderful strudel for the party. Put my poor sugar cookies to shame.

Anyhow, after a while Daddy calmed down and managed to get through the night without an argument, so I guess you can say that all's well that ended well.

Must run now, darling. Off to the clubhouse to play Scrabble.

Oodles of love from,
Mom

**To: Jausten**
**From: DaddyO**
**Subject: Foul Play**

Just got back from playing Scrabble at the clubhouse. I would've won, too, if your mom hadn't gotten the Q and the Z and both blanks. (Frankly, Lambchop, I think she marks the tiles.)

While we were there, we ran into Stinky Pinkus. I expected her to be her usual insufferable self, gloating about winning the trophy. But she was surprisingly quiet. Uneasy, even.

And then I noticed she was alone. No sign of Irma, her houseguest. When I asked where Irma was, Stinky got all shifty-eyed and mumbled something about how she got called away on a family emergency.

And right away I got suspicious. I remembered how the two of them were arguing at the punchbowl last night. And today, Irma's gone. Just like in *Rear Window* when Raymond Burr argues with his wife. And in the next scene, he's carting her chopped-up body to the East River in his valise!

Frankly, Lambchop, I suspect foul play.
Love 'n' hugs from,
Daddy

**To: Jausten**
**From: Shoptillyoudrop**
**Subject: Unbelievable!**

You're never going to believe this, sweetheart.

It seems that Lydia Pinkus' houseguest was called away on a family emergency, and now Daddy suspects "foul play." As in murder!

He swears he saw the two of them arguing last night, and he actually thinks Lydia may have done away with her best friend.

I knew Daddy would be mad about losing the Halloween decorating contest. I even expected him to accuse Lydia of cheating. But murder? That's a bit over the top. Even for Daddy.

Honestly, I blame it all on those horror movies he's been glued to. After weeks of watching people being hacked, stabbed, and chainsawed to death, his imagination has gone haywire!

I need to get Daddy an appointment with a good psychotherapist ASAP.

Your frantic,
Mom

**To: Jausten**
**From: DaddyO**
**Subject: Ridiculous!**

Your mom wants me to have my head examined! Did you ever hear anything so ridiculous? She can have my head examined by all the doctors she wants. And you know what they'll find up there? Nothing! Absolutely nothing!

XOXO,
Daddy

# Chapter 10

It's never a good sign when your attorney's office is above a massage parlor.

And indeed, that's where I found Raoul Duvernois, Esq.—right above Erotica Massages. ("Where fantasies come true for only $25 an hour!")

Both Raoul and the gang at Erotica were located in one of the seedier parts of Hollywood. I drove over at around ten the next morning and, after parking my car between two hookers, one of whom assured me she swung both ways, made my way to the address Lance had given me.

At first all I saw was the massage parlor and wondered if Lance had somehow screwed up. But then I stood back and saw a window on the second floor etched with the words, RAOUL DUVERNOIS, ATORNEY AT LAW.

(A second sign you're in trouble is when your lawyer spells attorney with only one "t.")

A flight of shabbily carpeted stairs took me past Erotica to Raoul's second-floor "suite." His receptionist, a perky sprite of a thing, sat in a tiny anteroom, engrossed in a copy of *Cosmo*, her lips moving as she read "How to Keep Your Man Happy in Bed."

(I didn't need *Cosmo* to tell me the answer to that one: Give him the remote.)

"Ahem." I cleared my throat to catch her attention.

"Oh, hi!" she said, looking up at me with enormous blue eyes. "May I help you?"

"I'm Jaine Austen. I have an appointment to see Mr. Duvernois."

"Right!" Beaming me a wide smile, she popped up from her desk with a tape measure. "Let me measure you for your neck brace."

"Neck brace? Why would I need a neck brace?"

"For your whiplash."

"But I don't have whiplash."

"You will," she giggled. "Sooner or later, all Raoul's clients wind up with whiplash."

A broad wink accompanied the quote marks she made when she said "whiplash."

Ah, it was good to know integrity was alive and kicking above Erotica Massages.

After having my neck measured, I was ushered to a plastic waiting chair and spent the next several minutes scratching a rash that seemed to have developed on my left forearm. Probably an allergic reaction to that damn ape suit.

As I sat there scratching, I pondered the e-mails from my parents I'd been foolish enough to read earlier that morning.

I was not at all surprised Daddy suspected Lydia Pinkus of foul play. Over the years, Daddy had accused the poor woman of everything from cheating at shuffleboard to rigging homeowner association elections. It was only a matter of time before he upped the ante to murder.

And not for one minute did I think Mom would get Daddy to see a shrink. Not after what happened the last time she tried. After just one session, high doses of sedatives were required. For the shrink, that is. Daddy just drove off to the Dairy Queen and had a banana split.

In the midst of my musings, Raoul Duvernois's door swung open and the great man himself came sweeping out from his office to greet me. A grand entrance if I ever saw one.

"Bonjour, Mamselle Austen!" he gushed, reeking of aftershave.

Lithe and rail thin, his black hair slicked back to a patent-leather shine, he looked like he should've been dancing the tango with a rose clenched between his teeth.

His offices may have been in one of the seedier sections of Los Angeles, but Raoul certainly hadn't stinted on his clothing budget, clad in a designer suit and silk tie that no doubt cost more than my Corolla.

I guess the wages of whiplash really paid off.

"What a pleasure to meet you!" he said, tucking my arm into his and ushering me into his office.

He must've run out of money when he finished buying his tie, because his office looked like it came straight from the Goodwill—with a battered desk, corroding metal file cabinet, and two upholstered visitors' chairs, both sporting a dubious assortment of brownish stains.

"Have a seat," he said, pointing to one of the chairs.

He nimbly sprinted behind his desk and lowered himself into a swivel chair that had probably last been used by Clarence Darrow.

I sat down on what I fervently hoped was not a wad of chewing gum, and glanced around. Over in the corner I noticed a pile of neck braces and, on Raoul's desk, a pile of Handicapped automobile placards. Peeking out from under a stack of papers was a copy of the *Daily Racing Form*.

"Can I get you anything?" he asked, shooting me an oily smile.

*Another attorney would be nice.*

"No, thanks, I'm fine."

"Lance tells me you're in trouble with the police."

"I'm afraid they think I may have murdered Cryptessa—I mean, Eleanor Jenkins."

"What makes you say that?"

I told him the whole story, about leaving my ape suit on Peter's bed and getting trapped in the Tummy Tamer and then finding out that Cryptessa had been killed by someone in an ape suit.

As I talked, Raoul nodded sympathetically, taking copious notes.

A ray of hope began to glimmer on the horizon. Maybe this guy knew his stuff after all.

When I was through, he put down his Erotica Massage ballpoint pen and shot me a confident smile.

"Have no fear, Jaine. I think we have a lawsuit here."

"A lawsuit?"

"Yes!" He jumped up and grabbed a neck brace from the pile in the corner. "When you were struggling out of that Tummy Tamer, I bet you sprained your neck. We'll sue those bastards for all they're worth!"

"But what about the murder charge?"

"Oh, that," he said with an airy wave of his hand. "I'll think of something to get you off the hook."

This guy had to be kidding.

"Are you actually licensed to practice law?" I finally had the guts to ask.

"In Guatemala, yes."

"But we're in Los Angeles now."

"What the judge doesn't know won't hurt him," he replied with a throaty chuckle. "Now, c'mon. Let's get you fitted for that brace."

Needless to say, I did not take Raoul's neck brace. Or his business card. Or his $10 Off coupon for an Erotica Massage.

What a colossal waste of time this had been, I thought as I stomped back to my Corolla. Raoul Duvernois would be as much help to me in court as a zit on prom night.

Heading home, I turned on the radio, checking the news stations for stories on Cryptessa's murder. But all I heard was chatter about a fire in El Segundo, a robbery in Bel Air, and the Scandal du Jour at City Hall.

I'd been afraid Cryptessa's murder would be splashed all over the newspapers that morning—a front-page story with my ghastly driver's license photo beneath the headline:

FREELANCE WRITER GOES BERSERK,
KILLS AGGRAVATING NEIGHBOR

But stuck as she was at the bottom of the Hollywood food chain, Cryptessa did not rate page one coverage. The story of her murder had been tucked away on page five of the metro section. Just a few sentences about how former sitcom actress Eleanor Jenkins had been stabbed outside her home by an assailant in a gorilla costume.

According to the story, the police were following several leads and were asking anyone with information about the identity of the assailant to contact Detective Brian Casey of the Beverly Hills Police Department.

Thank heavens there'd been no mention of *moi*.

But that still didn't mean I was off the hook. Far from it.

I remembered that fishy glare Detective Casey

had lobbed me when he warned me not to leave town.

I was a hot suspect, all right. And I certainly could not depend on Raoul, my Franco-Guatemalan ambulance chaser, to clear my name.

It looked like I'd just have to do a little investigating on my own.

(You should know that I've solved a bunch of homicides in my day—stirring sagas of murder, mayhem, and Chunky Monkey binges. All of which you can read about in the titles listed at the front of this book.)

As I told Lance, I'd pretty much ruled out Peter's friends and coworkers as suspects. Which left the small band of neighbors who'd shown up at the Halloween party. All of them had grudges against the former sitcom zombie. All of them had witnessed my blowup with her at Peter's house-warming. And all of them had access to my ape suit.

So which one of them decided to take advantage of my fight with Cryptessa to frame me for her murder?

I decided to start my investigation with the Hurlbutts.

Hadn't Mrs. Hurlbutt been the one who raced into Peter's house with the news of Cryptessa's murder? What had she been doing outside anyway? Driving a stake in Cryptessa's heart, perchance?

After a pit stop at my apartment for a pizza bagel and minced mackerel guts (the mackerel guts were for Prozac—and so was a good chunk of the pizza bagel), I headed across the street and rang the Hurlbutts' bell.

Mrs. Hurlbutt came to the door in a turquoise jogging suit, her impossibly red hair sprayed into a stiff *Here's Lucy* bob.

Her eyes widened in surprise at the sight of me.

"Jaine, what are you doing here? You out on bail?"

"No, I'm not out on bail. I was never arrested."

"But I saw the cops taking you away last night."

"They just wanted to ask me a few questions, and then they let me go."

"Oh." It was clear from her tone of voice she thought the cops had made a major mistake.

"Well?" she said, making no move to invite me in.

"I was hoping I could talk to you and Mr. Hurlbutt for a few minutes."

"All right," she said, grudgingly. "But we were just in the middle of lunch, and I don't have enough for you."

Emily Post, eat your heart out.

I followed her into her 1970s kitchen with its avocado-green appliances and a dishtowel from the Grand Canyon hanging from the oven door.

Mr. H. was seated at a table for two in the corner, eating what looked like a most delicious tuna noodle casserole. A huge dish of the stuff sat in the center of the table.

Mrs. Hurlbutt plopped down across from him, leaving me standing there.

"Can I get you a seat?" Mr. Hurlbutt had the decency to ask.

"No, Harold," Mrs. H. decreed. "She's just staying a few minutes."

I must have been staring at his casserole because Mr. Hurlbutt then asked, "You want some?"

Mrs. Hurlbutt shot him a withering glare.

"If we give her some, we won't have enough for lunch tomorrow, and I want it to last two days."

"Really, that's okay." I smiled a smile meant exclusively for Mr. Hurlbutt. "I'm fine."

"So what did you want to talk about?" Mrs. Hurlbutt asked.

"Cryptessa's murder."

"If you ask me," Mrs. Hurlbutt said with a righteous sniff, "it's karma. Payback for Cryptessa killing my tulips."

The scary thing is she meant it. She actually thought that tulip-o-cide was grounds for capital punishment. Which made me wonder once again if Mrs. H. was indeed the killer.

I suddenly flashed on the day I was cleaning my car and saw Mrs. H. stabbing the slugs in her garden. How ferociously she'd gone at them with her hoe. All because they'd had the temerity to invade her flower bed. Had she gone after Cryptessa in a similar rage?

"I'm afraid the police think I did it," I said.

"Did you?" she asked, with her usual sledge-hammer tact.

"Of course not!"

"I told you she didn't do it," Mr. H. piped up.

"That's the trouble with you, Harold. You always think the best of people."

"Last night at the party," I said, wrenching the conversation back on topic, "I left my ape suit on Peter's bed, and someone else wore it to kill Cryptessa."

"So that's your story, huh?" Mrs. H. smirked, oozing skepticism.

It was all I could do not to shove that tuna noodle casserole up her wazoo.

"Anyhow, I was wondering if either of you saw anybody going into the hallway to Peter's bedroom?"

"Yes, of course," Mrs. H. said, scooping up a forkful of casserole. "I saw you. You hightailed it there right after you saddled us with that gasbag Lila Wood. Which I didn't appreciate one little bit, I don't mind saying."

"Did you see anyone aside from me go down the hallway?"

"No, it was hard to see much with Lila yapping in my face."

"What about you, Mr. Hurlbutt?"

But Mrs. Hurlbutt cut him off before he could get a word in.

"Harold, the traitor, ran off to the buffet and left me stranded with Lila. Said he'd be right back with some cold cuts, but that was the last I saw of him until after Cryptessa was murdered."

Very interesting. So the Hurlbutts had been separated. Which meant that either one of them could have slipped away to kill Cryptessa.

"I told you I got caught up in a conversation with Matt Moore," Mr. Hurlbutt said, blushing a deep red. "And no," he added, turning to me, "I didn't see anyone go down the hallway. Aside from you, that is."

"Can you two think of anyone—*other than me*—who might have killed Cryptessa?"

"If I had to guess," Mrs. Hurlbutt said, "I'd say Emmeline Owens. She hated Cryptessa with a passion, ever since Cryptessa threw that lemon at her dog."

"But Emmeline couldn't have done it," Mr. Hurlbutt said. "She wasn't even at Peter's party. How would she have gotten hold of Jaine's ape suit?"

"Oh, Harold. You're so naïve. Who's to say the killer was even wearing an ape suit?"

Mrs. H. was right of course. We only had Emmeline's word for that. For all we knew, Emmeline could have made up that whole ape suit story to save her own fanny.

"Yes," said Mrs. Hurlbutt, nodding, "the killer could very well be Emmeline Owens. Isn't that right, Harold?"

She turned and shot him a look of such steely intensity I thought she'd drill a hole through his skull.

"Right, dear," Mr. H. nodded, squirming in his seat.

Beads of sweat had broken out along his brow, and glancing down, I saw he'd torn his paper napkin into tiny shreds.

Mr. Hurlbutt was clearly not a happy camper.

Was it because he knew Cryptessa's killer was his own wife?

Or, worse, because he'd done the dirty deed himself?

# Chapter 11

I had a hard time believing Emmeline was the killer—mainly because she weighed about ninety-two pounds soaking wet. I doubted she had the strength to open a pickle jar, let alone plunge a stake in Cryptessa's heart.

And yet Cryptessa had hurled a lethal lemon at her beloved Lana Turner. Surely that might be a motive for murder. What's more, I remembered how furious Emmeline had been when she'd accused Cryptessa of eating her birthday chocolates. She certainly seemed ready to kill her then.

So I decided to pop by her house and question her. At the very least, maybe I could pick up some leads.

Unlike Mrs. Hurlbutt, Emmeline welcomed me with open arms.

"Why, Jaine! How lovely to see you!"

She stood there in the doorway, a china doll in a gingham Capri set, her silvery hair framing her face in a Dutch bob.

"What perfect timing!" she cried. "I just took a batch of sugar cookies from the oven."

Indeed I could smell the heavenly aroma of vanilla wafting through the house.

She led the way to her living room, a white wicker-and-chintz affair, replete with tiny footstools and silk flowers sprouting from teapots—all very Tea Time at Laura Ashley's.

Dominating the room was a large oil portrait hanging over the fireplace. In it, a much younger Emmeline sat alongside a handsome Tyrone Power-esque man.

"That's me and my dear, departed husband, Xavier," Emmeline said, following my gaze.

"You make a beautiful couple."

"Thank you," she said, her eyes lingering on her handsome husband. "Xavier was the love of my life."

At which point, the ball of white fur that had been snoring on the sofa sprang to attention and gave a petulant yip.

"Aside from you, Lana, darling!" Emmeline hastened to assure her bichon. "You're the love of my life, too."

Having mollified Lana, she turned her attention back to me.

"Make yourself comfortable, Jaine," she said, waving me to a hibiscus-covered armchair, "while I fix us some tea."

"Let me help."

"No, no. You just stay here and make friends with Lana Turner."

With that, she picked up the dog and dumped it in my lap.

"Don't worry," she trilled as she trotted off. "She hardly ever bites."

Alone with the dog, I smiled feebly.

Lana growled in return, baring a set of rather frightening little fangs.

"Nice doggie!" I simpered, wondering if rabies shots were as painful as people said.

Then, to my surprise, she rolled over in my lap and offered me her belly.

Tentatively I reached down to pet her, hoping I wasn't about to lose a finger or two. I needn't have worried. With the first stroke, she gave a moan of doggie ecstasy.

It took Emmeline a good ten minutes to rustle up that tea, every second of which I spent stroking Lana. If I dared to stop, she bared her teeth and growled at me most unpleasantly, Cujo with a hair bow.

At last, just as carpal tunnel syndrome was about to set in, Emmeline came trotting back with the tea and cookies and swooped Lana from my lap, relieving me of belly rub duty.

"Have a cookie, dear!" she urged, nodding at a plate of golden, sugar-dusted cookies.

I was more than happy to oblige.

One luscious, buttery bite and my aching wrist was quickly forgotten.

I happily chomped it down and reached for another.

It felt good to break away from chocolate for a change and give other calories a chance to frolic on my hips.

I was having such a good time ingesting empty calories that I almost forgot why I'd stopped by. Until Emmeline, smiling brightly, said:

"So you're out of jail already! I knew you couldn't have killed Cryptessa."

I did not bother to correct her. Clearly Mrs. H. had been working overtime, spreading the word about my "arrest" to anyone with half an earlobe.

"If you ask me," Emmeline said, feeding a morsel of cookie to Lana, "the killer is Helen Hurlbutt."

I wisely refrained from mentioning that Mrs. Hurlbutt had just been saying the same thing about her.

"Helen went absolutely crazy when she thought Cryptessa poisoned her tulips. Came tearing over to her house, screaming bloody murder. I couldn't help overhearing, of course."

"Of course," I murmured.

I could just see Emmeline standing at her front window catching the action with a pair of binoculars.

"I honestly thought Helen was going to kill Cryptessa right then and there. *I'll get you for this,* she told her, shaking her fist. *Just wait. One day you'll pay for what you did!*"

Well, how do you like that? If one were inclined (and I sure was), one could interpret that as a death threat.

"But Cryptessa just snickered and slammed the

135

door in her face. If only she'd apologized, she might still be alive today." A pregnant pause to scratch Lana behind her ears. "Although confidentially," she added, "I can't help thinking that life will be so much more pleasant without her. You can't imagine how miserable it's been having Cryptessa as a neighbor—stealing my chocolates, throwing lemons at Lana. And that godawful typing of hers, at all hours of the day and night. Working on that silly novel of hers.

"Yes," she sighed, "it's a tragedy she's gone, but I can't say I'll miss her."

By now Lana had gotten her fill of love scratches and had ambled under the coffee table where she was hard at work gnawing on a chew toy.

"It must have been terrible for you, though," I said, coaxing her back to the murder, "witnessing Cryptessa's death."

"Oh, yes," she assured me, biting down on a sugar cookie with gusto. "Just terrible."

"Did the killer say anything at all before killing her?"

"No, not a thing. Just took aim and stabbed her in the chest."

"So you couldn't even hear if it was a man or a woman?"

"No, like I told the police, all I know is, it was someone in an ape suit."

So much for leads.

"Well, thanks for the cookies," I said, getting up to go. "They were delicious."

At which point, Lana started yipping angrily at the sofa.

"Naughty Lana," Emmeline said, springing up from her chair. "You pushed your chew toy under the sofa again, didn't you? Now Mommy has to get it out."

"I'll get it," I offered.

The last thing Emmeline needed was to be crawling down on her knees. Not at her age.

I kneeled down in front of the sofa to reach in and get the toy—hoping it wasn't drenched in dog spit—but it was just out of my grasp.

"Not a problem," Emmeline said. "This happens all the time."

And then, with the strength of a sumo wrestler, that little slip of a woman lifted one end of the very heavy sofa so I could grab the toy.

Good heavens. Emmeline Owens was a lot stronger than she looked. Strong enough, certainly, to have rammed that stake in Cryptessa's heart. But, no. Someone who baked such delicious sugar cookies couldn't possibly be capable of murder.

Could she?


"Jaine, honey. I've got the most exciting news ever!"

I was sitting across from Kandi in the living room of her Westwood condo.

Kandi lives in one of the many New York–style high rises that line Wilshire Boulevard, like Park Avenue with palm trees. On a clear day, you can see the Pacific from her living-room window.

She calls it the condo that *Beanie & The Cockroach* built.

I'd received a call from her late that afternoon summoning me to her place for a pizza dinner, where she promised she'd share a late-breaking news bulletin. She'd refused to breathe a word of her good news, however, until I was settled on her plush chenille sofa, a glass of cabernet in hand, a box of pizza between us.

Her half of the pizza, ordered from one of those upscale Italian restaurants Kandi's so fond of, was a ghastly combo of arugula and sun-dried tomatoes. Mine, thank heavens, was a gooey mozzarella and barbeque chicken, studded with sweet red onion slices.

She knew me well.

"I'm so excited," she said, practically bouncing off the ceiling, "I can hardly eat."

A state of mind I've yet to experience.

"I've waited long enough," I said, popping a piece of onion in my mouth. "Are you going to tell me your news before or after I reach menopause?"

"Madame Vruska was right!" She grinned in triumph.

"Madame Vruska?"

"The fortune teller."

Ah, yes. The seeress right next to Kandi's nail salon.

"Remember how she predicted I'd meet my true love in the arts?"

"Vaguely," I said, tearing myself away from a particularly luscious glob of mozzarella.

"Well," she beamed, "her prediction came true! I met him!"

Before you go shopping for a wedding present, I should tell you that Kandi, like Lance, meets Mr. Right with the frequency of a public radio pledge drive.

"How nice." I smiled wanly. "What's he like?"

"His name is Steve and he's a podiatrist at the Santa Monica Foot and Ankle Institute."

"Wait a minute. How is a podiatrist an artist?"

"Madame Vruska didn't actually say he'd be an artist. All she said was that I'd meet him *in the arts*. And I did. I met him in the parking lot of the county art museum. Even though, technically, Steve wasn't going to the museum. He was just parking his car there while he grabbed a burger at the restaurant across the street. But the thing is, we did meet in the arts. Right?"

"Right."

I was not about to be the one to bust her bubble. Life would take care of that soon enough.

"I'm telling you, Madame Vruska is sheer genius. Which is why I've set up an appointment for you."

"Me?"

"Yes, you. You need some guidance to get your life on track. And don't worry. It's my treat."

"That's very thoughtful of you, but I don't want guidance from someone who sees the future in a cup of Lipton's."

"Madame Vruska doesn't read tea leaves," she said, sniffing in disdain. "She reads coffee grounds."

"Oh. Coffee grounds. That makes all the difference."

She failed to detect my irony.

"Really, Kandi, it's very sweet of you, but I don't want to—"

"Enough!" She held up a hand. "You're going. I insist! Say yes," she commanded, grabbing the pizza box, "or you don't get any more pizza."

"I'm not going to see Madame Vruska, and if you think you can bribe me with a piece of pizza, you're sadly mistaken."

And if you believe I really said that, go straight to the back of the class and put on your dunce cap.

"Okay, okay, I'll go," were the words you should've guessed I uttered.

Kandi smiled, satisfied, and released the pizza from captivity.

"Now enough about me," she said. "How did everything work out at Peter's Halloween party? Did you make a big impression in your Tummy Tamer?"

"Oh, I made a big impression, all right. Not on Peter, but on the Beverly Hills Police Department."

"What on earth happened?"

And I told her all about it. How Lance double-crossed me and rented me an ape suit instead of my flapper outfit and how I got trapped in the Tummy Tamer and left my ape suit on the bed and how the killer wore it to stab Cryptessa and how the cops thought I did it because Cryptessa was suing me in small claims court for the death of her parakeet.

When I was finished, she shook her head, aghast.

"You cut yourself out of the Tummy Tamer? Why on earth would you do that? It takes inches off your hips and thighs!"

"Forget the damn Tummy Tamer, Kandi. The cops think I killed Cryptessa."

"That's absurd," she said, dismissing the charge with a wave of her as-yet-uneaten arugula and sun-dried tomato pizza. "And we can prove you didn't do it."

"We can?"

"Absolutely!"

"How?" I asked, wondering if she'd had a Sherlock Holmesian burst of insight into the case.

"Madame Vruska, of course. With her amazing psychic gifts, she'll figure out who the killer is."

And to show you how desperate I was, for a minute I allowed myself to hope that Kandi was right.

Could Kandi's fortune teller possibly lead me to the killer?

If not, at least she could grind me a good cup of coffee.

# Chapter 12

Bright and early the next morning, while I was still in my robe and jammies, the police showed up with a search warrant.

Soon a team of Beverly Hills's finest were rifling through my apartment doing their best to re-enact a small tornado. I figured they were looking for the ape suit, which—I gleaned from bits and pieces of scattered cop chat—seemed to have vanished into thin air.

Needless to say, they didn't find the ape suit in my apartment, but they were treated to the unforgettable sight of my *Bottoms Up!* undies, which Prozac was thoughtful enough to retrieve from my hamper and drop at their feet.

All in all, a most depressing experience.

And things were about to get worse.

Because no sooner had the cops left than the phone rang.

"Ms. Austen?" A raspy, cigarette-clogged voice came on the line. "This is Estelle Santos calling."

"Who?"

"Estelle, from Estelle's Costume Shop. According to my records, you were supposed to return your ape suit yesterday. Any chance you can bring it back this afternoon?"

"I'm afraid that won't be possible. You see, it's . . . um . . . missing."

"Whatever. Accidents happen. Not a problem, hon."

Gee, she was being awfully sweet about this.

"I'll just charge your credit card two hundred and sixty-five dollars for a replacement ape suit."

"Two hundred and sixty-five dollars?"

"It says right on your credit card receipt: If you lose it, you replace it."

Frantically I rummaged through my purse till I found the credit slip from Estelle's Costume Shop. There it was in tiny letters at the bottom of the receipt: *Any lost costumes to be replaced at customer's expense.*

"Well, enjoy the rest of your day!" And with a raspy chortle, Estelle hung up.

Oh, dear. The last thing my poor anemic credit card needed was another two hundred and sixty-five dollars on its back.

But I did not have time to sit around and stew about mounting credit card debt, because just then the phone rang with yet another piece of poop for my fan.

This time it was Marvin Cooper.

"Hey, Jaine. How're the Larry Lumbar spots coming?"

I hadn't touched them in days.

"I'm almost done," I fibbed.

"Good. Then fax 'em to me by the end of the day, okay?"

"Will do."

I hung up with a groan. I really had to knuckle down and get to work. And I would. Just as soon as I fortified myself with a nutritious breakfast of Double Stuf Oreos.

I raced to my cupboard in the vain hopes that I'd find a package of the little darlings. But of course I didn't.

Here at Casa Austen, cookies tend to have a notoriously short life span.

For a brief instant I considered chowing down on leftover Halloween candy. But I could not allow myself to stoop that low. Mainly because, several days ago, I'd tossed said candy in the garbage, determined to be as sylphlike as possible for my grand entrance at Peter's party.

My cupboards, alas, were depressingly chocolate-free.

And so fifteen minutes later, I was at my local supermarket's cookie aisle, tossing the coveted Double Stuf Oreos into my basket. While I was there, I decided to pick up some lettuce, apples, and Chunky Monkey.

The lettuce and apples were only for show, of course, to convince the checker I was a sensible eater and not the kind of person who came charging into the market on emergency Double Stuf Oreo runs.

I was heading over to the produce section to pick up my decoy apples when I heard:

"Yoo hoo, Jaine!"

Looking up, I saw Lila Wood chugging my way, her stocky bod jammed into a polyester pantsuit, sensible low heeled pumps clacking on the linoleum.

Her cart, I saw, was stocked with low-fat cottage cheese and Healthy Choice dinners. Tucked away in a corner was what she'd really come for: a quart of fudge ripple ice cream.

"So glad to see you're out of jail!" she trilled.

Damn that Mrs. Hurlbutt and her big mouth.

"Did they actually book you and take your mug shot?" Lila asked breathlessly. "You don't have a criminal record, do you?"

"No, Lila. I was never arrested. And I haven't been charged with a thing."

"How wonderful!" she beamed. "So you can still vote?"

"Of course I can still vote."

"Great. Then I'll count on your support in the neighborhood council election. Remember: A Vote for Wood is a Vote for Good!"

With that she whipped out a flyer from her purse and shoved it in my hand.

"Here's some vital information about the unscrupulous developer who wants to build that dreadful mini-mall at the end of the street. Rumor has it he's going to rent out space to a tattoo parlor!"

I glanced down at the flyer and saw a grainy photo of a round-faced bald guy, under the headline: RALPH MANCUSO, BUILDER WITHOUT A CONSCIENCE!

"Here's some pictures of Mancuso's other properties," Lila said, shoving another piece of paper in my hand. "You can see for yourself what terrible buildings he puts up. Never properly maintained, always a blight on the neighborhood! We have to stop him before he ruins our block!"

"Of course," I said, tsking as if I cared.

As eager as I was to dig into my Oreos, I decided to take advantage of my meeting with Lila to question her about the murder.

"Speaking of bad things happening in the neighborhood," I said when her monologue about the Evils of Ralph Mancuso finally ran out of steam, "what a tragedy about poor Cryptessa, huh?"

She shot me a skeptical look. "I wouldn't go that far, dear. Unfortunate, maybe. Tragic, not so much. After all, the woman's house was a trip to trashy town. All it needed was a car parked on the front lawn."

"Still," I persisted, "her death was quite a shock."

"Oh, yes. I just hope our property values don't go down, what with a murder on the block."

Quite the sensitive soul, wasn't she?

"Did you happen to notice anyone leaving

Peter's party around the time of the murder?" I asked, wrenching the conversation away from property values.

"I saw you," she said, "sneaking down the hallway."

If she expected to get my vote, she certainly wasn't going about it the right way.

"Aside from me," I huffed.

"Let me think." She paused to scratch her head with a stubby finger.

"Now that I think of it, I did see someone leave the party."

At last! A lead!

"Who?"

"Your neighbor, Lance. Do you think he killed Cryptessa?" she asked, thrilled at the idea.

"No, he was just going out to get some ice. Can you think of anyone else who—"

"Oh, look!" she cried, staring over my shoulder. "It's the Franklins from around the corner. I really must run and say hello. Don't forget! Vote for Lila Wood—And Keep the Bad Out of the Hood!"

With that, she grabbed her cart and charged off to corner the poor, unsuspecting Franklins.

For a fleeting instant, I wondered if Lila could've possibly killed Cryptessa in a misguided attempt to beautify our block.

Nah. The woman was a crashing bore, but homicidal? I didn't think so.

Shoving her to the bottom of my suspect list, I trotted off to get my apples and lettuce—along with some cortisone cream for that itch on my arm. It still hadn't gone away.

Just another cursed memento of my Halloween from Hell.

# Chapter 13

Four hours and a disgraceful number of Oreos later, I put the finishing touches on the Larry Lumbar spots and faxed them off to Marvin.

"Thank heavens that's over," I said, leaning back in my chair.

Prozac, who'd spent most of the afternoon curled up next to my computer, her tail occasionally flicking across the keyboard (she likes being part of the creative process), rolled over on her back and gazed up at me lazily.

*Yes, now you can devote the rest of the day to rubbing my belly.*

"Sorry, Pro," I said, after giving her belly a couple of halfhearted swipes. "Mommy has to clean the apartment."

She narrowed her eyes into angry little slits.

*It's always about you, isn't it?*

Ignoring her baleful glare, I spent the rest of the afternoon cleaning the mess the police had so considerately left in their wake that morning.

Finally, when all was back in order, I settled down on my sofa with a much-deserved glass of chardonnay. As I sat there, sipping (okay, gulping) my wine, my mind kept drifting back to Cryptessa's murder and what I'd learned so far in my investigation.

Lila had been no help whatsoever. All she cared about was that silly neighborhood council election. But what a surprise about Emmeline, huh? Lifting up her heavy sofa like it was a feather duster. She certainly had the strength to plunge that stake in Cryptessa's heart. But had she really done it? Had she never forgiven Cryptessa for trying to kill Lana Turner?

And then there were the Hurlbutts. Mrs. Hurlbutt said she and Mr. Hurlbutt lost sight of each other at the Halloween party. Which meant that either one of them could have sneaked off and killed Cryptessa.

Mrs. Hurlbutt was the person I'd like most to see behind bars, but what about Mr. Hurlbutt? He said he'd been chatting with Matt Moore when he left Mrs. Hurlbutt. But I remembered how uncomfortable he looked when he said it.

Maybe it was time to pay a little trip to the Moores and check out his alibi.

I looked at my watch and saw it was after six. With any luck, they'd be home from work.

The Moores' house, like Cryptessa's, was a Spanish beauty. But unlike Cryptessa's, theirs was fastidiously maintained, with fresh paint, gleaming red-tiled roof, and a lawn fertilized to velvety perfection.

I rang the bell and heard the muffled sound of chimes from inside.

Seconds later, Kevin Moore came to the door,

still in her biz-gal togs, not a single ash-blond hair out of place.

She looked me up and down, clearly not impressed with what she saw.

"Sorry. We're not interested in any magazine subscriptions."

"I'm not selling magazines," I hastened to explain. "I'm Jaine Austen. Your neighbor from down the street. We met at Peter Connor's house-warming party."

Another once-over and recognition set in.

"Oh, right. You're the renter."

I looked for signs of neighborly hospitality, but I looked in vain.

Any second now, I'd be feeling the breeze of a door slamming in my face. And something told me Kevin Moore wasn't about to sit around answering questions about the murder. I had to think of another way to get past that front door.

"I was hoping to have a word with you—"

"Actually now's not a good time."

"—about buying a condo."

Just like that, she morphed from Ice Queen to Miss Congeniality.

"Come in! Come in!" she gushed, all smiles.

I followed her through her foyer to her living room, watching the bright pink soles of her Christian Louboutin shoes clack against her peg-and-groove hardwood floors.

There was a time I would not have known a

Louboutin from a lobotomy, but thanks to endless episodes of *The Real Housewives of Beverly Hills*, I happen to know what they look like. I also happen to know they cost about a thousand bucks a pop.

Either the Moores were doing a great job in real estate, or they were doing a great job faking it.

"Look who's here, Matt!" Kevin called out. "Our darling neighbor from down the street. Jean Austen."

Matt Moore looked up from where he was sitting on a sleek taupe sofa in their Ethan Allen showroom of a living room.

"But I thought you were in jail," he said.

"No, no," I assured them. "I'm free as a bird. Absolutely innocent. Had nothing whatsoever to do with Cryptessa's death."

He shot me a skeptical look, quickly snatching up a tiny knife from a plate of hors d'oeuvres on the coffee table.

Good heavens. Did he honestly think I was going to stab him with a cheese knife?

"Jean wants to buy a condo!" Kevin announced.

The magic words. Suddenly Matt was all smiles. Who cared if I was a suspected murderer, as long as I could sign the escrow papers?

"Fabulous!" he beamed. "We can get you into a one-bedroom Beverly Hills Adjacent for only four hundred grand!"

Yikes. For four hundred grand, I could buy a city in the Czech Republic.

"And just forty thousand down," Kevin added.

"Quite the bargain," I said, not bothering to mention I was about $39,950 short on the required cash.

"Sit down, won't you?" said Kevin, guiding me to an armchair across from the sofa. "Have some sashimi."

She picked up the plate of hors d'oeuvres from the coffee table and held it out to me. On it, I now saw, were nothing but blobs of slimy raw fish.

"No, thanks," I gulped. "They look dee-lish, but I just ate."

"Have some wine, then," Matt said.

And before I knew it, he was pouring me a glass of a pinot grigio that I'd seen at Costco for twenty-seven bucks a bottle. And if it cost twenty-seven bucks at Costco, heaven only knew how much it cost in real life.

Needless to say, I would have no trouble chugging that stuff down.

"So what are you looking for?" Matt asked.

I was on the verge of saying, "Cryptessa's killer" when I realized he was talking about the condo I supposedly wanted to buy.

"Let's see," I mused. "One bedroom, with a balcony, granite countertops, stainless steel appliances, working fireplace."

As long as I was lying, I might as well lie with stainless steel appliances.

"We'll get on it right away," Kevin assured me. "And we'll call you as soon as we've lined up some properties."

Oh, dear. A sinking sensation came over me as I realized I'd just unleashed a pair of realtors into my life. Once they think they've got a potential sale, Los Angeles realtors have been known to cling to their clients like crazed Tummy Tamers.

"Take your time," I demurred. "There's no rush. Honest."

"Oh, no!" Matt said, shooting me a buttery smile. "We'll get you into that condo by Christmas."

"Well, it's been great talking to you, Jean," Kevin said, starting to get up. "Thanks so much for stopping by."

My cue to leave. But I couldn't go. Not yet. Not until I questioned them about the murder.

"Maybe I will have one of these sashimi," I said, reaching for a slimy pink glob.

"It's absolutely fabulous," Matt said.

I took a tiny bite.

Now, I've never actually eaten one of Mrs. Hurlbutt's slugs, but I'm guessing they taste a lot like the Moores' sashimi. With great effort, I managed to swallow.

"Yum!" I smiled weakly.

Then, holding the sashimi aloft as if poised to

take another bite, I said, "Such a shame about Cryptessa."

"A real shame," Matt echoed.

"She certainly didn't deserve to die the way she did," Kevin tsked.

To my surprise, they both seemed to mean it.

"She was an impossible neighbor," Kevin said, "but she was a human being, after all."

"Well, almost," Matt added with a chuckle. "I still can't believe she cut down our hedges while we were away on vacation."

I looked for signs of rancor in their eyes, but I saw none.

"Do you have any idea who could have killed her?"

"Not a clue." Matt shrugged.

"The police seem to think it was someone from Peter's Halloween party," Kevin said. "That's what they said when they came over to ask us some questions."

"Speaking of Peter's party," I piped up, grateful for the opening, "Mr. Hurlbutt mentioned he had a nice chat with Matt that night."

"Mr. Hurlbutt?" Matt seemed puzzled.

"You know, honey," Kevin said. "The bald guy with the gossipy wife."

"Oh, that guy," Matt said. "No, I didn't talk with him at the party. Gee, I wonder if they want to sell their house."

Whoa. If Mr. Hurlbutt hadn't been chatting with

Matt during the time he'd left his wife, what *had* he been doing?

Slipping into my ape suit, perhaps?

"I guess I'd better be shoving off," I said, getting up to go.

"Aren't you going to finish your sashimi?" Kevin asked.

Oh, hell. I was still holding the damn thing.

"No, it's too good to eat all at once. I'll save it for later."

And with that, I hustled out the door, wondering if mild-mannered Mr. Hurlbutt was indeed the killer.

# Chapter 14

Okay, so Mr. Hurlbutt had been AWOL for several pivotal minutes at Peter's party. During which time he could have easily nipped across the street to kill Cryptessa.

But why?

He didn't seem like the type who'd go ballistic over some dead tulips. Was he acting on orders from his wife? If so, why had he lied to her about chatting with Matt? Why not just say, "Honey, I was across the street killing Cryptessa like you told me to. Now can we get some shrimp puffs at the buffet?"

These were the questions bouncing around in my brain as I headed down my front path early the next morning.

My questions came to a screeching halt, however, at the sight of Peter Connor walking toward me, looking très adorable in a T-shirt and shorts.

For a bordering-on-skinny guy, he had marvelously muscular thighs.

Reluctantly I wrenched my eyes away from his bod. I really had to get a hold of myself. I didn't stand a snowball's chance in hell of dating this guy. Aside from the obvious difference in our Desirability Rankings, there was the pesky little matter of me being a murder suspect. Not to mention the fact that I'd recently decapitated his Limoges Buddha figurine.

(Which, in all the hoo-ha of the murder, I'd forgotten all about replacing.)

"There's something I need to talk to you about," he said, looking very solemn.

Oh, Lord. What if he'd found the busted Buddha and figured out I'd done it? What if he'd seen me dashing into his office? What if he'd been coming to my apartment to demand reparations?

"Oh?" I said, affecting an air of stilted nonchalance.

"I heard how the cops brought you in for questioning," he said, "and I just want you to know I can't believe you had anything to do with Cryptessa's death."

Thank heavens. He hadn't found the Buddha! And he didn't think I was a homicidal maniac!

"That's very kind of you to say."

Aside from Emmeline, he was the only one on the block who hadn't assumed I was guilty.

My heart, already gooey, was on the verge of completely melting when I suddenly remembered my duties as a part-time semi-professional PI. No one, not even Peter, could be ignored as a potential suspect. Could Peter himself be the killer?

It hardly seemed likely. He barely knew Cryptessa. And I had a tough time believing he'd kill her simply because she caused a ruckus at his housewarming party. After all, I was part of that ruckus, too, and I was still alive.

"You going for a run?" he now asked, eyeing the sweats I was wearing.

*Moi*? Going for a run? Let's all pause for a round of hearty chuckles.

Of course I wasn't going for a run. I was going to the corner Starbucks for a mocha latte espresso and blueberry muffin.

But so overcome was I by Peter's vote of support (and fabulous thighs) that I found myself saying:

"Oh, yes. I love to run. I go running all the time."

"Great," Peter said. "Let's run together."

"Now?" I blinked, an out-of-shape deer in the headlights.

"Yes, now. How about it?" he grinned, flashing me that yummy cleft in his chin.

Oh, groan. No way could I possibly keep up with him. I'd have to make up some excuse. I'd tell him I just remembered an important phone call I had to make. Or a doctor's appointment I had to keep. I'd make up something—anything.

But much to my annoyance, the words that actually came out of my mouth were:

"Sure, why not?"

What the heck was wrong with me? Clearly my proximity to his fabulous thighs was playing havoc with my powers of speech.

"Okay, let's go!" he said.

And with that, he took off, his fab t's churning like pistons.

As I hurried to catch up with him, I forced myself to think positive thoughts. I could do this if I really put my mind to it. Absolutely. I'd be the Not-So-Little Engine that Could.

*I can do it,* I told myself. *I can do it. I can do it!*

And you'll be happy to know that my positive thinking worked—for a whole block and a half. After that I was wheezing like an asthmatic Edsel.

"Am I going too fast for you?" Peter asked, slowing down.

"Sprained ligament," I managed to gasp. "Got it hiking over at Griffith Park." (Would these lies never stop?) "It's slowed me down a bit."

"If you'd rather," he offered, "we can walk."

*Oh, God, yes!*

"It probably would be best."

We began walking and eventually I was able to breathe without making ugly gurgling noises.

"So what was it like being questioned by the police?" Peter asked.

"Not too awful."

(A lot easier, in fact, than that block and a half of running.)

"I suppose you know that the killer was wearing my ape suit," I said.

"That's what I heard."

"But I swear I wasn't in it."

"I believe you, Jaine."

He patted my shoulder reassuringly, sending a small jolt of excitement down my spine.

"I don't suppose you noticed anyone going into your bedroom the night of the murder?" I asked when I'd recovered my composure. "Anyone who could have slipped into my ape suit?"

"No, I'm afraid I was busy talking with my guests. I'm just sorry," he said, shooting me a sidelong glance, "that I didn't get to spend more time with you."

My heart, which was still pounding from his touch, now did a flip-flop. I only hoped I'd live through this walk to possibly date him someday.

"By the way," Peter said, "I never did thank you properly for those brownies you baked for my housewarming. True confession," he added with a sheepish grin. "I ate one that fell on the rug. Just dusted it off when everyone was gone and popped it in my mouth."

He picked up food from the floor and ate it???

A sure sign we were meant for each other.

"Anyhow, it was fantastic," he said. "The best I ever ate."

I should have confessed right then and there that it was from Mrs. Fields, but did I? Of course not.

"Oh, it was nothing," I said instead. "I love to cook."

Was I mad? First I'd lied about the running, and now this??

Clearly some demon had gotten control of my tongue.

And it got worse.

Because then, with a simpering Martha Stewart smile, I found myself saying, "Someday I'll have to have you over for dinner."

"Great," he replied, not missing a beat. "How about tomorrow?"

Yikes. I never thought he'd take me up on it. Not so soon, anyway. I needed at least a couple of weeks (possibly years) to learn how to turn out an edible meal. No way could I fake it by tomorrow night.

I absolutely, positively had to dream up an excuse to get out of this.

So naturally, the words that came out of my mouth were:

"Sure. See you at seven."

What can I say? I blame it all on those thighs.

# Chapter 15

By the time I got home, I was in a much better mood. That's because I stopped off for my espresso latte and blueberry muffin. Nothing, I find, lifts one's spirits like a jumbo blueberry muffin with a high-voltage caffeine chaser.

How foolish I'd been to panic over fixing dinner for Peter. How difficult could it be? Surely with a little help from the Internet, I'd be able to find a nice, easy main course recipe. That, plus a salad, a loaf of crusty French bread, and some of my famous "homemade" brownies for dessert and—voilà—dinner would be served!

Checking in with my good friends at Google, I soon found the perfect recipe—Goof-Proof Meatloaf. Only six ingredients. And ten minutes' assembly. Even I couldn't screw that one up.

Feeling quite proud of myself, I then proceeded to search online for a figurine to replace Peter's busted Buddha. And as luck would have it, I located one just like it on eBay for only thirty-five dollars. Eagerly I sent away for it. This was my lucky day.

Well, not quite.

Because just then I got a phone call from Marvin Cooper.

"Jaine, sweetheart," he said. "I got the Larry Lumbar spots."

Right away I smelled trouble.

"And?" I asked.

"And I loved 'em. I just want to make a few tiny tweaks."

For those of you non-writers out there, that means: *Batten down the hatches. Page One rewrite ahead.*

"First tweak," he said. "I want you to dump Larry Lumbar."

What did I tell you?

"He's a great character, but I've been talking with my marketing team (*the guys at his golf club*), and they say the bad back approach has been done to death. So I took it to my research team (*his brother-in-law Sid*), and guess what they found out?"

"Previously undiscovered lint in Sid's navel?"

Okay, so I didn't really say that.

"The average ten-year-old mattress is swarming with dustmites. You can only see 'em with a microscope, but they're ugly little critters. So I want to do a campaign featuring a dustmite named Danny whose mattress is about to be replaced by a brand-new Mattress King mattress."

"Danny the Dustmite?"

"Great idea, huh?"

J. Walter Thompson, eat your heart out.

"Think you can get me some ads by tomorrow?"

"Sure thing, Marv."

I hung up with a groan and opened a new file on

my computer. Thanks to the remaining caffeine in my system, I was soon deep into the adventures of Danny Dustmite. I was just at the part where Danny was warning his fellow dustmites, *Oh, no! A brand-new Mattress King! Get ready to bite the dust!* when I was brought back to reality by a racket at my front door.

I opened it to find Lance, breathless with excitement.

"You'll never guess what I've been doing!"

"Going to med school in Heidelberg? Reading Marcel Proust in the original French? Knitting wine cozies for the homeless?"

"Ouch," he winced, stabbing himself in the heart with his fist. "What have I done to deserve such sarcasm?"

"Estelle called from Estelle's Costume Shop. It seems I owe two hundred and sixty-five dollars for a missing ape suit—an ape suit that wouldn't be missing if you hadn't pulled a fast one and rented it for me in the first place."

He had the good grace to look ashamed.

"I still don't know what came over me," he said with big puppy dog eyes. "I plead temporary insanity."

"Only temporary?"

"Honest, Jaine. I'm sorry. I'll pay the bill."

"If it hadn't been for you and that stupid ape suit," I sputtered, "I wouldn't be a murder suspect today!"

"But I tried to make it up to you. Didn't I set you up with one of the finest lawyers in L.A.?"

"No, in fact, you did not. For your information, Raoul Duvernois is not licensed to practice law in California."

"Oh, that," he said with a careless wave. "A mere formality."

"Maybe in Guatemala. But here in L.A. it's considered a bit of a no-no."

"Not only have I set you up with a legal mastermind," he said, ignoring my objections, "but I've taken it upon myself to investigate the case."

"You have?"

"I've been scouting around like mad, digging for evidence!"

"Find anything?" In spite of myself, I was interested. Was it possible Lance had found a clue that would point me to Cryptessa's killer?

"I've found scads of hot info!" he nodded eagerly, plopping down on my sofa and grabbing one of the decoy apples I'd picked up at the supermarket, now in a bowl on my coffee table.

"Like what?" I asked, plopping down next to him.

"Like for one thing, Mr. Hurlbutt has had *three* failed hair transplants! And Kevin Moore owns twelve pairs of Christian Louboutin shoes, none of which she bought from me, the stinker. And get this: Lila Wood has been stealing her neighbor's newspapers for the past fifteen years! Apparently she gets up at the crack of dawn, reads the paper, and then puts it back in the driveway. She even bought a professional sealer to reseal the plastic wrapping. When you think of all the money she spent on that sealer, she could've been buying the papers. Well, maybe not fifteen years' worth—"

"You call that evidence?!" I screeched, snatching the apple from his hand. "How is any of that supposed to get me off the hook for murder?"

"If you'll just be patient," he said, grabbing the apple back, "I'll get to the stuff about the murder."

"I ran out of patience three hair transplants ago. Just tell me what you learned about Cryptessa."

"Well," he said, taking a deep breath, "you know how Cryptessa was always accusing her cleaning lady of stealing from her?"

I thought back to the day I paid my condolence call, and how Cryptessa had claimed Rosita was robbing her blind.

"About a week before she died, Cryptessa set a trap for Rosita and left some money out on her dresser. When it was gone at the end of the day, she confronted Rosita on her front lawn, reading her the riot act. Mrs. Hurlbutt just happened to be walking by and overheard the whole thing."

"Yeah, right. If I know Mrs. Hurlbutt, she was hiding in the bushes, taking notes."

"Anyhow, when Cryptessa threatened to report Rosita to the police, Rosita got furious and said, *Try it, and you'll be very sorry.*"

Damn that Mrs. Hurlbutt. Why the hell hadn't she told me this little nugget when I was questioning her?

"For all we know," Lance was saying, channeling his inner Hercule Poirot, "Rosita killed Cryptessa to keep her from blabbing to the cops."

Sure sounded like a motive for murder to me. Especially if Rosita was an illegal immigrant. Her whole life would be destroyed if Cryptessa sicced the cops on her. Who's to say she didn't take a break from her serving duties at Peter's party to slip into my abandoned ape suit?

"I got you Rosita's phone number," Lance said, holding out a slip of paper, "in case you wanted to talk to her."

I have to admit I was touched. True, Lance could be a royal pain in the fanny, but when push came to shove, he had my back.

At times like this, I just wanted to give him a hug.

"I stopped by Peter's house this morning to get it," he said, waving the slip of paper. "Peter told me he'd been out running with you. 'Running?' I said. 'With Jaine? The woman gets winded brushing her teeth!' We both had a jolly laugh about that. Anyhow, here's Rosita's number. No need to thank me. I'll just take a few more of these apples."

Apples in hand, he went sailing out the door.

Okay, cancel that hug.

When I gave Rosita a call, there was no answer. No big surprise in the middle of the day. I was guessing, and hoping, that she was busy working at a new job. So I whiled away the rest of the afternoon with my good buddy Danny Dustmite, and at around six o'clock, I gave her another try.

This time, she picked up.

"*Hola?*"

In the background, I could hear a TV playing, with raucous bursts of canned sitcom laughter.

"Rosita? This is Jaine Austen."

"Who?"

"Cryptessa's neighbor from down the street."

"Oh, right. The lady who killed Van Helsing."

"I did not kill that bird. It was just an unfortunate parakeet heart attack."

"How can I help you?" she asked, a wary note in her voice.

"I need to talk to you about something."

"If it's about Cryptessa's murder," she said firmly, "I've said all I'm going to say to the police."

Oh, foo. Time for Plan B.

"Actually, I wanted to talk to you about cleaning my apartment."

"I can give you Wednesday afternoons," she said, noticeably perkier.

"I'm afraid I can't afford your services on a regular basis. I just need a one-time cleaning."

"All right. How about next Wednesday?"

I didn't want to wait that long. Who knew where I'd be next Wednesday? Sharing a prison cell with a gal named Duke, perhaps?

"Do you think you could do it sooner?"

"I'm pretty booked up."

"How about tonight?" I asked.

"Tonight?"

"Yes, it's a bit of an emergency. I'm having a dinner party tomorrow and I'd really like the place to look nice."

Which was no lie.

"I don't usually work nights."

"It won't take long. It's just a small one-bedroom apartment. You'll be through in an hour, an hour and a half, tops."

"I'll have to bring Jennifer, my little girl. I can't leave her home alone."

"That's fine."

"And it'll cost you fifty dollars."

Ouch.

"Of course!" I chirped. "See you at seven?"

Rosita showed up promptly at seven, with her little girl in tow. A skinny ten-year-old with her mother's huge brown eyes, Jennifer wore the plaid skirt, white blouse, and navy crew neck of a local parochial school. Slung across her back was a hot pink book bag.

She graced me with her mother's shy smile, and then suddenly her eyes lit up.

171

"Look, Mom!" she cried, catching sight of Prozac lounging on the sofa. "A cat!"

"Be careful," I said as she raced toward her. "Sometimes she scratches."

But Prozac, as she often is with strangers, was a perfect angel, letting Jennifer pick her up and cuddle her.

(I guess she saves all her scratches for me.)

"Oh, Mom," Jennifer cooed. "She's so cute!"

Prozac gazed up at her with big green eyes.

*So I've been told.*

"Time to do your homework, honey," Rosita said.

Prozac shot her a dirty look.

*Party pooper.*

Reluctantly Jennifer let Prozac go and settled down at my dining room table with her books.

"I guess I'd better get started cleaning," Rosita said.

I'd been hoping to work in a bit of chat time, but Rosita was in no mood to gab.

"Where's your vacuum?" she asked briskly.

I dug it out from my closet where it had been vacationing for an embarrassing number of weeks, and the next thing I knew, Rosita was whirling around the apartment, cleaning my floors, kind enough not to gasp at the dust bunnies the size of Chihuahuas under my bed.

When every square inch of the floor had been zapped clean, she snapped on rubber gloves and began scrubbing my bathroom till it twinkled. I don't know how she did it, but she even got rid of those ghastly lime deposits on my shower door.

Having worked her magic in the bathroom, she headed for the kitchen.

"*Dios mio*," she said, running her finger along the range. "This is the first time I've ever had to dust a stove."

"I don't use it very much," I confessed, shamefaced. "Don't even bother cleaning the oven. It hasn't been on in years. I just use it to dry my undies in emergencies."

I hung around the kitchen, hoping to start a conversation, but Rosita studiously ignored me as she scoured down the counters.

When at last she was through, my apartment sparkled like a diamond.

I only wished I could afford this on a regular basis. Heck, I wished I could afford it just this once.

I wrote her a check for fifty dollars, wincing with every digit.

Snapping off her rubber gloves, she pocketed my check and called out, "Come on, Jennifer. We've got to go."

Jennifer, who'd finished her homework and was now sitting on the couch petting Prozac, looked up wistfully.

"Mom, I want a cat."

Prozac took time out from purring to shoot me a demanding glare.

*And I want a kid. Somebody to pet me when you're busy with your silly writing assignments.*

"Cats are not all they're cracked up to be," I said, lobbing Prozac a snippy look of my own.

Then with a bright smile, I turned to Rosita. "You must be hungry after all that work. I insist that you and Jennifer stay for a snack."

"No, no," Rosita said. "We've got to get going."

"Wait." I dashed into the kitchen and seconds later came out holding my bait. "I've got Double Stuf Oreos."

"Please, Mom," Jennifer pleaded.

"Well, okay," Rosita said. "It's really very kind of you, Ms. Austen."

Wasting no time, I brought some cookies on a plate to Jennifer.

"Why don't you eat them in the bedroom with Prozac and watch TV?" I said, gunning for some alone time with Rosita.

"Can I, Mom?" Jennifer asked.

"Okay, sure. But don't get any crumbs on the bedspread," she called out as Jennifer scampered off.

I put some more cookies on a plate for Rosita and me in the dining room. A far cry from my usual straight-from-the-bag approach. I even boiled water for tea in my freshly polished teakettle.

"Jennifer's such an adorable kid," I said.

And I meant it.

"She's smart, too." Rosita nodded with pride. "She's going to go to college. Someday she's going to be somebody. No cleaning houses for her."

At that moment, hearing all the love and pride in her voice, I fervently hoped Rosita wasn't the killer. She seemed way too nice for homicide.

Nevertheless, I couldn't rule her out. Not without questioning her.

"So," I said casually, "have you lined up a new job to fill Cryptessa's days?"

"Oh, yes," Rosita nodded. "A very sweet lady in Westwood."

"What a nice change, huh?"

"I'll say. Why I stayed with Ms. Eleanor as long as I did, I'll never know. I suppose I was afraid I wouldn't find anything else. If I'd known how easy it was going to be, I would have left her a long time ago."

"I bet she was impossible to work for."

"You have no idea."

"I heard she accused you of taking some money from her dresser."

"Has Mrs. Hurlbutt been talking again?" she said with an angry snap of her Oreo. "What a gossip."

Amen to that.

"Ms. Eleanor was always accusing me of stealing from her. Just like she accused the gardener of dumping motor oil in her backyard and accused the IRS of spying on her. The woman was loco! And that ten dollars she left out on her dresser? I never touched it. She probably took it herself and forgot all about it."

"Weren't you afraid when she threatened to report you to the police?"

"No," she said with a defiant tilt of her chin, "I wasn't afraid. I knew she'd never go through with it. I told her if she tried it, she'd be sorry. She'd never get another cleaning lady to put up with her nonsense."

So that's what Rosita meant when she warned Cryptessa she'd be sorry if she went to the police. Maybe it wasn't a death threat but merely a warning that Cryptessa would never find anyone to replace her.

I wanted to believe Rosita was innocent.

But who knew? Maybe behind that defiant chin, she'd been scared silly that Cryptessa would report her to the authorities and shatter her world to pieces.

What's more, I couldn't help noticing that all the while she'd been talking, Rosita had been scratching her arm. Just like I'd been scratching my arm for the past several days. Now I saw she had an ugly rash just below her elbow. Just like mine.

She saw me staring at it.

"I just tried a new brand of rubber gloves," she

said with a nervous smile. "Must be allergic to something in them."

Maybe.

Or maybe, just maybe, she got the rash from wearing an itchy ape suit.

# Chapter 16

The next day dawned bright and, inside my apartment, squeaky clean. Rosita may or may not have been a killer, but she was one heck of a house cleaner. In the early morning sun, my apartment positively sparkled.

I walked around, touching dust-free surfaces, plumping already-plump pillows, and gazing at my reflection in my high-gloss tea kettle.

I should have been a nervous wreck, of course. Lest you forgot, tonight was the night Peter was showing up for dinner. But somehow my freshly cleaned apartment gave me confidence. Surely I could whip up a simple dinner for two, I thought as I nuked my morning bagel and sloshed some Hearty Halibut Innards into a bowl for Prozac.

After breakfast (during which I was careful not to spill even the weensiest crumb on my gleaming hardwood floors), I wrote out my grocery list, then got dressed and headed over to the supermarket.

"Hi, doll!" A greasy biker dude, parked atop a monster cycle, gave me a broad wink as I got out of my car in the parking lot. "Nice wheels."

Following his gaze, I realized I still had that silly plastic skeleton skull clamped to my grill. I made a mental note to get rid of it ASAP. If there was one thing my eyesore of a Corolla could not afford, it was another eyesore.

"Wanna go for a spin?" Mr. Greasy asked, patting his cycle.

Not without a hazmat suit.

"Maybe some other time," I said, skittering away.

Inside the market, I strolled the aisles with a spring in my step, wheeling my cart past other efficient early morning shoppers, Andy Williams crooning "Moon River" in the background.

With my shopping list as my guide, I picked up the ingredients for my meatloaf and salad, as well as a fabulous loaf of crusty French bread and some yummy sesame crackers for my cheese-and-crackers hors d'oeuvres.

It was when I strolled over to the cheese display that I saw the answer to my culinary prayers: a great big beautiful cheese ball, studded with pecans. I'd been meaning to pick up a chunk of Havarti, but the minute I laid my eyes on that cheese ball, all thoughts of Havarti flew out the window. How festive a cheese ball would be instead, surrounded by a fan of crackers.

Yes, nothing says fine dining like a pecan-studded hunk of cheese. It would take my modest little meatloaf dinner and turn it into a meal to remember!

True, it was a tad pricey, but what the heck. I wanted to make a good impression on Peter. I tossed it in my cart and headed for the checkout counter, imagining many such shopping trips in the future, me cooking intimate cheese ball dinners for two, Peter aglow with admiration.

After paying for my groceries, I made a pit stop at the nearest Mrs. Fields for some of my "homemade" brownies, then headed back home.

As much as I would've liked to, I couldn't spend all day fantasizing about future dinners with Peter. I still had to finish that Danny Dustmite campaign. So once I put my groceries away, I hunkered down at my computer to hammer out some commercials. When Danny had finally bitten the dust, I sent the spots off to Marvin.

By now it was 3:00 p.m. and I still had scads of time left before Peter showed up at seven.

I spent a good hour of it online, learning how to fold a napkin into a swan.

It's not as easy as it sounds. But after about fourteen tries, I'm proud to say I finally managed to create two lovely swan napkins.

I then proceeded to clear all my office paraphernalia from my dining room and set the table, using my good "Waterfjord" dishes (a Home Shopping Club gift from my mother, complete service for four, only $59.99). The swan napkins made quite an elegant touch, I thought as I placed them carefully on the Waterfjords.

Then, the moment of truth. I headed into the kitchen to start cooking.

As I began assembling the ingredients for my Goof-Proof Meatloaf, Prozac wandered in from the living room. She saw me standing at the counter in cooking mode and blinked in amazement.

*Just FYI. That boxy thing with the knobs is called an "oven."*

I'm happy to report that I managed to assemble the meatloaf without mishap. My Goof-Proof recipe had not let me down. It was every bit as easy as it had claimed to be. When it was all neatly patted down into my brand new meatloaf pan, I put it in the oven. Then I quickly assembled the salad. I'd cheated and bought prewashed lettuce, which I just dumped in a bowl, along with some cherry tomatoes and store-bought croutons. Later I'd toss it with some creamy Caesar dressing. After cutting my French baguette in half lengthwise, I slathered on some butter I'd softened in the microwave. Then I wrapped the whole thing in tin foil and put it aside, to be slipped into the oven about ten minutes before serving. Finally, I got the cheese ball out from the fridge and left it out on the counter so it could warm to room temperature.

Things were going so well, I felt like I was ready for my own show on the Food Network.

Really, I had to try this cooking thing more often, I thought as I trotted off to reward myself with a nice relaxing soak in the tub.

Ten minutes later, I was up to my neck in

strawberry-scented bubbles, lost in a most delicious daydream of my life as Mrs. Peter Connor, with me whipping up gourmet meals in our chef-quality kitchen, and Peter in the den, editing my Great American Novel.

I spent a good half hour soaking in fantasyland. Finally, when all my strawberry-scented bubbles had popped and I had won the Pulitzer Prize, I dredged myself out of the tub and slipped into my robe.

Before I got dressed, I decided to zip into the kitchen to check on my meatloaf.

But the minute I set foot in the living room, I froze in my tracks. There, all over my freshly vacuumed floors, was a trail of sticky white goo. On closer inspection, I saw it was cheese! Accompanied by shards of pecans.

Oh, hell. I'd left the cheese ball out on the kitchen counter, never dreaming Prozac would be interested in it. After all, Prozac doesn't care for cheese. Or nuts.

But, alas, I had forgotten that she loves *balls*.

At which point she came barreling out from behind the curtains, nudging what was left of the cheese ball. With one final swat of her paw, she sent it skidding across the room, where it landed at my feet.

*Touchdown!*

Oh, for heaven's sake! I grabbed the ball, now deeply cratered with Prozac's paw prints, missing most of its nuts, and coated with the few puffs of dust that had managed to escape Rosita's vacuuming.

Racing into the kitchen, I frantically scraped away the craters and dust till it was clean again, then reshaped it into a ball. By now it was the size of a Ping-Pong ball, but it was all I had and I was sticking with it.

Bereft of pecans, I rolled it in some smashed-up crackers and—voilà—the world's first Mini-Cracker Ball.

Taking no chances, I stowed it in the fridge, away from Prozac's calamitous clutches.

Then, as Prozac daintily licked her paws clean, I scurried around on my hands and knees, mopping up nuts and cheese from my floor.

All as I can say is thank heavens I have hard-wood.

I was standing there, surveying the room, looking for any cheese blobs I might have missed, when I glanced over at my dining table and groaned to see that my beautiful swan napkins had been mauled to within an inch of their lives, their mangled corpses lying limply on my Waterfjords.

"Prozac!" I screeched. "Look what you've done!"

She gazed up at me, quite proud of herself.

*I know. Aren't they great?*

I tried to restore them to their former swanlike glory, but it was hopeless. Unfortunately they were the last of my cloth napkins, so I took two bargain paper napkins and tossed them on the table, folded in half, cafeteria style.

So much for setting a beautiful table.

By now I had less than ten minutes to get dressed before Peter showed up. I dashed into my bedroom, tossing on my elastic-waist skinny jeans, a black silk blouse, and fabulous tan suede boots I got half off at Nordstrom's annual shoe sale. With no time to blow out my mop of curls to silken perfection, I corralled them into a messy ponytail.

Makeup? A luxury I could only dream of.

Because at that minute, there was a knock on door. Oh, hell. Peter was here. Three minutes early!

And I was just about to answer it when I suddenly realized I didn't smell anything cooking. Shouldn't my apartment be filled with the yummy aroma of meatloaf?

Quickly, I dashed into the kitchen and opened the oven door. To my horror, I saw that the meatloaf was still ice cold, totally uncooked.

Oh, hell. Cancel that gig on the Food Network. I'd forgotten to turn on the oven!

No need to panic. I'd just bump up the temperature so it would cook faster. It would give Peter and me more time to linger over our wine and cracker ball.

Taking a deep breath and forcing myself to be calm, I made my way to the front door and opened it.

Peter was standing there, looking très adorable in khakis and a baby blue oxford shirt.

"Hi, there," he said, holding out a bottle of wine. "For you."

Whatever semblance of calm I'd been able to work up was gone with the wind.

"Um, thanks," I managed to say, with all the grace and vivacity of a robot on downers.

Prozac, who had been napping on the sofa, resting up from her playdate with the cheese ball, now sat up, giving Peter the once-over.

*Hubba hubba, hot stuff!*

Like a flash, she was off the sofa and rubbing herself shamelessly against his ankles.

"Who do we have here?" Peter said, bending down to scratch her under the chin.

*Your future love slave, if you play your cards right.*

She tore her eyes away from him long enough to look in my direction.

*Forget what I said about getting me a kid. I want one of these!*

"Make yourself comfy on the sofa," I said to Peter, "while I get the hors d'oeuvres."

I hurried to the kitchen and grabbed my cracker ball from the fridge, then tossed it on a plate with a handful of crackers. Opening the bottle of cabernet Peter had brought over, I poured out two glasses and put everything on a tray.

When I came out from the kitchen, I found

Prozac in Peter's lap, behaving in a most disgraceful manner. I won't go into details, but let's just say that if she'd been wearing a G-string, Peter would've been slipping a twenty-dollar bill in it.

"Don't let her get her paws on this," I warned as I set the cracker ball down on the coffee table. "She'll destroy it in no time."

"Not this little angel?" Peter asked in disbelief.

Prozac looked up at him with big green eyes.

*Don't listen to a word she says. I went nowhere near that cheese ball. That pecan in my tail has been there for weeks!*

"You've got such a nice place here," Peter said as I joined them on the sofa.

"Thanks," I said, surreptitiously snatching up a glob of cheese from a throw pillow and wrapping it in a cocktail napkin.

"Here's to good neighbors," he said, clinking his glass against mine. "And good times," he added, with a most appealing grin.

I took a healthy slug of my cab, which slid down my throat like velvet. Yum!

"So how did you get that fabulous cleft in your chin and would you mind awfully if I kissed it?"

Okay, so I didn't really say that. Two drinks later I might have, but not then. Instead I just asked him how he was liking his new house, and he said he was liking it very much indeed.

We started chatting about this and that; I think

Peter was talking about his job and the difference between New York and L.A., but I can't really swear to it; I was too busy trying not to stare at his chin.

By now, thanks to my good friend, Mr. Cabernet, I was feeling quite mellow, snuggled on the sofa, Peter just inches from my thighs.

I was beginning to think the evening might be a success after all, when I was jolted from my dreamy state by a loud knocking on the door.

I'd know that knock anywhere.

"Yoo hoo! Jaine! It's me! Lance!"

"Aren't you going to get it?" Peter asked as I sat there, praying Lance would give up and go away.

With a sigh, I got up and opened the dratted door to find Lance standing there, all spiffed up and moussed to perfection.

"Why, Jaine!" he cried in mock surprise. "I had no idea you had company!"

Oh, please. He probably had his ear glued to the wall for the past fifteen minutes.

"Yes, indeed. I do have company," I said, resolutely blocking his path.

But that wasn't about to stop him.

"Hi, Peter!" he said, shoving me aside and barging into the room. "What are you doing here?"

"Jaine invited me for dinner."

"Jaine? Making dinner?" Lance said with a

most annoying trill of laughter. "The woman who needs MapQuest to find her kitchen? What's she making? Reservations?"

"Oh, Lance. How very droll. I've always loved that joke. Ever since I first heard it on my grand-pappy's knee."

Ignoring my jab, he sprinted over to the sofa and sat down next to Peter, the cushion no doubt still warm from my tush.

"Isn't Jaine's place quaint?" he cooed. "Who says you can't find stylish pieces at Goodwill?"

I was *thisclose* to hurling my cracker ball at him, but my innate good manners (and poor aim) made me think better of it.

Then Lance wrinkled his nose, sniffing.

"Ick. What are you cooking? Old gym socks?"

I had to admit, it did smell sort of funny. I couldn't imagine why. I'd followed the Goof-Proof Meatloaf recipe to a tee. It was nothing, I assured myself. Lance was just trying to throw me off my game, and I couldn't let him get away with it.

"Get me a martini, will you, hon?" he now ordered, practically snapping his fingers. "Extra dry, with a twist."

Where did he think he was, anyway? The Algonquin Bar?

"Come and help me make it, Lance dear," I said, grabbing his elbow and hauling him off to the kitchen.

"What the hell do you think you're doing?" I hissed when we were alone.

"Just popping by for a friendly visit."

"Well, you just pop on out again, mister."

"Try and make me," he said with a taunting smile.

And then, off my look of fury, he sailed back into the living room.

Okay, he asked for it. This was war!

I stomped back into the living room, just in time to see Lance cutting off a sliver of my cracker ball.

"I simply must try some of this yummy cheese ball," he said, snuggled on the sofa next to Peter. "Jaine is so clever in the kitchen. You should try her Hungry-Man dinners. Sometimes she even defrosts them. Hahahahaha!"

Two could play at this game.

"So sorry I can't make you a martini, Lance. I'm out of gin. You must have finished it the last time you were on one of your benders."

Score one for Jaine.

Making no effort to pour him some wine, I sat down in the armchair across from him and Peter.

"So, tell us, Lance," I said, a phony smile plastered on my face, "all about your med school days in Heidelberg."

I watched in delight as he squirmed in his seat.

"Not much to tell," he said with a nervous smile.

"Don't be modest," Peter jumped in. "Lance told me he graduated first in his class."

"Oh, my! I never knew that. You must be fabulously fluent in German."

"Very," Peter said. "He wrote his dissertation in German."

"Did he, now? Well, go ahead, Lance. Say something in German."

Lance's eyes darted between us like a trapped rabbit.

"Do you happen to speak German, Peter?" he finally managed to say.

I could see the wheels spinning in his devious little brain. He was hoping against hope Peter spoke no German, so he could fake it.

"Yes, I speak a little German. Our company has an office in Berlin."

*Wunderbar*!

"How much fun!" I cried. "Now you and Lance can gab away! Go ahead, Lance."

His smile turned sickly.

"Would you look at the time," he said, shooting me a dagger look. "As much as I'd love to stick around and *sprechen sie Deutsch*, I really must be tootling."

"Must you?" I said with a fake moue of disappointment. "And I was so looking forward to hearing you *sprechen*."

"Yes, I must," he said through clenched jaws.

"Well, ta-ta!" I said, swallowing the urge to shove him out the door.

"Good night, all!" Lance replied with a carefree wave for Peter and a snarl for me.

After shutting the door firmly behind him, I returned to my perch on the sofa, feeling quite elated.

The battle was over. And I had won!

"So where were we?" I asked, plopping down on the sofa.

*In the middle of a very important belly rub.* Prozac yawned. *So hands off, sister.*

I flashed Peter what I hoped was a marginally seductive smile, but he was paying no attention to me.

"Do you smell something burning?" he asked.

And indeed I did.

"Look!" he said, pointing to where smoke was billowing from the kitchen.

Holy Moses! I raced to the kitchen and opened the oven door to see my meatloaf up in flames.

In a moment of idiotic panic, I tossed my wine onto the fire, which just made it fan higher.

Thank heavens Peter kept his cool in my culinary crisis and doused the flames with the sensible choice—water. When the fire was out, he reached into the oven with a pot holder and pulled out my "Goof-Proof" meatloaf, now blackened beyond recognition.

(And what have we learned from this little

episode, class? That's right. In my hands, nothing is ever goof-proof.)

I stared at my would-be entrée miserably as Peter threw the whole soggy mess into the sink.

"Hey, what's this?" he said, reaching back into the oven.

I almost died of shame when he pulled out the charred remains of a pair of old gym socks.

So Lance really *had* smelled gym socks burning! I suddenly flashed back to a day last rainy season when I got caught in a downpour and put my socks in the oven to dry. If only I'd used my oven once in a while like a normal person I would have discovered them ages ago.

By now I had given up any and all attempts at impressing Peter. Not only had I set fire to my own kitchen, but now Peter knew I was the kind of woman who kept gym socks in her oven.

He tossed the socks on top of the meatloaf in the sink.

Prozac, who had been a happy witness to this whole ghastly affair, sniffed at the sodden mess in the sink, then gazed up at Peter.

*And this is one of her better meals.*

# YOU'VE GOT MAIL!

**To: Jausten**
**From: DaddyO**
**Subject: I Knew It!**

I knew there was something fishy going on with "Stinky" Pinkus and I was right!

Last night I got the munchies for some Rocky Road ice cream, but all we had in the freezer was that low-fat ice milk your mom buys when she's on a diet. So even though it was after midnight, I got in my car and headed over to the market.

I hadn't gone three blocks when who did I see but Stinky Pinkus creeping out from her house with a duffel bag! I pulled over and watched in amazement as she got into her car and sped away.

I ask you, Lambchop, where was Stinky going with a duffel bag in the middle of the night?

And what the heck was inside? I'll tell you what was inside. The murder weapon! Maybe a fireplace poker. Or a butcher knife. Or a bloody ax! Clearly Stinky was on a mission to get rid of it.

After years of honing my skills watching *Law & Order*, I've got a nose for sniffing out trouble. "The Nose" knows.

Stinky Pinkus killed that friend of hers, all right. And I intend to prove it!

Love and kisses from
Your daddy,
Hank "The Nose" Austen

**To: Jausten**
**From: Shoptillyoudrop**
**Subject: Upsetting News**

Most upsetting news, sweetheart. Last night Daddy went out on a midnight run for ice cream—although why he went out for ice cream when we had some perfectly delicious low-fat ice milk, I'll never know—and he saw Lydia Pinkus getting into her car with a duffel bag.

He insists she was getting rid of the murder weapon she used to kill her friend Irma. Which sounds absurd, of course.

But I can't help wondering. What *was* Lydia doing with a duffel bag after midnight? She's usually asleep by 10:30 at the latest.

Oh, dear. Daddy couldn't possibly be right, could he?

XOXO,
Mom

# Chapter 17

I stood in my robe and pj's the next morning, staring bleary-eyed at the disaster area formerly known as my kitchen, still cringing at the memory of last night's Flaming Meatloaf Fiasco.

"Oh, Pro," I sighed. "How will I ever live this down?"

She looked up from where she was inhaling her morning mackerel guts.

*You could always scratch my back for the next half hour or so. That should make you feel better.*

After putting out the fire, Peter had offered to take me to a restaurant for dinner, but I'd been way too embarrassed to accept. Instead I just mumbled my thanks and said something about having to stay home and scrub my oven.

Of course, I had no intention of doing any oven scrubbing. Not then, anyway. Instead, I just swallowed my shame, along with a Mrs. Fields brownie or three, and trundled off to bed.

Now, in the cold light of day, things looked even worse than they had the night before. There in my sink were the charred remains of my Goof-Proof Meatloaf, topped with my barbequed gym socks. Watching Peter fish those socks out of the oven last night had to have been one of my Top Ten Most Humiliating Moments ever.

Clearly, I'd blown it with Peter. I'd simply have to cross him off my "To Marry" list and get on with my life.

Starting with this godawful kitchen.

So, after a nutritious breakfast of Folgers Crystals and brownie crumbs, I rolled up my pajama sleeves and spent the next hour scrubbing my oven and washing soot from my walls.

When all evidence of last night's disaster had been washed away, I nuked myself another cup of coffee and settled down to check the latest e-mails from my parents.

I have to admit I was a tad taken aback. Was it possible that for once in his life Daddy was right? Was something fishy going on with the heretofore irreproachable Lydia Pinkus? Was it possible she had committed some deed of the dastardly order?

But I couldn't afford to spend valuable time worrying about Daddy's would-be murder. Not when I had a very real one of my own to solve.

Time to get back on track and focus on my investigation.

So far, I'd talked to all the neighbors who were at Peter's party. All except Amy, the shy grad student. So after hosing myself down in the shower, I trotted across the street to knock on her door.

She answered it in jeans and a UCLA sweatshirt, her hair swept up in girlish pigtails, tortoise shell glasses perched on her tiny nose.

"Hi, Amy!" I said in my perkiest voice. "Sorry to bother you, but I was wondering if we could have a little chat."

"About what?" she asked, blinking into the sunlight.

For once I decided to stick with the truth.

"Cryptessa's murder."

"Gosh, that was awful!" she said, shaking her head. "I still can't believe it happened here on our block. I told my parents, and now they want me to get an alarm system."

She leaned against the doorjamb, showing no intention of asking me in.

"Would you mind if I came inside for a few minutes? It's sort of awkward talking about it here on your front steps."

"Actually," she demurred, "I'm right in the middle of studying for a big exam."

"It won't take long. I promise."

"Well, okay."

I followed her into her living room, an Early Ikea affair, with cinder-block bookshelves, a futon, and two folding chairs as the only guest seating. Textbooks and papers were scattered on the futon, a laptop propped on a coffee table. Gazing around the room, I wondered how a student like Amy could afford the rent. True, we were on the cheaper end of the street, but still, one needed some sort of income to survive on this block. I figured her parents were probably footing the bills.

"Have a seat," she said, clearing away some papers from one of the folding chairs.

She sat across from me on the futon, her legs tucked neatly under her. Next to her on an orange crate end table was a half-eaten English muffin. After my brownie crumb breakfast, it was all I could do not to reach out and grab it.

But I had to forget about English muffins with butter melted in the nooks and crannies and concentrate on the task at hand.

"How can I help you?" Amy asked.

"I suppose you heard that the police questioned me about Cryptessa's death."

"Yes, the Town Crier told me."

Okay, she didn't actually call Mrs. Hurlbutt the Town Crier, but it's such an accurate description, I thought I'd throw it in.

"I've been doing some investigating on my own," I said, "hoping to clear my name. And I was wondering if on the night of Peter's party you saw anyone acting suspiciously."

"Gee, Jaine. It was a Halloween costume party. Lots of people were acting suspiciously. I saw at least three Draculas trying to bite their dates' neck."

"Did you see anyone leave the living room to walk down the hallway?"

"No, I only stayed at the party for about fifteen minutes. I chatted a bit with one of the gals from Peter's office; then I grabbed a cookie and went home."

I had no doubt that all she grabbed was one measly cookie. But did Amy really go home? Or did she slip down the hall to put on my ape suit? And if so, why? As far as I knew, Cryptessa and Amy had virtually no dealings with each other.

Or had they? Time to find out.

"So did you know Cryptessa very well?" I asked as casually as I could.

"Not at all," she replied, just a tad too quickly. "We never even spoke."

Up until that moment, she'd been looking straight at me, but now she started fussing with some papers on the futon, avoiding eye contact.

Amy may or may not have been an excellent student. But she was one heck of a rotten liar. She'd spoken with Cryptessa, all right. But about what?

"I'm sorry," she said, jumping up from the futon, "but I've really got to get back to my books."

Was that a flicker of fear I saw behind those tortoise shell glasses?

"Sure, I understand. Thanks for your time."

Just as I got up to go, the phone rang. Amy let her machine get it, eyeing me nervously, eager for me to leave. Which made me all the more determined to stay.

Heading for the door, I accidentally-on-purpose dropped my keys and then fumbled to pick them up, stalling for time, hoping to hear who was calling.

My curiosity paid off. A man's voice came on the line. From the sound of his voice, an older man.

"Amy, babe," I heard him say, "I'll be over tonight at eight. Later, honeybun."

I looked over at Amy, who was blushing furiously.

So shy little Amy had a boyfriend. And an older man at that. Very interesting.

Little Amy was full of surprises, wasn't she?

What exactly had gone on between her and Cryptessa? Who the heck was Mr. Honeybun? And how on earth could she forget to finish an English muffin?

I was heading down her path, pondering these questions (and whether to get Chicken McNuggets or a Quarter Pounder for lunch) when I looked up and saw a rusty old heap of a car pulling up in front of Cryptessa's house.

Seconds later, Cryptessa's nephew Warren emerged from its depths.

Wasting no time, I scooted over to join him.

When last we saw Warren, if you recall, Cryptessa was threatening to cut off financing for some franchise he wanted to buy. And suddenly I wondered if he'd knocked her off before she got the chance.

"Hey, Warren!" I called out, hurrying to his side.

"Oh, hi!" he waved, his bald spot shining in the sun. "So good to see you again!"

For someone who'd just lost a dearly departed relative, he was certainly in a chipper mood.

"I just wanted to offer you my condolences."

"Right," he said, suddenly solemn, as if remembering he was supposed to be in mourning.

"Do the police have any idea who did it?" I asked, hoping he knew something I didn't.

"Last I heard, it was you."

The Town Crier strikes again.

"I can assure you it wasn't."

"I believe you," he said. "You look much too nice to be a killer."

He smiled broadly, revealing a most disconcerting gap between his two front teeth.

"Any idea who could have done it?" I asked.

"Take a number. My aunt spent her whole life making enemies."

"Do you suppose any of them were at Peter's Halloween party?"

"Beats me," he shrugged. "I wasn't even there."

I wasn't so sure about that. After all, Warren had known about the party. Peter had invited him, along with Cryptessa, the day they stopped in at his housewarming. Maybe Warren had shown up in costume, unrecognized by anyone. Maybe he hadn't even planned to kill his aunt that night. Maybe he'd just come for the free buffet. But then he'd seen my ape suit lying there and heard opportunity knocking.

Maybe the reason he believed me when I

said I didn't kill Cryptessa was because *he* did.

"Well, it's been great talking to you," he said, "but I've got to get started sorting through my aunt's things. It's going to be a nightmare. She's got electric bills from the Eisenhower administration."

"Let me help," I offered, hoping to find a clue to the killer among Cryptessa's possessions.

"Gee, that's awfully nice of you," he said, treating me to another glimpse of his gap-toothed grin.

Sorting through Cryptessa's stuff turned out to be a fairly hellish affair. Warren wasn't kidding about those ancient utility bills. I was soon to discover that Cryptessa had been a world-class hoarder, every closet and drawer in her house jammed to capacity. And unfortunately I couldn't do much snooping, since most of the time Warren insisted we work together side by side, the better to regale me with tales of the new business venture he was about to embark on—a fast-food franchise called Falafel Land.

"Falafel is the fast food of the future!" he informed me with pride.

I sincerely doubted that a deep-fried chickpea patty was going to give Mickey D's any serious competition, but I smiled and nodded as if I believed him.

"I'm going to have chicken falafels. Steak falafels. And instead of wrapping them in pita bread, I'm thinking of putting them in waffles. And calling it a Waffle Falafel. How does that sound?"

Like something destined for a barf bag.

But of course I did not tell him that. Instead I just forced out a pallid, "Dee-lish."

Eventually I managed to escape from his side when I volunteered to sort through the things in Cryptessa's bedroom.

Like every other closet in her house, the one in her bedroom was stuffed to the gills. But I was surprised to discover that most of the clothing was beautiful. True, it was decades old, but I could see it had cost a bundle in its day. How sad to think Cryptessa spent her last years in that dreadful ketchup-stained sweat suit when she had all these lovely outfits.

"Help yourself," Warren said, creeping up behind me. "If you see anything you like, take it."

"Thanks, that's very kind, but I don't think so."

I was sorely tempted by a chic little black cocktail dress, but Cryptessa had been such an unhappy soul, I was afraid of catching her bad karma.

While Warren started bagging Cryptessa's clothing, I nipped over to her night table, still hoping to find a clue. But all I unearthed were some long-expired prescription drugs and a stash of mini vodka bottles.

"Hurray! Something I can use!" Warren had once again snuck up on me and was now jamming the vodka bottles in his pockets.

I managed a quick glimpse in Cryptessa's lingerie drawer (always a favorite hiding place) but found nothing but raggedy panties and more vodka bottles.

In the top drawer of her dresser, I came across a faded fabric jewelry box. Most of the pieces inside looked like they'd come from the bottom of a Cracker Jack box—junky stuff whose mystery metals had long ago turned green. But lying amid the dross was a shiny gold locket. I turned it over and saw the inscription:

*To Eleanor with Undying Love*
*XOXO*

At last, I'd found someone who'd liked Cryptessa. Loved her, actually.

I was glad she'd had that in her life.

"Most of it looks like junk to me," Warren said, peering over my shoulder into the jewelry box. "But I'll take it to an appraiser just in case."

Finished in the bedroom, we hit the kitchen, plowing our way through mismatched dishes, burned pot holders, and drawers stuffed with a colorful assortment of plastic forks.

I was hoping to get a chance to look through Cryptessa's desk drawers in the den, but Warren beat me to it, sweeping all her papers into a trash bag.

"This might be worth something," he said,

pointing to Cryptessa's old Underwood typewriter. I thought of Emmeline next door and how happy she'd be to have it silenced forever.

In the hall closet, we found a vintage camera with a telephoto lens, as well as a stack of old *I Married a Zombie* scripts, which Warren eagerly put aside, hoping to sell them on eBay.

The scripts, the camera, the jewelry and typewriter—not to mention the mini vodka bottles—those were the items Warren kept.

Everything else was either bagged for Goodwill or earmarked for the trash. Warren and I made endless trips to the garbage cans out back, hauling Hefty bags bursting with the detritus of Cryptessa's life, careful not to step in the gardener's oil slicks.

By now I was kicking myself for volunteering to help. With Warren practically glued to my side, I hadn't been able to unearth a single clue. And why the heck was he so reluctant to let me out of his sight anyway? Was he afraid I'd find something connecting him to Cryptessa's murder?

We were tossing our last load into the garbage when I saw that Warren was about to get rid of Cryptessa's scrapbook, along with Bela the Bat.

"You're throwing these out?" I asked, remembering how fond she'd been of both mementos of her long-ago career.

"Yeah," he shrugged. "Who on earth would want a scrapbook and a moldy old bat?"

"I'll take them."

"They're all yours."

I cringed at the thought of keeping a stuffed bat in my apartment but didn't feel right about tossing Bela into the dumpster. Maybe I'd give it to Lance for his birthday. He deserved it, after the way he'd horned in on my dinner with Peter.

Finally the last piece of trash was tossed and the last Goodwill box was taped shut. My ordeal was over. I felt like I'd just spent the past several hours moonlighting on a Viking slave ship.

I was beyond exhausted, and so hungry I was ready to eat the wallpaper.

"Thanks so much for all your help," Warren said, his bald head glistening with sweat.

"My pleasure," I lied.

"Can I buy you some lunch? I know a great falafel joint over in Westwood."

"Thanks, but I'll grab a bite at home."

I left him on the phone, calling a camera store, asking how much he could get for Cryptessa's vintage camera.

He sure wasn't wasting a second cashing in on her estate, was he?

# Chapter 18

*It's me or the bat!*

I'd just walked in the front door with Bela, and Prozac was having a full-fledged hissy fit. Tail swishing, teeth bared, eyes blazing—the whole enchilada.

"Don't be such a drama queen," I said, shoving Bela out of sight on the top shelf of my hall closet. "There." I slammed the closet door shut. "You can't see it anymore. Happy now?"

*Are you mad? Don't you realize the minute we're asleep, it's going to creep out and start sucking our blood?*

She followed me as I headed for the kitchen, practically glued to my heels, yowling with disapproval.

*I refuse to live under the same roof as that moldy creature! I intend to fight this, I tell you! All the way to the Supreme Court if need be. Nothing will stop me! Absolutely nothing!—Hey, is that Luscious Lamb Guts in Savory Sauce?*

It was indeed. In times of kitty crisis, I find lamb guts are often the answer.

Bela totally forgotten, Prozac was now rubbing against my ankles in a feeding frenzy.

*Don't be stingy with the savory sauce!*

Seconds later, her little pink nose was buried in

lamb guts while I scarfed down extra-chunky peanut butter straight from the jar.

It's a toss-up as to which of us inhaled our food faster.

Having put somewhat of a dent in my hunger, I was heading for the tub to soak my aching muscles when the phone rang.

Wearily I picked up, and Kandi's voice came on the line.

"You haven't forgotten, have you?"

"Forgotten what?"

"I knew it. You did forget. Your appointment with Madame Vruska. It's this afternoon at four o'clock."

Damn. It was already after three.

"Oh, gee," I moaned. "Do I have to go?"

"Yes, you have to go. Madame Vruska's amazing psychic skills will undoubtedly change your life. And besides, I already paid for you in advance."

And so instead of soaking in the tub, up to my neck in strawberry-scented bubbles, I spent the next forty minutes grinding my teeth in snarled traffic as I inched out to Madame Vruska's salon in Culver City.

The "salon" turned out to be a no-frills storefront on Venice Boulevard. A giant hand in the window advertised RARE INSIGHTS AT "MEDIUM" PRICES.

I walked into a small anteroom, separated from the main space by a beaded curtain. A cute, freckle-faced blonde in cutoffs, Ugg boots, and an I ♥ THE BEACH sweatshirt was sitting in one of the waiting chairs, reading a copy of *Surfing Today.*

How very annoying. I couldn't believe I'd slogged through all that traffic to be on time for my appointment when Madame V already had someone else waiting to see her.

The blonde, whose thick mane of hair was swept up in a ponytail, looked up at me through a fringe of sun-bleached bangs.

"You Jaine Austen?" she asked, putting her magazine aside.

"Yes."

With that, she got up and held open the beaded curtains.

"Right this way."

"Don't tell me you're Madame Vruska?"

"That's me!" she grinned. "It's not my real name, of course. I just think it sounds so much more exotic than Gidget Donovan, don't you?"

Gidget?? Leave it to Kandi to find the world's only Surfer Psychic.

"Have a seat," Gidget said, gesturing to a round table in the center of the room.

I was expecting the place to be dark and dim with dusty thrift shop furniture, but on the contrary, it was clean and modern—with tasteful toile fabric covering the table, pretty floral prints on the wall, and lemon-verbena scented candles scattered throughout the room. All very Gidget Goes to Pottery Barn.

"Cappuccino?" she asked, pointing to an espresso maker in the corner.

"No, thanks, I'm fine."

"Well, then, let's get down to business," she said, sitting across from me.

Between us on the table was a round glass thingie, which I could only assume was a crystal ball.

Gidget ignored the ball, however, and held out her hands.

"Let's see that palm of yours."

I gave her my palm, wishing that I'd had time to at least take a shower. My fingernails were embarrassingly grubby.

"Excuse my nails. I was just helping somebody clean out his house. But I guess you already knew that. Haha!"

She wasn't laughing.

"If you don't take this seriously," she said with a bit of a pout, "it's not going to work."

I tried my best to plaster a solemn look on my face.

Somewhat mollified, she stared down into my palm.

"I can see you've been eating peanut butter."

"You can?"

"Yes, you've got a blob of the stuff on the cuff of your sweatshirt."

And indeed, I looked down and saw a smear of peanut butter on my cuff.

I can't take me anywhere.

"Now for my actual reading," she said, examining the wrinkles in my palm, her brow furrowed in concentration. "I see you are under a cloud of suspicion. You are a suspect in a murder case."

"Did Kandi tell you that?"

"She may have mentioned something along those lines," Gidget conceded, "but I can also see it in your palm. Along with some melted chocolate."

Okay, so I ate some Hershey's Kisses with my peanut butter.

"Hold on!" She dropped my palm and clutched the crystal ball, gazing into its depths. "Someone is coming through to me. Yes, yes!" she said, squinting through her bangs. "I see the woman who died."

"Cryptessa?"

"She dresses badly. Sort of like you."

Well! Of all the nerve.

"She's wearing a sweat suit. It's got a stain on it. Not peanut butter. Something red. Maybe barbeque sauce. Or ketchup."

Omigosh. I never told Kandi about Cryptessa's stained sweat suit. And it wasn't in the papers. Maybe Gidget really did have psychic powers.

"Can you tell me who killed Cryptessa?" I asked eagerly.

"No, but maybe Cryptessa can."

"What do you mean?"

"Let's try contacting her."

I expected her to dim the lights and hold hands, séance-style, or maybe shout into the crystal ball. But she did nothing of the sort. Instead she took out what looked like a cell phone from her pocket.

"What's that?"

"A Soul Phone. Picked it up at a paranormal convention I went to in Aspen a couple of weeks ago. It's a conduit to the Other Side. It lets you text the dead."

"Text the dead?" I blinked in disbelief. She had to be kidding. My faith in her shot back down to zero.

"Do you know the deceased's birth date?"

"No."

"How about her address?"

Oozing skepticism, I gave her Cryptessa's address, which she typed on her silly Soul Phone.

Then she put the contraption down on the table and held her hand over it, her eyes squeezed shut.

"I've got a connection!"

I refrained from asking if there were roaming charges in hell.

"Is this Cryptessa?" she called out.

After a beat of silence, her eyes sprang open. Underneath her freckles, her face was flushed with excitement.

"Yes! She's saying yes!" Then, calling out into

the ether, "What have you got to say to Jaine Austen?"

With her hands on the phone and her eyes shut, she sat waiting for an answer from the Other Side. I was about to get up and put an end to this nonsense when Gidget announced:

"She forgives you for what you did to Van somebody. Van Johnson? Van Halen? Vivian Vance?"

A chill ran down my spine. She was talking about Van Helsing. And I'd never mentioned the parakeet's name to Kandi.

"What else does she say?" I asked, now gripping the table with white knuckles.

"She wants you to take care of someone. Berna? Bertha?"

"Bela??"

"That's it! Bela. Take care of Bela."

I couldn't help myself. I was impressed.

"This is important, Gidget. Ask her who killed her."

Omigosh. Any minute now, Kandi's Surfer Psychic would be solving the case!

"Who killed you, Cryptessa? Who killed you?"

We both sat there, waiting with bated breath. But then, shoulders slumped, Gidget shook her ponytail in defeat.

"Damn it. I'm losing her."

"Oh, no," I groaned.

So much for answers from the great beyond.

Gidget urged me not to give up hope.

"Now that a connection has been made," she said, "we might even be able to get her to cross over from the Other Side and materialize in human form."

I left Madame Vruska aka Gidget in a state of confusion, my mind abuzz with questions. Had she really made contact with Cryptessa? Or had she dug up all that information about Bela and Van Helsing on the Internet? Maybe a fan site devoted to Cryptessa trivia.

Was my Surfer Psychic legit, or was the voice on the other end of her "Soul Phone" just a dial tone?

# Chapter 19

The minute I got home, I headed straight for the tub and spent the next blissful hour up to my neck in those longed-for strawberry-scented bubbles. By now I had given up trying to decide whether or not to put my trust into Gidget, the Surfer Psychic, and was concentrating on the far more momentous decision of whether to order Chinese or pizza for dinner.

Chinese won.

Dredging myself from the tub, I threw on my robe and called my neighborhood Chinese takeout place, The Mandarin Kitchen.

"Hey, Barry," I said to the owner when he picked up. "It's me. Jaine."

Yes, I'm on a first-name basis with my Chinese takeout guy. And with my pizza delivery guy, too, if you must know.

"What'll it be?" he asked. "The usual?"

"The usual," I confirmed.

Which—in case you ever want to have me and Prozac over for dinner—happens to be wonton soup, chicken pot stickers, and shrimp with lobster sauce (Prozac's favorite).

I was on the living room sofa, nursing a glass of chardonnay and waiting for my chow to show up, when I happened to notice Cryptessa's scrapbook on the coffee table where I'd left it earlier that day.

Picking it up, I began leafing through her meager showbiz triumphs. There she was in her cameo from *Hawaii Five-O*. And her supporting role in a paper towel commercial. Another page held a program from her star turn in a dinner theater production of *Hello, Dolly!*

Most of the album, not surprisingly, was taken up with photos from *I Married a Zombie*.

In spite of her ghoulish black togs and over-the-top bat wing eyeliner, Cryptessa was beaming in every picture. Never had I seen her so radiant, so alive. Those were her glory days, all right. Too bad they'd lasted only a season.

I was about to snap the book shut when I spotted something peeking out from behind the fabric lining of the back cover. Looking closely, I saw that the seam had been ripped and that a photo had been shoved underneath the lining.

Pulling it out, I gasped in surprise.

It was a snapshot of sweet little Amy Chang sitting on Mr. Hurlbutt's lap! Clad in nothing but a black lace teddy and fishnet stockings!

I recognized where they were sitting—on the futon in Amy's living room. But I could tell by a window sash in the foreground that the picture had been shot from outside the house, through Amy's front window.

And then I remembered Cryptessa's camera with the telephoto lens. The one Warren and I had found in her hall closet. Good heavens. It looked like Cryptessa had been using it to spy on her neighbors. And what a jackpot she'd hit. Mild-mannered Mr. Hurlbutt, having an affair. With Amy, of all people!

So *he* was the older man who'd called her on the phone this morning. Mr. Honeybun. The one who said he'd stop by at eight tonight.

Well, I sure hoped Amy was in the mood for company.

Because Mr. Hurlbutt wasn't the only one about to pay her a visit.

At ten of eight, after a delicious Chinese dinner (marred only by Prozac trying to hog all the shrimp in the lobster sauce), I marched across the street and rang Amy's bell.

"Coming, sweetie!" she called out from inside.

Seconds later, I heard high heels clacking across her hardwood floors.

She opened the door in her teddy/fishnet ensemble, tottering on stiletto heels, her glossy black hair flowing down past her shoulders. She'd assumed a pose straight out of a *Playboy* centerfold, hand on her slim hip, mouth in a sexy pout.

A pout that froze, however, at the sight of *moi*.

"Jaine!" she cried, crossing her arms over her exposed boobage. (Not that there was much to expose.) "I was expecting somebody else."

"I know exactly who you were expecting."

"You do?"

"Yes, I know all about your affair with Mr. Hurlbutt."

"Mr. Hurlbutt?" Her false eyelashes fluttered in surprise. "But I'm not having an affair with Mr. Hurlbutt."

"Then how do you explain this?" I said, whipping out the photo of Amy on Mr. H.'s lap.

"Oh, that," she said, eyeing the picture with a sigh. "Come on in, and I'll tell you."

I followed her into the living room, averting my gaze from her half-exposed tush, and took a seat on one of her folding chairs. I wanted to keep my distance from the futon; heaven only knew what had gone on there.

"These teddies are so darn flimsy," she said, pulling on a clunky woolen cardigan. "One of these days, I'm going to catch my death of a cold."

Swathed in the cardigan, she sat down across from me on her futon.

"So," I asked. "What's going on?"

She took a deep breath and plunged in. "The truth is . . . I've been working part-time as a call girl."

Little Amy? A call girl?! You could've knocked me over with a fishnet stocking.

"Somehow Mr. Hurlbutt found out about it and made an appointment to see me. I felt sort of funny about it, what with us being neighbors, but he seemed so darn unhappy, I couldn't say no. He came over for his session, but when the time came to head for the bedroom, he couldn't go through with it. You can see in the picture how uncomfortable he looks."

I glanced down at the photo in my hand, and sure enough, now that I took a closer look, I could see Mr. Hurlbutt sat stiff and unsmiling, not at all like a guy who was about to be swinging from the chandeliers.

"I guess he and Mrs. Hurlbutt were having marital problems," Amy was saying. "And he thought I'd be the answer. But as soon as he got here, he realized what a mistake he'd made. I swear, absolutely nothing happened that night. Mr. Hurlbutt has been nothing to me but a good neighbor."

Now anger flashed in her eyes. "But Cryptessa, the nosy witch, had been spying on us! Can you believe the nerve of that woman? Standing outside my apartment and taking our picture with a telephoto lens!"

I could believe it, all right.

"She said it was a disgrace the way I was carrying on and that it was her civic duty to tell my parents. I thought I'd die. My parents didn't even let me date until I was eighteen. Can you imagine what would happen if they found out I was a call girl? My mom would literally have a heart attack."

She wrung the hem of her cardigan, frantic at the very thought.

"She even threatened to post the picture on Facebook. Or as she called it, 'Face Page.' My life would have been ruined!"

"Lucky for you," I said, "somebody bumped her off when they did."

"Wait a minute!" she gasped. "You're not implying I had anything to do with her murder, are you?"

"Sort of."

And indeed I was. After all, Amy had the perfect motive for killing Cryptessa.

"You've got to believe me," Amy cried. "I never went near her. I'm terrified to cheat on a test, let alone kill somebody."

She sat there huddled in her cardigan, a waif in fishnet stockings, and I had to admit she looked the picture of innocence.

"Omigosh!" she said, checking her watch. "My eight o'clock client should be here any minute. You've really got to go."

"Sure thing," I said.

I left her in the living room, fluffing her hair and applying lip gloss.

Outside at the curb, a dapper silver-haired guy was getting out of his Mercedes, a bottle of champagne in hand.

"Lovely night," he said, nodding to me.

I watched him stroll up the path to Amy's front

door, my mind still boggled at the thought of Amy working her way through college as a call girl.

Honestly, hadn't the girl ever heard of student loans?

# Chapter 20

Later that night, I was cuddled in bed with Prozac, watching Gloria Swanson and William Holden in *Sunset Boulevard*. Well, Prozac was watching (she has a thing for William Holden), but my mind was wandering, flooded with images of waiflike Amy Chang thrusting a DO NOT TRESPASS sign in Cryptessa's heart.

I was lying back against the pillows, wondering if maybe Mr. Hurlbutt had been in on the action, when I suddenly heard the unmistakable sound of my front door opening.

I bolted up in bed.

Someone was breaking into my apartment!

I told myself not to panic. Maybe it was Lance, using the key he knows I keep under my flowerpot. But why would he be barging in like this? Why wouldn't he just knock?

"Lance? Is that you?"

But there was no answer. Just the sound of footsteps in my living room.

Omigod! It was a burglar. Or worse, the killer!

What if Amy was an accomplished lock-picker, as well as collegiate call girl, and had broken into my apartment to shut me up forever?

Once again, I told myself not to panic. Surely I could take on teensy-weensy size 0 Amy. But what if it wasn't Amy? What if she'd sent Mr. Hurlbutt to bump me off? Or what if it was the two of them? I'd never be able to fight both of them at once.

Now the footsteps were in the hallway, getting closer and closer.

I couldn't just sit there. I had to do something!

I reached over to the phone on my night table and, with trembling fingers, punched in 911.

And with lightning efficiency, they put me on hold.

Damn L.A. and its municipal budget cuts.

I dropped the phone and raced to the closet where I crouched in the corner behind some old boots. Which unfortunately left most of my body still exposed. So I frantically pulled my chenille robe from a hook and draped it over me, hoping I could pass myself off as a pile of unwashed laundry.

At which point I heard someone stomping into the bedroom.

"Where the hell are you?"

I recognized the voice. But couldn't believe my ears. No, it simply couldn't be.

The next thing I knew, the closet door was being jerked open.

"There you are!"

I sat there, frozen, as my robe was ripped off me, and looked up to see a wild-eyed woman in a ketchup-stained sweat suit.

Holy Moses! It was Cryptessa!

Eyes blazing with fury, she held a molting Bela in her arms.

"This is your idea of taking care of Bela?" she screeched, holding out the bat. "Sticking him in a stuffy closet?

"You poor darling," she cooed to the critter. "Mommy's here now, and everything's going to be all right."

Then she turned back to where I was still huddled behind my boots. "You're supposed to be guarding Bela with your life. Don't you realize what a treasure he is?"

I'm afraid all I could do at that juncture was gulp in reply. So amazed was I to see Cryptessa alive and well in my bedroom, I seemed to have lost my powers of speech.

"I thought you were dead," I finally managed to croak.

"Not to my legions of fans," she sniffed. "To them, my memory will live on forever."

"Your memory? Does that mean you *are* dead?"

"I prefer to think of it as skeletally challenged," she said, perching down on the corner of my bed with Bela in her lap.

Omigosh. Was I actually talking to a ghost?

Then I remembered what Gidget had said—that once a connection had been made to the Other Side, it was possible for the not-so-dearly-departed to materialize in human form. Could my Surfer

Psychic have been right? Was I looking smack dab at the ghost of Cryptessa Muldoon?

Gingerly I crept out of the closet and sat across from her on my bedspread.

"I guess you could say that I've passed on to that great Sound Stage in the Sky. Which is not all it's cracked up to be, let me tell you. For one thing, they don't have TiVo. Or bagels. Or reruns of *I Married a Zombie*."

I tsked in sympathy, wondering if my hand would go through her if I reached out to touch her.

"That's what I hear, anyway," she said. "I haven't actually made it to heaven yet. They won't let me in until I take an anger management course. Did you ever hear of anything so silly? Me? With anger issues?—Hey, get your crummy paws off my bat, you little monster!" she hollered at Prozac, who was scratching at Bela's fur.

"But what are you doing here?" I asked, my mind still grappling with the idea of a ghost on my bedspread.

"I keep getting messages on my Soul Phone from some gal named Gidget that I'm supposed to get in touch with you. So here I am."

Wow, I really had to get myself one of those Soul Phones. Just as soon as I paid my Verizon bill.

"Well? Whaddaya want?" Cryptessa asked impatiently.

This was it. The moment I'd been waiting for. I

was about to find out exactly who murdered Cryptessa Muldoon.

"I need to know who killed you."

"Oh, *that* rat! It was—"

And just as she was about to tell me who the killer was and solve the whole darn mystery, a phone started ringing. She reached into the pocket of her sweatpants and whipped out her Soul Phone.

"Yeah?" she growled into the device. "Oh, okay." A smile lit her face. "I'll be right up.

"Gotta run," she said to me, jumping off the bed. "There's a sing-along on Cloud 237. Bet you never knew I could sing, did you? One of my many underappreciated talents. I was once the second understudy in the southwest touring company of *Mame*."

"How lovely," I said. "But changing the subject just a tad, who killed you?"

I wasn't about to find out. Because by now she'd started fading away.

"Just remember," she called out faintly, "to take care of Bela!"

"But I need to know who the murderer is!"

It was too late; she'd disappeared into the ether. All that was left was her Soul Phone, which had now starting ringing again. I tried to answer it, but it just kept ringing. Over and over again. Until finally I woke up and realized what you probably realized several pages ago—that it was all just a dream.

All except for the sound of my phone, which was jangling away on my nightstand.

Groggily I picked it up.

"Who is it?"

"It's me," a perky voice replied. "Kevin Moore. Sorry to call so late, but I wanted to let you know I've lined up some fantastic properties for you to see."

Oh, hell. I'd forgotten all about my tiny fib about wanting to buy a condo.

"How about I pick you up tomorrow at one o'clock and we'll go house hunting?"

"Gee, tomorrow's an awfully busy day."

"I promise it won't take long. And I did spend a lot of time lining up those listings."

Some people sure know how to play the guilt card.

"Okay, fine," I sighed. "See you tomorrow."

After brushing my teeth and doing my nightly beauty regimen (splashing some cold water on my face), I climbed back into bed and looked over at the spot where Cryptessa had been sitting in my dream.

How odd. There was an impression on the bed, as if someone really had been sitting there. That was nuts. I'd probably left it myself earlier that night when I sat down to kick off my sneakers. But a chill ran up my spine as I now noticed something else: a small clump of fur. I reached across and picked it up. It was stiff and gray, not at all like

Prozac's fur. No, it was bat fur. Bela's fur, to be precise.

But how on earth had it gotten on my bedspread?

I told myself there had to be a logical explanation.

I probably got some on my clothing when I brought the bat home earlier that day.

That had to be it.

I mean, my meeting with Cryptessa was just a dream.

Wasn't it?

# Chapter 21

When I woke up the next morning, I half expected to see Cryptessa perched on the edge of my bed.

She wasn't, of course. And I told myself quite sternly that she'd never been there, that her appearance last night was a nothing but a vivid dream, brought on no doubt by the Double Stuf Oreos I'd eaten before climbing into bed.

Just to reassure myself, I checked the hall closet and was relieved to find Bela the bat exactly where I'd left it, no signs whatsoever of having been moved.

Surely the bat fur I'd found on my bed came from my own clothing. The ancient stuffed critter was molting like crazy and undoubtedly left a trail of fur on whoever picked it up.

"There are no ghosts in this apartment," I said to Prozac, dishing her breakfast into her bowl. "Except maybe the ghosts of some dead mackerels."

She looked up from where she was weaving between my ankles in her usual feeding frenzy.

*Hurry it up, will ya? I can't wait all day. I've got important body parts to scratch.*

After scarfing down my own breakfast (a cinnamon raisin bagel nuked to perfection), I was determined to focus my attention here among the living and have a little chat with the newest addition to my suspect list, Mr. Harold Hurlbutt.

For all I knew, Cryptessa had shown him the incriminating photo of him and Amy, and he'd killed her to shut her up.

I ambled over to the Hurlbutts' house and, in a stroke of luck, found Mr. Hurlbutt working out front, repairing the fence separating his property from Amy's duplex.

How symbolic, I thought as I watched him hammer nails into the cedar planks, that he was hard at work enforcing the barrier between the two of them.

"Hi, there," I said.

His face fell at the sight of me. "I was waiting for you to show up," he sighed. "Amy told me you found the picture."

He was facing me now, and I could see he was wearing a sweatshirt that said, I'M THE BOSS. MY WIFE SAID I COULD BE.

He glanced at his house, probably to make sure Mrs. Hurl-butt wasn't watching. Then he lowered his voice to a near whisper. "Look, Mrs. Hurlbutt and I had been going through a pretty bad patch, and I guess I went a little crazy. But I swear on a stack of Bibles, nothing went on between me and Amy."

"I believe you."

And I did. But that still didn't mean he didn't knock off Cryptessa to shut her up.

"As much as Helen drives me crazy at times, I love her very much, and I couldn't bring myself to cheat on her. End of story."

He picked up his hammer and whammed a nail into the fence as if to drive home his point.

"But Cryptessa didn't see it that way," he said, hammering with gusto. "She threatened to show the picture to Helen. I had to pay her five hundred dollars to keep her mouth shut. Then she asked me for another five hundred. She would've kept on blackmailing me for the rest of my life."

"But don't you see, Mr. Hurlbutt? That gives you a perfect motive for wanting to kill her."

"That's ridiculous," he blinked, seemingly shocked at the thought. "I hated the old bat. But I'd never kill her."

"Then where were you the night of Peter's Halloween party when you left your wife? You told me you were talking with Matt Moore. But he said he never spoke with you."

"I was talking to Amy," he confessed with a sigh. "I tried to convince her to give up her extra-curricular 'job.' She's such a sweet kid; it's a shame to see her selling herself like that."

Just then we heard the sound of a screen door banging. Mr. Hurlbutt quickly resumed pounding the fence as Mrs. Hurlbutt came out on the lawn with a plate of fresh-baked corn muffins.

My salivary glands, napping after their recent bout with my cinnamon raisin bagel, sprang into action.

"Hi, Mrs. Hurlbutt!" I chirped.

"Oh, it's you," she snapped, ever the gracious hostess. "What are you doing here?"

Mr. Hurlbutt shot me a pleading look.

"Um . . . I was just wondering if you guys are having trouble with your mail. My delivery has been awful lately."

"Ours is just fine."

Mr. Hurlbutt smiled at me gratefully.

"Here, Harold." Mrs. Hurlbutt held out the plate. "I brought you some corn muffins."

I waited for her to offer me one, but I waited in vain.

"I guess I should be trotting along," I said, eyeing the plate hungrily.

"Oh, go ahead," Mrs. Hurlbutt grunted, following my gaze. "Take one."

"If you insist." I grabbed a muffin before she could change her mind. "Bye now."

I started back across the street, and when I got to the other side, I turned around and saw Mrs. Hurlbutt giving Mr. Hurlbutt a peck on the cheek. He squeezed her hand in return.

In spite of their problems, it looked like they really did love each other.

The million dollar question was: Had Mr. Hurlbutt killed for that love?

# Chapter 22

Okay, class. Time for today's real estate lesson. In most parts of the country, $400,000 will get you a really beautiful condo—granite countertops, stainless steel appliances, hardwood floors, walk-in closets—the works.

In West Los Angeles, $400,000 will get you granite countertops, stainless steel appliances, hardwood floors, and walk-in closets.

The rest of the condo, however, will cost you another $400,000.

I was about to discover the wildly overpriced West Los Angeles real estate market when Kevin Moore picked me up later that day in her shiny new BMW convertible.

"Wait'll you see the first place," she gushed as I got in the car. "It's got a fabulous ocean view!"

At that point, I was a property virgin, not fluent in real estate speak, and actually believed her.

We took off in the convertible, Kevin's blunt-cut blond bob miraculously not moving an inch in the wind. I, on the other hand, was a walking Brillo pad by the time we showed up at a distinctly seedy, semi-industrial section of Santa Monica, where graffiti sprouted like mushrooms on the building walls.

Kevin pulled into the parking area of what

looked like a former Motel 6—a flimsy two-story stucco affair, painted an appalling shade of doggie doo brown.

"You're going to love the neighborhood!" Kevin enthused, in full-tilt cheerleader mode. "It's got such an eclectic mix of people!"

She did not lie. Winos of all races and creeds were loitering on the street around us.

I followed the fuchsia soles of her Christian Louboutins up a flight of rickety stairs to the second floor of the building.

"Here we are," she said, swinging open the scuffed door to one of the units.

The first thing that hit me was the smell, a heady aroma of kitty piss and stale beer.

Whoever had lived there had already moved out, leaving a colorful assortment of stains on the carpet and nails in the walls. The stove in the "kitchenette" was crusted with grease dating back to the Pleistocene Era. And strands of what looked like dried spaghetti still clung to the ceiling.

"It just needs a little TLC," Kevin pronounced.

True. If by TLC she meant "tear down, level, and condemn."

"Here's the living room."

She gestured to the filthy cave next to the kitchenette, where empty beer cans had been piled high in a fake fireplace, then ushered me down a hallway where some imaginative child had drawn a series of swastikas in crayon.

"What do you think of this?" she said, opening the door to a dusty but rather large closet.

"A walk-in closet," I murmured, trying not to stare at a suspicious brown blob on the carpet. "How nice."

"Oh, this isn't a closet, hon," she trilled. "It's the bedroom."

"But there's no window."

"I know; it makes it nice and cozy, doesn't it? Now let's go see the master bath."

She proudly showed me a mold-infested bathroom.

"As you can see," she said, pointing to a gaping hole in the floor, "the previous owners took the toilet with them."

What a fitting souvenir.

"I've been saving the best for last," she now said, leading me back down Swastika Alley to the living room.

"Here it is. The pièce de résistance. Your ocean view." She pulled aside the rotting drapes at the window.

"Voilà!" She waved outside with a flourish. "Isn't it impressive?"

"Very," I nodded. "Over 200 billion sold."

"No, hon. Behind the McDonald's sign. If you crane your neck, you can see the ocean."

I craned my neck.

"That's another billboard. With a picture of the ocean."

"It's not the real ocean?" she asked, squinting into the distance.

"Afraid not."

"Damn. I've really got to get my contacts checked. Oh, well. It's still a lovely billboard, isn't it?"

Somehow I managed to nod yes.

"So," she chirped, her Ultra Brite smile beaming in the dingy room. "What do you think?"

I thought I'd rather live at the McDonald's.

"If you like it, you'll have to act fast. This one won't last."

I'll say. I gave it fifteen minutes before it collapsed.

"I'm afraid it really isn't for me."

"Not a problem!" she said, still beaming. "I've got plenty more properties to show you."

Indeed she did. She proceeded to drag me to a series of run down apartment-turned-condos last seen on a SWAT team drug bust. Kevin, however, oohed and aahed at each property, as if she'd just unveiled the Hope Diamond. For every flaw, she had a positive spin.

I'll spare you the ugly details of my House Tour from Hell, but here are a few snippets from our conversation, featuring Kevin in advanced spinmeister mode:

ME: Isn't that a hole in the wall?
KEVIN: A perfect spot for a planter!

ME: Omigosh. The basement is flooded.
KEVIN: The current owners are using it as a koi pond!


ME (SHOUTING OVER ROARING TRAFFIC): But the building's right next to the freeway.
KEVIN: I know. It's a commuter's dream!


We were driving home from our last stop (The Freeway Special), my mind still reeling at the hovels selling for four hundred grand. Alongside me, after two hours of architectural atrocities, Kevin's smile was undiminished.

"So what did you think of the last one?" she asked.

"I don't think I want to live so close to the freeway. The noise out on the balcony was pretty bad."

The balcony in question had been a perilously narrow affair with a wobbly railing and rusted hibachi.

"All you need are a few plants to baffle the sound and you'd never even know you were next to a freeway."

Oh, come off it. The only thing that would baffle the sound of that freeway was a nuclear bomb.

"Matt could help you do some landscaping," Kevin chirped, oblivious to my glaring lack of enthusiasm. "My hubby's got a fabulous green thumb. He did our own yard. And Cryptessa's, too."

"Cryptessa's?" I asked, happy to talk about something—anything—other than me forking over four hundred grand I didn't have for a hovel I didn't want.

"After the old witch had our hedges cut down, she had the nerve to ask Matt to help her plant some rosebushes."

"No!" I said, pretending to be outraged.

"But Matt, pussycat that he is, went ahead and did it. With Cryptessa standing over him the whole time, barking orders like a marine drill sergeant."

"That's exactly what she did to me!"

Eagerly I told her the saga of my adventures in Cryptessa's backyard, burying Van Helsing and planting petunias. I chattered on about how I broiled in the sun, broke my nails, and ruined my shoes in the gardener's oil slicks.

With any luck, I could keep this conversational ball bouncing and distract Kevin from the topic of me buying a condo.

"Would you believe she made me dig a grave three feet deep for a teeny tiny parakeet?"

"Bummer. So about those properties, hon? Which one do you feel like writing an offer on?"

So much for distraction.

I had to be firm and simply tell her I wasn't interested, that I'd rather move to a Siberian gulag.

"I'm afraid none of them really appealed to me."

Good. It was over. Now she'd leave me alone and I'd never have to look at grout mold again.

But like I said, I was a property virgin. Little did I realize that this was just the beginning.

"Not a problem," she chirped. "I'll just line up a whole bunch more."

Oh, foo. I had to put a stop to this. I couldn't possibly waste any more of her time or mine. Why on earth had I made up that stupid lie about being in the housing market in the first place? I didn't have the money to buy a welcome mat, let alone a condo.

I had to think of a way out of this.

And then an idea came to me. Not a particularly good one. But it was the best I could think of at the time, and I ran with it.

"Oops. My phone," I said, reaching into my purse.

"I didn't hear it ring."

"It's on vibrate."

"You can feel your phone vibrating through your purse?"

"Absolutely. It's a very strong vibration. Practically shiatsu."

I flipped my phone open and began my little charade.

"Hello? . . . Oh, hi, Uncle Willie. How's everything going? . . . You're out of the hospital? . . . They found a cure for your rare blood disease?

Oh, that's wonderful. How fantastic. Look, I'm with someone else right now. Let me call you the minute I get home."

I flipped my phone shut.

"You'll never guess who that was!"

"Your uncle Willie."

"Right. And you'll never guess what happened."

"They cured his rare blood disease."

"We all thought poor Uncle Willie was a goner. But it turns out he's going to live. Isn't that wonderful news?"

"Swell," she said, faking a perky smile, undoubtedly calculating her commission from my would-be condo purchase.

"Which means I won't be getting my inheritance," I said.

"Oh?"

"And sadly, I won't be able to buy a condo at this time."

Now she snapped to attention.

Her smile went bye-bye and anger flashed in her eyes. For a minute, I was afraid she was going to stop the car and make me walk the rest of the way home.

"Do you realize I've just wasted two hours of my life showing you crappy condos?"

Okay, she didn't really say that, but trust me. That's what she was thinking.

We drove the rest of the way home in an icy silence.

Which was awkward, of course. But definitely worth it.

From the look on her face, I knew I wouldn't be hearing from Kevin Moore any time soon.

I was walking up the path to my apartment—a virtual palace compared to the hellholes I'd just seen—when Lance came bounding out from his front door.

"I won!" he gloated.

"You won what?"

"Our bet. About Peter! It's official. He's gay! I've got a date with him tomorrow night. Dinner for two at Belle Reve out in Malibu."

I knew of the joint, one of those dimly lit love nests with candles on the table and the surf pounding outside the window. I'd been there years ago with my ex-husband, The Blob.

And it had indeed been a most romantic evening. For The Blob, anyway. He got our waitress's phone number while I was in the ladies' room.

"Peter actually asked you out?"

"Technically I may have done the asking," Lance conceded, "but he said yes."

"Maybe Peter agreed to go out with you as a friend."

"Oh, please. We're going to a restaurant Zagat calls one of the most romantic places west of the Rockies. It's got to mean something."

Alas, I feared it did.

241

Oh, well. I should've known Peter was gay all along. I mean, how many straight guys have Limoges figurines on their bookshelves?

"Have a nice time," I said feebly.

"I will. For sure!" Lance gushed with a most annoying wink. "And I'll let you know where I want you to take me for *our* dinner."

"What dinner?"

"The one you're going to buy me now that I've won the bet. Remember? Loser has to buy the winner dinner."

Oh, foo.

"Don't worry, hon. I won't choose anything expensive. Not very, anyway."

Cursing myself for making that silly bet, I let myself into my apartment, where my phone was ringing.

Prozac glanced up from where she was sprawled out on the couch.

*Answer that, will you? I'm in the middle of a very important nap.*

Ever her faithful servant, I hurried to get it.

It was Marvelous Marv, the Mattress King.

I prayed my Danny Dustmite spots had gone over well. I think we can all agree I was due for some good news.

"Great job with the Danny Dustmite spots!" Marvin boomed.

"So glad you liked them!" I said, visions of a nice fat check winging my way.

And then came those four little words I'd learned to dread:

"Just one little tweak."

Oh, hell.

"I need you to dump Danny Dustmite."

"What??"

"My research team tells me the dustmite approach is passé."

Damn his brother-in-law Sid!

"The hottest thing in mattress marketing is bedbugs. Everybody's scared of 'em. So I've decided to offer an exclusive Bedbug Protection Kit, free with every Mattress King mattress. And instead of Danny Dustmite, I want you to write a bunch of spots featuring a bedbug named Bernie."

"Bernie the Bedbug?"

"Great name, huh?"

"Peachy."

"I knew you'd love it. Anyhow, the deal is that Bernie's living the life of luxury in some poor sap's mattress, and then everything falls apart when his mattress is replaced by a brand-new Mattress King mattress. Dynamite idea, huh?"

"Dynamite," I agreed lamely, wishing I could shove a stick of the stuff up Sid's meddling fanny.

"Can you get me the spots by tomorrow?"

"Sure thing, Marvin."

I hung up with a sigh and shuffled over to my computer.

To think that Lance had a date with the man of my dreams while I was stuck with Bernie the Bedbug.

As Daddy would say, what a travesty of justice.

# YOU'VE GOT MAIL!

**To: Jausten**
**From: DaddyO**
**Subject: Hot on Stinky's Tail**

I'm kicking myself for not following Stinky Pinkus on her secret "duffel bag" mission the other night. I could've taken a cell phone picture of her dumping the murder weapon and gone straight to the police. But, confidentially, Lambchop, I still haven't quite figured out how to take a picture with my cell phone. And besides, I wanted to make it to the market for my Rocky Road before they closed.

But fear not! I've been making up for my missed opportunity. Big-time. Today I tailed Stinky to Macy's where, hiding behind a display of Martha Stewart quilts, I watched her buy a thick woolen blanket.

Lesser minds might not have figured it out, but I knew right away why she was buying it. To wrap the corpse, of course!

Elementary, my dear Lambchop!

Love 'n' hugs from

The Nose

PS. I'm off to Stinky's backyard to see if I can find evidence of a freshly dug grave!

**To: Jausten**
**From: Shoptillyoudrop**
**Subject: Distressing Phone Call**

Oh, dear. I just got the most distressing phone call from Lydia Pinkus. She looked out her window a few minutes ago and saw Daddy peeking over her back fence, staring into her yard. When she asked him what he was doing, he said he was looking for a lost golf ball!

Did you ever hear of anything so preposterous? The golf course is at the other end of Tampa Vistas. (Although the way Daddy plays, I guess it's not all that impossible.)

What poor Lydia must think of us!

I only wish I knew what she was doing with that duffel bag in the middle of the night.

Your anxious,
Mom

**To: Jausten**
**From: DaddyO**
**Subject: The Case Against Stinky P**

Slowly but surely, Lambchop, I am building my case against Stinky Pinkus. Guess what I saw in her backyard this afternoon? A shovel! Propped right up against her back door. She hasn't dug the grave yet, but she's going to. Any day now.

The body's got to be in her town house somewhere. Which leaves me no other alternative.

I'm going to have to break in and find it!
Your intrepid,
Daddy


**To: Jausten**
**From: Shoptillyoudrop**
**Subject: Gals' Night Out**

I'm off for a gals' night out at the movies with Lydia and Edna. I don't know how I'll be able to look Lydia in the face, what with Daddy peeking over her fence this afternoon. When he got home, he confessed he'd been looking for signs of a freshly dug grave!

I read him the riot act and told him he couldn't possibly go around looking for graves in my best friends' backyards. I expected him to put up a fight, but for once, he behaved like a normal human being and promised to put an end to his investigation. I guess he finally realized how silly he was being.

Still on his best behavior, he didn't make any fuss about my leaving him alone tonight with a Hamburger Helper casserole for dinner. Just told me to go out and enjoy myself.

I'd better sign off and get dressed before the girls show up. It looks like it's going to rain any minute. A perfect opportunity to wear my new water-resistant suede boots with faux fur trim. (Just $59.66 from the shopping channel, with FREE shipping and handling!)

Want me to send you a pair, hon? They're sold out of tan, but they've got a darling Electric Blue color that should look so cute in Los Angeles. How about it, sweetheart?

Love and kisses,

Mom

**To: Jausten**
**From: DaddyO**
**Subject: Tonight's the Night!**

Tonight's the night, Lambchop! Your mom's just left for the movies with Lydia and Edna. Leaving the coast clear for me to spring into action and find Lydia's hidden corpse!

While I was at Stinky's this afternoon, I very cleverly pretended Mom wanted to borrow one of her recipes. And while she was in the kitchen getting it, I dashed upstairs to her bedroom and unlocked the sliding door to her balcony.

That's how I'm going to let myself in!

Yes, tonight, I will shimmy up the drainpipe of Stinky Pinkus's town house, swing onto the balcony, and slip in through the sliding door, no one the wiser. I know Stinky's got a corpse hidden somewhere, and I'll leave no knick-knack unturned in my relentless quest to find it!

Oops. I'd better hurry. Looks like it's about to rain.

Love 'n' hugs,
Daddy

# Chapter 23

See? I told you Daddy was nuts. What sort of crazy person runs around investigating murders without a license or even an iota's worth of training?

Oops, wait. That's what I do, isn't it?

But at least I started out my investigation with a dead body. The closest Daddy got to a corpse was that Fang-tastic Dracula out on his lawn.

I checked out my parents' e-mails the next morning, shuddering at the thought of Daddy breaking into Lydia Pinkus's town house. I had no idea what Lydia had been doing with that duffel bag the other night, but I sincerely doubted she'd been toting around a murder weapon.

Shoving Daddy to the dusty corner of my brain reserved for root canals and Tummy Tamers, I decided to buckle down and get to work on Bernie the Bedbug.

I'd meant to tackle Bernie last night, but you know how it is with work assignments: one minute you're sitting in front of your computer, clear-eyed and brimming with determination, and the next you're sprawled in bed with your cat on your stomach, sucking down a carton of Chunky Monkey and watching re-runs of *Everybody Loves Raymond*.

But now, armed with a steaming cup of Folgers, I was up for the job. At this stage of the game, I was an old pro at mattress-dwelling insects, and so a scant five hours later (I took a few *Raymond* breaks) I finished the spots with Bernie's immortal last words: "Holy Innersprings! It's Mattress King! I'm doomed!"

(Hey, I never said I was Shakespeare.)

I'd just faxed them off to Marvin when the UPS guy came knocking on my front door with a package. A glance at the return address told me it was my replacement Buddha.

Eagerly I tore it open, digging out my treasure from the Styrofoam peanuts.

My face froze in dismay at the sight of the thing.

It was nothing like the one I'd ordered. A snow-white cherub with wide blue eyes, it looked like the Pillsbury Doughboy in a kimono.

I quickly dashed off an irate note to the e-tailer who'd sold it to me. He replied that he'd already sold the figurine I'd ordered and took the liberty of sending me this one because it was "practically identical" to my original choice.

I informed him in no uncertain terms that he needed to get his eyes examined and demanded a refund. After which I bid the doughboy a fond farewell and packed him back up in his peanuts.

Then I slumped down on my sofa with a sigh.

Maybe I should just tell Peter the truth and fess up that I'd broken his Buddha. No, it was bad enough I'd gotten brownie stains all over his rug. I couldn't possibly own up to this blunder, too.

I may have lost the Peter Wars, but Peter was still my neighbor, one who might possibly publish my Great American Novel someday, if I ever got around to writing it, and I didn't want him to think I was a complete nitwit.

So I went back online, determined to find a genuine replacement.

At first my Web search yielded nada. But then Lady Luck, who up till then had clearly been vacationing in the Bahamas, made a surprise re-entrance into my life. On the umpteenth page of Google listings, I came across what looked like an exact replica of the Buddha I'd decapitated.

Even better, it was right here in Los Angeles, at an antique shop over in West Hollywood.

Like a flash, I was on the phone with Gary of Gary's Fine Antiques, confirming that he did indeed have a genuine Limoges Buddha figurine just like the one I'd broken.

Gary assured me his Buddha did not bear the slightest resemblance to the Pillsbury Doughboy, and I told him to hold on to it for dear life.

"Whatever you do," I told him, "don't sell it. My name is Jaine Austen and I'll be right over!"

Seconds later, I was zooming out the door.

I stopped zooming, however, when I hit Olympic Boulevard, which was clogged worse than the toilets on yesterday's condo tour.

Teeth grinding, I inched along in traffic until I eventually made it to Gary's shop on a tiny street in West Hollywood. After pulling into the narrow parking lot at the side of the shop, I leaped out of my car, rushing past a sleek brunette reeking of money and designer perfume.

Gary's Fine Antiques turned out to be a dusty joint crammed with what I suspected were not actual antiques but upscale thrift shop offerings.

"Are you Gary?" I asked a pale bespectacled guy behind the counter.

"That's me," he nodded.

"I'm Jaine Austen, the woman who called about the Buddha."

"Sorry," he said with a careless shrug. "I just sold it to another lady."

"But I told you to hold it for me."

"Listen, hon. If I held everything for everybody who said they'd stop by and never showed, this would be a warehouse and not an antique store. So unless you give me your credit card number over the phone, it's up for grabs."

Damn!

I guess he could tell by the string of colorful curses I was muttering just how upset I was.

"Maybe the other lady will sell it to you. If you hurry, you can catch her. She's probably still in the parking lot."

I raced outside just in time to see the sleek brunette driving off in a hunter green Jaguar.

I waved at her frantically, but she was yakking on her Bluetooth and, totally oblivious to my antics, just kept going. Lord only knew where I'd find another Buddha, and I was determined to get my hands on this one. Jumping back into my Corolla, I started to follow her.

It turned out Ms. Jaguar was quite the kamikaze driver, weaving in and out of traffic with the ease of a Hollywood stuntman.

My idea of speeding is going 56 in a 55 mile zone, but I screwed up my courage and tried my best to keep up with her, coming perilously close to several fender benders in the process. At one rather harrowing point, I was almost rear-ended by a beige Camry behind me.

It was when we were driving north on Doheny that I caught a lucky break. Ms. Jaguar was stopped at a red light and, cutting in front of an irate Jeep driver, I managed to pull up beside her. Immediately I started honking my horn, gesturing for her to pull over. But that irritating woman was still yakking on her phone, still oblivious.

We continued this crazy car chase for a few miles until we were on Sunset Boulevard, driving out toward the ocean.

For a while I'd managed to stick right behind her, but now she was several cars ahead of me. As we headed west, I saw her turning right on Mandeville Canyon, a very tony enclave of town, favored by people with multiple brokerage accounts.

Speeding for all I was worth, I followed her up the winding canyon road until I saw the Jaguar pull into a huge gated estate.

By the time I got there, the gates had swung shut and Ms. Jaguar was heading up the path to her front door.

Then, in the distance, I heard the sounds of sirens wailing. Oh, rats. I hoped it wasn't the cops out to arrest me for speeding.

I rang the buzzer on the gate, but there was no answer.

That was ridiculous. I knew Ms. Jaguar was home. I just saw her walk into the house.

I rang the buzzer again. Still no reply.

By now the sounds of the sirens were coming closer. I wondered if someone here in The Land of the Rich was having a medical emergency.

I was about to ring the buzzer for the third time when suddenly what seemed like a whole platoon of police and private security cars came bombing up the hill and screeched to a halt around my Corolla.

"Don't move!" shouted one of the cops, a tanned tree trunk of a man. "Or we'll shoot!"

Holy Moses. What the heck was this all about?

"Hey, I know I was speeding, but this is America. We don't shoot people for that."

"We've got a report that you've been terrorizing

the resident of this house," the tree trunk said.

"Me? No, I was just trying to buy her Buddha."

"Her what?"

I calmly and rationally explained how I had been following Ms. Jaguar in the hopes of buying her Buddha figurine.

Okay, so maybe I wasn't so calm. Or rational. Maybe I babbled just a tad. To the best of my recollection, what I said went something like this:

"It all started when I decapitated Peter's Buddha, trying to cut myself out of my Tummy Tamer, and sent away for a replacement from eBay but when it showed up this morning it was the Pillsbury Doughboy so I raced out to Gary's Fine Antiques, only to discover that Gary had already sold it to Ms. Jaguar even though I expressly told him to hold it for me, which is why I'll never be going back *there* again, and surely you can understand that I had to follow the Jaguar and get the Buddha so Peter could publish my Great American Novel."

Eventually the cops were able to make sense of my story.

"So you followed this lady home," the tree trunk said, "hoping to buy her figurine."

"Right. But I don't understand why she called the police. I don't exactly look dangerous, do I?"

"No, but your car does."

He gestured to my Corolla.

And then I saw it. That damn Halloween skull! It was still clamped to the front of my car. I never did get around to taking it off. What's worse, in my bumpy car chase, somehow the skull's eyes had started blinking rather maniacally.

No wonder Ms. Jaguar had been scared.

The cops told Ms. Jaguar my story and, convinced that I was harmless, she came out to the front gate with the Buddha. I was thrilled to see it was the exact same figurine as the one I broke.

Taking pity on me, the generous woman let me have it for a mere hundred dollars more than she paid for it.

I wrote her a check, praying it wouldn't bounce, and then headed home, my prized Buddha nestled in bubble wrap on the passenger seat.

It wasn't until I was heading east on Olympic that I noticed the beige Camry behind me. How odd. It looked like the same Camry that had almost rear-ended me earlier that day. I squinted in my rearview mirror, trying to get a good look at the person behind the wheel.

Good heavens. It was Mr. Hurlbutt!

While I'd been busy chasing Ms. Jaguar, had Harold Hurlbutt been following me?

But that was absurd. There were zillions of beige Camrys all over town. I couldn't be sure that the one following me now was the same one that had almost rear-ended me.

Maybe Mr. Hurlbutt had been nowhere near me earlier and was behind me now simply because he lived on the same block I did and happened to be driving home at the same time I was. That had to be it. Chances are, he'd been out at the market, buying groceries for Mrs. Hurlbutt.

I turned onto my street and parked my car. Seconds later, Mr. Hurlbutt made the turn and pulled up in front of his house.

I sat locked in my car and watched as he got out of his Camry.

Not a grocery bag in sight.

It still didn't mean he was following me.

And yet, I couldn't help but wonder. Now that I knew about the incriminating picture of him and Amy, he had the perfect motive for wanting me out of the way.

Maybe Mr. Hurlbutt was the one who'd killed Cryptessa.

And maybe he'd been on my tail today, looking for an opportunity to do the same to me.

# Chapter 24

Never underestimate the calming powers of a hot bath and a cold chardonnay.

Honestly, sometimes I think if all the world leaders would just hop in a giant bubble bath with a glass of wine, there'd be peace in our time.

Early that evening, I was soaking in a mountain of strawberry-scented bubbles, sipping at a glass of chardonnay and thinking how crazy I'd been to worry about Mr. Hurlbutt. If he'd really been tailing me, would he have been foolish enough to stay right behind me where I could see his face in my rearview mirror? Of course not! Mr. Hurlbutt was a mild-mannered milquetoast who couldn't even talk back to his wife, let alone harm anyone. I'd been absolutely nuts to think otherwise. Clearly my imagination had been on overdrive, but that was all over now. I was calm. I was relaxed. I was—

Oh, gaaak!

I bolted up in the tub at the sound of a thunderous pounding at my front door.

Omigod! It was that demon Mr. Hurlbutt, come to do me in, once and for all!

So much for the curative powers of bubble baths and wine.

"Who is it?" I called out in a shaky voice.

"It's me!" I breathed a sigh of relief to hear Lance's voice. "Let me in! It's a matter of life and death."

Good heavens. Was Mr. Hurlbutt trying to kill Lance, too?

I leaped out of the tub and threw on my robe, leaving a trail of water and bubbles behind me as I raced to open the front door.

"My God, Lance. What's wrong?"

I looked around outside, grateful to see no signs of any would-be assassins lurking in the bushes.

"I need your advice, hon," Lance said, breezing into my apartment, carefree as can be, holding out two shirts on hangers for my inspection.

"Which shirt should I wear on my date with Peter tonight? The celadon check? Or the blue stripe?"

I could feel my blood pressure soaring.

"Are you mad?" I snapped. "Getting me out of the tub to look at your *shirts?* I thought this was a matter of life and death."

"Well, it is to me," he sniffed. "I want to make a good impression on my future soul mate, don't I?"

I shot him what I hoped was a withering glare.

"I do not care what you wear on your date with your future soul mate. And I highly resent your rubbing said date in my face when you know I have the warmies for that very same soul mate. Now if you'll excuse me, I've got a hot date with a bubble bath."

I turned to stomp off, but he latched on to my elbow.

"Aw, Jaine. I'm sorry if I seemed insensitive. I didn't mean to upset you. Really." He put on his most innocent puppy dog face. "And besides, I came to tell you something you might find interesting."

"And what might that be? What cologne you've decided to wear?"

"No, honey. I wanted to tell you that they're having a memorial service for Cryptessa tomorrow. Eleven a.m. at Hollywoodland Cemetery. I thought you'd want to know about it."

He was right. I made a mental note to be there and observe the mourners.

"I wish I could go myself," he said, "but I'll be working." Then another puppy dog look. "So are you still mad at me?"

"Yes, I'm still mad at you. But thanks," I added grudgingly, "for letting me know about the memorial service."

"Are you sure you won't tell me which shirt you like better?" He held up both shirts to his face. "I think the green goes better with my tan, but the blue brings out the blue in my eyes."

What the heck? He looked so desperate for my advice, I gave it to him.

"I like the blue."

"Great. Then I'll go with the green."

"What??"

"C'mon, sweetie. If you like it, it's *got* to be the wrong fashion choice."

"Lance!"

I can't swear to it, but I'm guessing tiny wisps of steam were coming out of my ears.

"You know what I always say: Moths come to your closet to commit suicide."

"Out!" I shrieked. "Out!"

And off he scooted.

"I'll let you know how things go with Peter," he called out as he sprinted back to his apartment.

Swallowing my irritation, I stomped back to the tub, but of course, by then it was cold. And I did not have the energy to drain it and start all over again. So I rinsed off in the shower and spent the next ten minutes mopping up the puddles of water I'd left when racing to answer the door.

Damn that Lance. Crowing about his date with Peter when he knew how much I liked him. And then literally adding insult to injury with his crack about moths coming to my closet to commit suicide.

When I thought of how he'd barged in on my dinner with Peter, I had a good mind to turn the tables and do the same thing to him. Yes, it would give me great pleasure to pop in on them at that restaurant in Malibu. Oh, how I'd love to see the look on Lance's face as I drew up a chair at their table and reached for a dinner roll.

But, of course, I could never stoop that low. After

all, I was an Austen. I had my pride. I had my dignity.

And for some strange reason, I had my best cashmere sweater in my hand.

What the heck was it doing there? And why was I putting on makeup? And my good Eileen Fisher slacks? And my one and only pair of Manolo Blahniks?

Somehow another Austen—one with no pride, no dignity, and a burning thirst for revenge—had taken over my body.

Which is the only explanation I can offer for why, twenty minutes later, I was dressed to the nines and roaring out to Malibu.

It was cold and raw in Malibu that night, an icy wind blowing in from the Pacific. Belle Reve's famed outdoor patio, with its spectacular view of the ocean, was deserted—save for one hardy couple huddled together under a heat lamp.

I hurried past them and went inside the restaurant, a warm oasis of candlelit tables. Across the room, a fire blazed in a stone fireplace, and over the sound system, Ella Fitzgerald was crooning about love gone wrong.

I scanned the restaurant but saw no signs of Lance and Peter. Maybe they were still at Peter's place having cocktails. I could just picture Lance, the little phony, sipping a martini and yakking about his med school days in Heidelberg.

263

"May I help you?"

I looked up to see a gorgeous young thing behind the hostess podium. Impossibly tall and blond, no doubt killing time as a hostess until her first movie role came along.

"I ... um ... I'm waiting for my party to show up."

"Do you have reservations?" she asked.

In fact, I was beginning to have quite a few, wondering if perhaps I'd been a tad hasty in my decision to crash Lance's date with Peter. But then I thought of Lance getting me out of the tub to look at his stupid shirts, and I got angry all over again.

"Yes, we have reservations," I said. "Under the name of Lance Venable. Or Peter Connor. Party of two, but I want to change that to a party of three."

She checked the reservations book and shook her fabulous blond head.

"Sorry, I don't seem to have anything."

"Do you have anything for a *Doctor* Venable?"

"No, nothing."

Looking around the restaurant, I noticed quite a few empty tables. Lance probably hadn't bothered to make a reservation. At this time of the year, with this kind of weather, the beach wasn't all that popular a destination.

"Would you care to wait for your party at the bar?" the hostess asked, indicating a sleek marble-topped bar off to the side of the room.

"Thanks, I will."

At the bar, I hoisted myself up on a barstool,

never a graceful proposition. As I struggled, I was aware of an old coot down at the end of the bar, giving me—or I should say, my tush—the eye.

"Can I get you something?" a stunning hunk of a bartender asked. The hostess's acting partner, no doubt. He beamed me a high-wattage smile, just in case I was somebody who could get him a part.

One look at their wine prices, and I knew what my choice would be.

"Just a water, please."

With a curt nod, he sloshed some water into a glass and shoved it at me.

Well! I sure wouldn't be going to any of *his* movies.

Suddenly I smelled a blast of peppermint breath on my neck.

I whirled around to see that the old coot at the end of the bar had sidled next to me.

For an old coot, he sure moved fast.

Silver-haired and blue-eyed, he'd clearly been a handsome man at one time, but he was decades beyond his sell date. The man had liver spots the size of quarters and rather frightening white teeth that I suspected had been purchased online.

"Come here often, honey?" he asked with a most unappetizing wink.

"Only when my hepatitis is acting up," I replied with a wink of my own.

Like I said, for an old guy, he sure could move fast. Like that, he was back at the other end of the bar.

I spent the next few minutes staring at the entrance, waiting for Peter and Lance to show up, practicing what I was going to say. (*Oh, hello, you two! What a surprise running into you like this! Nice shirt, Lance, honey, but I'm not sure green's really your color. And I see you finally got your watch back from the pawnshop!*)

When staring at the entrance did not make them materialize, I turned my attention to the other diners, most of whom seemed to be couples in love, or at least, lust. Everywhere I looked, I saw lots of hand-holding and smoldering smiles.

When was I ever going to get in on any of this action? I wondered. When would it be my turn to fall madly, deeply, insanely in love?

As the gods would have it, just two seconds later—when I saw a waiter coming out from the kitchen with the most amazing basket of crispy golden fries.

Yes, it was love at first sight as I watched the shimmering beauties sail past me.

I hadn't had any time for dinner and I was starving.

I summoned my actor/bartender with a wave.

"How much are your fries?" I asked when he finally bothered to saunter over.

"Eight dollars."

Forget it! Absolutely not! No way was I spending eight bucks on fries. Heck, I could get a whole meal for eight bucks.

You know where this is going, right?

"I'd like them extra crispy, please."

He nodded, this time gracing me with a glimmer of a smile, sensing there might be a tip at the end of his rainbow.

Minutes later, he came trotting out from the kitchen with a heaping basket of golden beauties. I couldn't wait to dive into them.

I just hoped Peter didn't walk in and catch me stuffing my face.

No danger of that. Because just as I was about to chomp down on my first fry, the stunning hostess drifted over to my side with a piece of paper in her hand.

"Are you Jaine Austen?" she asked.

"Yes."

"I just found this message for you buried under the reservation book."

She handed me one of those pink phone message slips.

It's a good thing I wasn't actually eating when I read it or I would've choked on my fry for sure.

I still seethe when I think about what it said:

Jaine, sweetie—
I knew you'd try something like this. Which is why I sent you to the wrong restaurant.
Love and kisses,
Lance

Why, that bum! Sending me here on a wild goose chase. I was so darn angry I totally lost my appetite.

For about three and a half seconds.

Then, as it often does, it came roaring back with a vengeance.

"Ketchup!" I shouted to the bartender, who, seeing the bloodlust in my eyes, promptly scooted over with a bottle of the stuff.

I poured myself a generous pool and proceeded to dunk each and every fry, inhaling them with gusto.

As I ate, I looked around the room at the lovebird diners, so smug in their togetherness. I fervently hoped they all got into knock-down, drag-out fights before the night was over.

I was just licking the last dollop of ketchup from my fingers when I happened to glance outside at the couple I'd passed on the patio when I first showed up. They were still there, huddled together under the heat lamp. The man, a squat fireplug of a guy, was nuzzling the neck of his date, a chunky brunette.

Wait a minute! I knew that chunky brunette. It was Lila Wood, my neighborhood politico!

My mind boggled at the thought of Lila as a love object.

But what almost knocked me off my barstool was her partner in whoopie. When he finally came up for air, I got a good look at his face and recognized him right away from the flyers Lila had given me the day I ran into her in the supermarket.

The nuzzler in question was none other than Ralph Mancuso, the evil developer Lila had sworn to oppose with her dying breath.

But Lila was putting up no resistance now as he leaned in to land a smacker on her lips. Yikes. It looked like Lila Wood was having an affair with her sworn enemy!

And suddenly I remembered Cryptessa's penchant for poking her nose into other people's business. Had she somehow found out about Lila's clandestine affair?

Had she threatened to expose her and destroy her political campaign?

And had Lila stabbed her in the heart to stop her?

These are all questions I pondered as I paid my bill and drove over to the nearest McDonald's.

(You didn't really think I was going to have fries without a burger, did you?)

# Chapter 25

I was nuking myself a cup of coffee the next morning, still haunted by the image of Lila locking lips with Ralph Mancuso. Not the most pleasant image on an empty stomach, I can assure you. Just as I was reaching into the freezer for a cinnamon raisin bagel, I heard Lance banging on my front door.

"Jaine. It's me. I need to talk to you."

"Go away!"

The last thing I wanted to do was talk to that miserable traitor.

"I'm sorry I sent you out to Belle Reve last night," he called out. "I just wanted to be alone with Peter."

"Good. You got your wish. Now go away."

I popped my bagel into the microwave.

"Can't we please talk?"

"Nope."

"I brought cheese Danishes," he crooned.

Usually a surefire way back into my heart, but not that morning.

"Forget it, Lance."

"I'll come back later, sweetie, when you're in a better mood."

"Try some time next decade."

If he thought I was going to sit there and hold

his hand while he oohed and aahed about Peter, he was nuts. Honestly, the guy had all the sensitivity of a bath mat. He'd blab on and on about how cute he'd looked on his dinner date, expecting me to be his cheerleading squad, never once considering my broken heart.

No, I was in absolutely no mood to put up with Lance's nonsense.

On the other hand, I couldn't just sit around and let my resentments fester. Not for more than a half hour anyway. After all, if Lance hadn't sent me on that wild goose chase to Malibu, I would've never discovered Lila's secret affair with Ralph Mancuso.

Indeed, it was a most valuable lead, one I intended to pursue just as soon as I finished scarfing down my cinnamon raisin bagel.

Lila lived up at the other end of the block, in a cute little California bungalow, painted lemon yellow with a bright red door and clusters of lush pink roses peeking out through a white picket fence.

Such a sweet house for such a tough cookie.

Birds chirped merrily in her magnolia tree as I rang her bell and waited for her to come to the door. Which she did, still in her bathrobe, her hair tousled from sleep, pillowcase creases on her cheek.

"Oh, hello, Jaine," she said, rubbing sleep gunk

from her eyes. "Excuse my appearance. Usually I'm dressed by now, but I slept in today. I was up really late last night."

I just bet she was.

"Come in, hon," she said, waving me inside, all smiles.

I looked around for signs of a steamy sexcapade—Ralph's socks balled up on the floor, maybe, or his tie hurled over a lampshade—but I saw nothing that indicated a man's presence in the house.

"So you've decided to work on my campaign!" Lila beamed.

Uh-oh. Time to nip that idea in the bud.

"I just got a bunch of flyers in from the printers," she was saying, "and now you can help me hand them out."

She shoved a glossy flyer into my hands. Lila's face beamed up at me from the cover, photoshopped to within an inch of its life. All wrinkles, jowls, and burgeoning double chins had been magically banished to Uglyland.

"So how many flyers do you think you can hand out? Two hundred? Three?"

"Actually, I'm a bit tied up with work right now."

"You mean, you can't work on my campaign?"

Eagle-eyed investigator that I am, I couldn't help but notice a blip of annoyance flit across her face.

"Afraid not," I said with an apologetic shrug.

*Then what the hell are you doing here?* were the words I could tell she was dying to utter. But the woman was running for political office. So instead she swallowed her irritation and plastered on a phony smile.

"Well, I'm so happy you could drop by to say hi. And I certainly hope I can count on your vote. Remember. A Vote for Wood is a Vote for Good!"

Just the opening I was waiting for.

"I'm not so sure about that. I'm thinking maybe a vote for Wood is a vote for Ralph Mancuso."

"How can you say that?" she said, suddenly flushing. "You know I'm staunchly opposed to Mr. Mancuso."

"It didn't look like you were all that opposed to him last night at Belle Reve."

"I have no idea what you're talking about."

Her phony smile had long since bit the dust.

"It's no use, Lila. I saw you two on the patio, playing kissy face."

"That's an outrageous lie! And if you repeat it to anybody, I'll deny it. After all," she huffed, "it's your word against mine."

"Not really," I said. "I happen to have a photo of you and Mr. Mancuso in a very compromising position. Some might even call it X-rated."

Of course I had no such photo, but she didn't know that.

"I found it among Cryptessa's possessions."

At this, she lost any remaining shred of composure.

"Why, that bitch!" she bellowed. "I paid her a thousand bucks to destroy that picture. I had a feeling she'd try to double-cross me."

So I was right! Cryptessa *had* been poking her nose into Lila's life.

"Is that why you killed her?"

By now, Lila's face had turned a most unbecoming shade of puce.

"You're crazy, Jaine. I had nothing to do with Cryptessa's death. And if you tell anyone I did, you'll be extremely sorry."

Suddenly I felt a frisson of fear.

Lila's fists were clenched into angry balls; the veins on her neck stuck out like lanyards. If she'd killed Cryptessa to shut her up, who's to say she wouldn't do the same to me?

Slowly she forced her face back into a semblance of a smile.

"Okay, I admit I've been having an affair with Ralph. And no, I haven't exactly been honest with the neighbors about his mini-mall. You know how people are. Nobody wants commercial property near their houses. So I pretended to be opposed to the project, hoping to change their minds once I was in office. And yes," she sighed, "Cryptessa was blackmailing me. But I swear I had nothing whatsoever to do with her death."

By now the anger had drained from her face, and all I saw in her eyes was weariness.

Was it possible she was telling the truth?

Perhaps.

But remember, class. Lila was a politician.

So we can't really trust her, can we?

# Chapter 26

Bidding Lila adieu, I headed home to get dressed for Cryptessa's memorial service.

I was almost tempted to wear a stained sweat suit in her honor, but in the end good taste prevailed and I put on a simple black slacks-and-sweater outfit. Thus appropriately clad, I drove over to the Hollywoodland Cemetery, Cryptessa's final resting place.

Boasting the famous Hollywood sign as its backdrop, Hollywoodland has long been known as the "in" cemetery for showbiz luminaries. An "A" list roster of actors, directors, and even a few lowly writers are buried in its hallowed grounds.

At last, after decades of obscurity, Cryptessa would be back in the business.

It was an overcast day in the middle of the week, and the place was pretty much deserted when I got there. So I had no trouble finding a parking spot.

As I got out of my Corolla, I noticed a bright orange Falafel Land van parked directly in front of the chapel.

It looked like Warren's new business was up and running.

I made my way into the small chapel and saw that only a handful of people had shown up for the service. There was Warren, of course, sitting in the front pew, looking suitably mournful in an ill-fitting suit. Mr. and Mrs. Hurlbutt sat behind him, Mrs. Hurlbutt craning her neck, checking out the mourners. The Town Crier was not about to miss a beat of the action.

I cringed to see Matt and Kevin Moore, decked out in their Gucci/Armani/Louboutin togs. I just hoped they wouldn't pull out condo spec sheets in the middle of the eulogy.

A couple of weirdo fans dressed à la Cryptessa in long black wigs and slinky satin dresses sat in the back row. (Which wouldn't have looked quite so weird if they hadn't been guys.)

Rounding out the mourners was a family of tourists—Mom, Dad, and teenaged son—dressed in jeans and I ♥ L.A. sweatshirts. As I slid into the pew behind them, I could hear the son, a sullen teen with floppy hair, whining:

"Why are we here? And who the heck is this Cryptessa lady anyway?"

"Can't you stop complaining for one minute, Kyle?" sighed his mother, a harried woman with aggravation lines deeply etched into her face. "Cryptessa is the lady who used to star in *The Munsters*."

The poor thing was having a rough day, so I didn't bother to correct her.

"I hate *The Munsters*," Kyle muttered.

"Well, I don't," snapped his mother. "And besides,

my feet are killing me and I need to rest for a while."

"I think I once saw her in a toilet bowl commercial," Dad chimed in.

"Oh, God," moaned Kyle. "Even the La Brea tar pits were better than this."

Like Kyle, I was beginning to wonder what I was doing at Cryptessa's memorial service. Exactly what did I expect? That the killer would show up and be so moved by the eulogies that she (or he) would leap up and confess?

Damned unlikely. Especially since my hottest new suspect, Lila Wood, wasn't even there.

Waiting for the service to begin, I looked around the chapel, with its white plaster walls, Moorish arches, and intricately carved wooden pews. In a small alcove beyond the minister's podium, an ornate fountain was tinkling softly. It was all very Hacienda Exotica—all except for the giant flat-screen TV mounted at the front of the room.

Part of the shtick at Hollywoodland was that you got to make a video before you died so that your loved ones could have something to remember you by. The fact that Cryptessa had no loved ones hadn't stopped her from making a video, as we would all soon discover.

Right now, the rent-a-reverend Warren had hired stepped up to the podium.

A tall, thin, lugubrious guy, looking for all the

world like one of Cryptessa's TV zombie relatives, he launched into a highly fictional speech about what a swell dame Cryptessa had been—"beloved by all who knew her, an actress whose comic performances will go down in the annals of television history." (I later found out that the speech had been written by none other than Cryptessa herself, tucked away in her safe-deposit box in the event of her death.)

The whole thing would've been a lot more believable, I suspect, if the rent-a-rev hadn't kept calling Cryptessa "Morticia."

"And now," he said, "a word from the dearly departed."

With a click of a remote, Cryptessa suddenly came to life on the flat-screen TV. There she was, sitting in her living room in a slinky black dress, which, I couldn't help noticing, was straining a bit at the seams. Her hair looked like it had been washed for the occasion and was lying in limp waves at her shoulders. Chalky powder coated her face, blood red lipstick seeping into the wrinkles around her mouth.

Behind her, Van Helsing was alive and chirping in his cage, and Bela the bat loomed over her shoulder on the fireplace mantel.

"First," she said with a theatrical flourish, "I want to thank all my many fans for showing up at my final Bon Voyage party."

I glanced at the three "fans" in the back of the

chapel. Two of them were texting; the third was busy teasing his hair.

"We've come here today not to mourn my passing," she intoned, "but to celebrate my life."

She threw out her arms in a celebratory gesture, damn near splitting the seams on her dress.

"It all started on a small farm in Iowa where I was born . . ."

Cryptessa started yakking about her humble beginnings, milking cows and putting on plays for the farm animals. The next twenty minutes creaked along as she spun a stultifying tale of how she rose from obscurity to become the fourth most popular mom in sitcom history.

By the time she'd landed her very first part (as that corpse in *Hawaii Five-O*), Mr. Hurlbutt was out like a light, snoring to beat the band.

"God, he's so lucky," Kyle sighed. "I wish I could sleep through this slop."

Indeed, it was all a royal snoozefest. But then everything took a turn for the interesting when, after trashing all three of her ex-husbands, Cryptessa started talking about "the one true love of my life."

She clasped her hands and put them over her heart, very Lillian Gish in *Birth of a Nation*.

No wonder she hadn't worked more often.

"Ours was a love that had to be kept secret," she said, looking wistfully into the camera. "But now that we're both gone, I can tell the world about the man who meant everything to me, who loved me with all his heart."

"That had to have been one nutty dude," muttered Kyle.

"Yes," Cryptessa said, "now I can tell the world about my own true love—my Xavier."

I sat up with a start.

Xavier? Where had I heard that name before? And then I remembered. Emmeline Owens's husband was named Xavier, wasn't he?

Then, as if in answer to my question, Cryptessa held up a framed eight-by-ten glossy of the same elegant gent I'd seen in the oil painting over Emmeline's fireplace.

And suddenly I flashed back on the locket I'd found in Cryptessa's jewelry box. What had it said?

*To Eleanor, with Undying Love*
*XOXO*

At the time, I just assumed XOXO stood for kisses and hugs. But now I realized that it meant a kiss and a hug from Xavier Owens!

Good heavens! Cryptessa had been having an affair with Emmeline's beloved husband! Had Emmeline found out about it? After years of suffering in silence, had she finally plunged a stake in the heart of the woman who had been boffing her husband?

. . .

By now the video had come to an end.

Cryptessa had bid us all a weepy farewell, and we adjourned to the alcove with the tinkling fountain to offer Warren our condolences.

A small buffet of wine and falafel balls had been set up to feed the mourners. A placard on the table informed us that the chow we were eating was "Catered by Falafel Land."

The tourists were chomping down eagerly.

"What yummy dumplings!" Mom exclaimed as she and Dad debated whether to go to Universal Studios or Grauman's Chinese Theatre.

"Why can't we go back home to Toledo?" Kyle whined. "I hate L.A. All I got to see was this crummy Munster lady and some stupid tar pits."

Behind them, the three fans were taking pictures of themselves with Cryptessa's urn. And next to me, Mrs. Hurlbutt was reading Mr. Hurlbutt the riot act for falling asleep during the service.

"Honestly, Harold. I can't take you anywhere anymore."

"Is that a promise?" he grumbled.

Off to the side of the buffet table, Matt and Kevin Moore were chatting earnestly with Warren. I was glad to see that at least some people were actually there to pay their condolences.

I stepped up to nab a falafel just in time to hear Matt say, "So let us know what you think, Warren. We're ready to buy your aunt's house whenever you give us the word. In fact, I've taken the liberty of drawing up a contract.

"As you can see," he added, handing Warren a sheaf of papers, "it's a most generous offer."

So much for condolences.

"We're even waiving our usual broker's fee," Kevin chimed in.

At which point, she glanced around and saw me standing there. If I thought she was going to welcome me with jolly hellos, I was sadly mistaken.

I'd seen friendlier looks on cranky pit bulls.

She must've still been ticked off at me for not buying that condo.

When she and Matt had finished their sales pitch and walked off, I stepped up to Warren.

"I'm so sorry, Warren," I said.

"For what?"

"Your loss."

"Right," he said, remembering his role as the grieving relative.

"She's gone on to a better place," he intoned solemnly, a line I was confident he'd picked up from *Mourning for Dummies*.

"It's so nice of you to drop by, Jaine. I certainly hope you'll come visit me at the grand opening of my new Falafel Land franchise."

And with that, he actually handed me a flyer for the grand opening.

Oh, Lordy. Even Cryptessa didn't deserve this.

I grabbed another falafel for the road and made my way outside.

As long as I was there, I decided to take a look around the Cemetery to the Stars. But as I wandered among the gravestones, I didn't do much stargazing. I couldn't stop thinking about Cryptessa's bombshell about her affair with Xavier Owens. Had Emmeline found out about it and killed Cryptessa in a crazed act of revenge? Did she lie to the police and tell them the killer was wearing an ape suit to frame me for the murder?

But if so, whatever happened to the ape suit? The cops never did find it, and if the killer wasn't wearing it, why on earth would anyone take it?

These were the questions flitting through my brain when I came across an open grave—a deep cavity in the ground, freshly dug, awaiting its new tenant.

Little did I realize that new tenant was about to be me.

Because just then I felt a powerful shove in my back. Before I knew it, I was hurtling into the muddy abyss.

I landed with a thud, my heart pounding. And looked up just in time to see the iconic pink soles of a pair of Christian Louboutins beating a hasty retreat.

# Chapter 27

Good heavens. Kevin Moore had just shoved me into an open grave! And she had not been alone. Alongside her Louboutins, I'd seen the supple leather of Matt Moore's Gucci loafers.

For a minute I just sat there in a stupor.

But that all ended when I saw a hideous black spider crawling across the arm of my sweater.

Aaack! I had to get out of there—now!

Springing to action, I tried to claw my way up to freedom. But the grave was at least six feet deep, and I couldn't get a toehold in the crumbly dirt walls.

Oh, God. What if they closed the cemetery and I was stuck there all night? I tried not to think of all the other creepy crawlies I'd be bunking with.

I screamed for help, but all I heard was silence in return.

I told myself not to panic. I'd simply use my cell phone to call 911. But the contents of my purse had scattered in the fall, and I groaned to see my phone lying near a rock, shattered in two, dead as a doornail.

Time to go back to Plan A: Screaming at the top of my lungs.

Which I proceeded to do with gusto, all the while my mind spinning with questions.

Why had Matt and Kevin pushed me into the grave? It couldn't be because I didn't buy a condo. That was ridiculous. If every looky-loo in L.A. got shoved into an open grave, there'd be no more space for dead people. No, it had to be more than that.

Something told me I'd just gotten a love tap from Cryptessa's killers.

But why would Matt and Kevin want to kill Cryptessa? They were practically the only ones on the block who didn't hate her. In fact, Matt had even helped Cryptessa doing yard work, planting rosebushes. No small act of kindness.

I thought back to my own day doing slave labor in Cryptessa's backyard, hacking through her cement-like soil in the broiling sun and ruining my Reeboks in the oil slicks from her gardener's lawn mower.

Then suddenly I had a wild idea. What if Cryptessa had been wrong about those oil slicks? What if they weren't from the gardener's lawn mower? What if it was real oil? The kind that turns Arabs into zillionaires. Lots of oil had been discovered in Southern California over the years. Why, there was an oil rig right behind the grounds of Beverly Hills High.

What if Matt and Kevin realized Cryptessa had oil on her property and killed her to get their hands on it? Either one of them could have slipped into my ape suit at the party. And they each had the other to give themselves alibis.

No wonder they'd been so eager to buy Cryptessa's house!

And no wonder Kevin had been giving me the evil eye at the buffet table. The day we'd gone condo hunting, hadn't I rambled on about ruining my sneakers with the oil from Cryptessa's backyard? The minute I'd opened my mouth about the oil, I'd put myself in jeopardy. The last thing the Moores wanted was for me to put two and two together and come up with a motive for murder.

By now I was convinced Matt and Kevin were the killers. True, just this morning I thought Lila had done the dirty deed, and fifteen minutes ago I was ready to arrest Emmeline. But Lila and Emmeline hadn't just shoved me into a grave, had they?

My thoughts were interrupted just then by the sound of footsteps approaching. Oh, Lord. What if it was Matt and Kevin, coming to finish me off for good?

Relief flooded my body as I looked up and saw a round-faced Hispanic worker peering down at me.

"You okay, lady?" he asked.

"I'm fine. Just get me out of here, please!"

Minutes later, he was back with a ladder, which he lowered down into the grave. Eagerly I clambered to freedom.

"You want to call a doctor?" asked the worker, a darling man whose name, according to his work shirt, was Cesar. "Check for broken bones?"

"No, I'm fine. Really." And I was. At times like these, my extra pounds come in quite handy.

"Okay. I'll just take you to the boss's office," Cesar said, ushering me to his golf cart.

"The boss's office?"

"I gotta do that every time I find somebody in an open grave."

I blinked in amazement.

"You mean, this has happened before?"

"Lots of times. Usually it's fraternity kids from USC."

Their parents must be so proud.

After chauffeuring me past a slew of celebrity mausoleums, Cesar pulled up to Hollywoodland's art deco administration building. I followed him inside and down a thickly carpeted corridor to an office at the end of the hall. The nameplate at the door announced that I was in the hallowed presence of Earl Pomeranz, Chief of Funeral Operations.

A balding, slightly portly gent in an expensive black suit leaped up from his desk to shake my hand.

"Good afternoon," he said solemnly. "How may we at Hollywoodland meet your needs today? Planning for the future? If so, we've got a very attractive plot near the actress who played Ethel Mertz's cousin on *I Love Lucy*."

"She's not here to buy a plot, Mr. Pomeranz," Cesar pointed out. "She fell into a grave."

"I didn't fall. I was pushed."

Mr. Pomeranz's mournful smile disappeared, replaced by a look of mild chagrin.

"The grave was clearly roped off," he pointed out.

Indeed it had been, but the Moores had shoved me right past the flimsy twine that had been strung between wooden gardening posts.

"So if you're thinking of calling an attorney," Mr. Pomeranz added, "I can assure you, you have no grounds for a lawsuit. In fact, I have right here a release form that I'd like you to sign, absolving Hollywoodland of any responsibility for bodily harm you may have suffered."

"I don't want an attorney. I just want the police."

"Why on earth would you want the police?"

"I already told you. I didn't fall in that open grave. I was pushed. The killers were out to get me!"

His eyebrows shot up.

"The killers?"

I calmly explained what happened. Okay, maybe I wasn't so calm. You know how I tend to babble in times of stress.

"Yes, the killers! Matt and Kevin Moore! Don't you see? When Matt planted those rosebushes, he must've realized there was oil on the property and made an offer on the house, which I'm sure Cryptessa turned down just to be obstinate and besides she'd never want to uproot Bela and Van

Helsing, so of course the Moores had to kill her with that DO NOT TRESPASS sign and they must've thought I was onto them because they pushed me into the grave and I know for a fact it was them because I saw the pink soles on Kevin's Christian Louboutins."

When I was through, Mr. Pomeranz's jaw was hanging open just a tad.

"Call an ambulance," he said to Cesar. "I think she may have suffered a concussion."

"I don't need an ambulance," I shouted. "I just need the police."

I was on the verge of sending Mr. P. to an early grave himself when suddenly the door burst open and Mrs. Hurlbutt came hurrying in, followed by Mr. Hurlbutt and—in answer to my prayers—the police!

"Jaine!" Mrs. Hurlbutt cried. "Are you okay? I saw the Moores shove you into that grave. And I took the liberty of phoning the authorities."

Thank heavens for the Town Crier! For once I was thrilled she'd been poking her nose into someone else's business.

Somehow I managed to explain to the cops what happened, and—with Mrs. Hurlbutt backing me up—the Moores were arrested on an assault charge. After which I made my way home, where I found Prozac hard at work clawing a throw pillow.

I was too wiped out to even yell at her.

Glancing over at my answering machine, I saw the light blinking. Wearily, I pressed the PLAY button.

"Jaine, sweetheart!" Marvin Cooper's voice boomed over the speaker. "Got those Bernie Bedbug scripts, and they're great. Just great!"

Victory, at last!

"Only one tiny problem."

Ouch.

"Research tells me everybody loves me as the Mattress King. So I'm going back to eating my crown."

Grrrr! All that work for nothing! At times like this, I wished I'd listened to my mother and become a dental hygienist.

Disgusted, I peeled off my mud-caked clothing and made a beeline for the bathtub, where I soaked in a chardonnay-enhanced stupor for the next forty-five minutes. When my skin had reached the consistency of stewed prunes, I dredged myself out and slipped into my chenille bathrobe and bunny slippers.

Padding into the living room, I plopped down on the sofa. And as a reward for all my suffering, Prozac was generous enough to climb on my lap and let me rub her belly.

"Oh, Pro," I moaned. "Mommy's been through hell and back. You can't imagine how awful it was being shoved in an open grave. My God, I saw a spider there the size of a baseball!"

*Yeah, right. Whatever. Is that falafel I smell on your breath?*

With that, she began yowling full throttle, her gentle way of reminding me it was dinnertime.

After feeding my faithful feline some Hearty Halibut Innards, I sent out for Chinese food—chow mein and wonton soup, which I slurped at halfheartedly, my eyes growing heavier with each bite. Believe it or not, I did not even begin to finish it.

Instead I got into bed and fell into a deep, comalike sleep.

I guess premature burial tends to tucker a gal out.

# YOU'VE GOT MAIL!

## *TAMPA VISTAS TATTLER*

### Nude Man Breaks into
### Tampa Vistas Town House

*A nude man was spotted breaking into the town house of Tampa Vistas resident Lydia Pinkus last night.*

*When Ms. Pinkus, along with two of her friends, returned to her townhome at around 10:00 p.m., they found the intruder, Mr. Hank Austen, passed out on her recliner, wearing a pink charmeuse bathrobe, a bowl of English trifle in his lap.*

*Ms. Pinkus has declined to press charges.*

*"I've come to expect things like this from Hank,"* *she said. "The poor man can't help himself."*

**To: Jausten**
**From: Shoptillyoudrop**
**Subject: Big Fat Lie!**

I'm so mad I could spit! Daddy's promise to give up his "murder investigation" was nothing but a big fat lie! The minute I left the house to go to the movies with the gals, he was hotfooting it over to Lydia's to search for Irma Decker's "corpse"!

By the time he got there, it was pouring rain

and pitch dark. With visibility near zero, Daddy proceeded to fall smack dab into Lydia's "Ghost Moat," which in the rain was a muddy mess.

But that didn't stop him. No, that crazy man hoisted himself out of the moat and shimmied up the drainpipe to Lydia's second-floor balcony to let himself in through her sliding glass door. Never mind that he could have broken his neck. Up the downspout he went. By the time he climbed over the balcony railing, he was dripping wet and covered with mud.

Not wanting to track any muck onto "the scene of the crime," he stripped down naked. Right there on the balcony! Where anyone could see him!

Naturally he was freezing to death, so he headed to Lydia's closet to find something to wear. Of all things, he chose her brand new pink charmeuse robe. She hadn't even had a chance to wear it, and now Daddy's got it all stretched out!

The way Daddy tells it, he decided to start his search for Irma's corpse in the refrigerator. Why on earth he thought he'd find a corpse in the refrigerator, I'll never know. If you ask me, he just wanted something to eat. That man can't go anywhere without a snack.

Anyhow, he looked in the refrigerator, and of course, Irma wasn't there. But what he did find was a big bowl of Lydia's fabulous English trifle. You may or may not know this, but Lydia Pinkus happens to be famous throughout Tampa Vistas for her English trifle. She'd whipped one up that afternoon, planning to serve it to me and Edna after the movies.

Daddy took one look at those layers of whipped cream and pound cake and strawberries and bananas and couldn't resist. He told me that all he intended to eat was just one spoonful. Well, one spoonful led to another and the next thing you know, he was sitting in Lydia's living room recliner, with the trifle bowl in his lap.

What Daddy didn't realize, of course, was that the trifle was loaded with rum. By the time he got to the bottom layer, he was out like a light.

And that's how we found him when we came home from the movies. Stretched out on the recliner in Lydia's brand new pink charmeuse robe, the bowl of trifle in his lap, whipped cream on his nose, snoring like a foghorn.

Honestly, honey, I thought I'd die!

And things only got worse, because just then the police showed up. Apparently Lydia's neighbor saw Daddy breaking into the town house buck naked and called them.

Lydia was an angel and declined to press charges. But I wasn't nearly so gracious.

"What on earth were you thinking?!" I screeched the minute the police had gone.

"I came to search for your best friend's dead body," Daddy said, scowling at Lydia.

Lydia blinked in amazement. "I have no idea what you're talking about."

"You can't fool me, Stinky—I mean, Lydia. I saw you sneak out of your house the other night with that duffel bag. The Nose knows. You were getting rid of the murder weapon!"

"That duffel bag was Irma's!" Lydia said. "It contained all her prescription medications. She left in such a hurry to visit her sick aunt over in Sarasota, she forgot to take it. She called me in a panic when she realized she didn't have it, so I got in the car and brought it over to her."

A perfectly logical explanation. But was Daddy satisfied? Of course not.

"A likely story," he sneered.

Just when I was ready to bop him over the head with the trifle bowl, the doorbell rang. And guess who it was?

Irma Decker! In the flesh.

The crisis with her sick aunt had passed and she'd come back to resume her stay with Lydia. You'd think Daddy would have the good grace to be embarrassed, but no, he actually asked Irma for a photo ID!

Before he could humiliate me any further, I grabbed him by the belt of Lydia's pink charmeuse robe and dragged him right out of there.

I may never speak to him again.

Your furious,

Mom

**To: Jausten**
**From: DaddyO**
**Subject: A Slight Glitch**

I suppose Mom told you what happened last night at Lydia's house. Due to a slight glitch, my search effort didn't go exactly as planned.

What a fuss everybody made just because I happened to have a bite or two of Lydia's English trifle. You would've thought I'd just stolen the British crown jewels.

It turned out Lydia didn't kill her friend, after all. Not this time, anyway. But I wouldn't put anything past old Stinky. She's trouble with a Capital T.

Speaking of trouble, I'm in a bit of hot water with your mom right now. Time to woo my way back into her good graces.

More later—
Daddy

**To: Jausten**
**From: Shoptillyoudrop**
**Subject: Sweet as Pie**

You'll never guess what Daddy just sent me. A dozen of the most beautiful roses! He's been as sweet as pie all morning. And tonight he's taking me out to dinner at Le Chateaubriand, my favorite restaurant, for a steak dinner!

And best of all, he put that awful Dracula creature away in the garage.

Daddy may be impossible at times, but when all is said and done, he can be awfully charming when he wants to be.

XOXO,

Mom

**To: Jausten**
**From: DaddyO**
**Subject: Out of the Doghouse**

Well, Lambchop, I'm happy to report I'm out of the doghouse with Mom. Roses and a steak dinner did the trick.

Your mom really is a wonderful woman. I know sometimes I can be a bit of a handful, and she's an angel for putting up with me.

Love 'n' snuggles from,

Daddy

PS. Just sent away for the most amazing Thanksgiving centerpiece: A Pooping Turkey! You just press down on the turkey's tail feathers, and out pops a Tootsie Roll! Isn't that a hoot? I can't wait to see the look on your mom's face when she sees it for the first time!

# Chapter 28

I woke up the next morning feeling perky and refreshed, and—after removing Prozac's tail from my nose—ready to face the day.

Not even the news about Daddy's disastrous visit to Lydia Pinkus's town house could dampen my spirits.

I was in the middle of a nutritious cold chow mein breakfast when I heard Lance's familiar knock on my front door.

"Jaine! It's me. You've got to let me in."

With a sigh, I got up to open the door.

"Have you heard?" he cried, rushing in. "The Moores have been arrested!"

"I know all about it, Lance. They pushed me into an open grave. I was the one who filed the assault charge."

"But that's not all!" His blue eyes grew wide with excitement. "They've just been charged with killing Cryptessa! It's on TV right now!"

We raced into my bedroom and turned on the news.

A smiling picture of Matt and Kevin, taken in happier days, was in the top right corner of the screen as a toothy anchorette breathlessly reported, "Test results just released by the police department show Matt Moore's fingerprints on the murder weapon, a DO NOT TRESPASS sign."

Over footage of Matt and Kevin in handcuffs, being marched to a police van, the anchorette informed us, "Kevin Moore, Mr. Moore's wife, has also been arrested as an accessory to the murder. Police are speculating that the Moores plotted the murder of the faded sitcom actress to gain access to oil rights on her property."

Yippee! I'd told the cops my theory about the murder, and they'd obviously taken me seriously.

"Police say they owe their break in the case to one of the Moores' neighbors."

How nice of them. They were going to give me credit.

"Yes," said the anchorette, "according to the police, a Mrs. Helen Hurlbutt alerted the authorities when she saw the Moores assaulting a woman who'd previously been a suspect in the case."

Of all the nerve! Here I solved the murder for them, and the cops were still referring to me as a former suspect.

Now Mrs. Hurlbutt was on the screen, talking to an on-the-spot reporter.

"It was nothing, really," she said, gloating into the camera. "I just did what any concerned citizen would do."

I clicked off the TV in disgust.

"I'm the one who found the killers, and she's getting all the credit!"

"Life's just not fair, hon," Lance said, lying back on my bed with a pained sigh.

I knew that sigh only too well. I felt a sob story coming on.

"My heart's been broken in a million pieces," he said, blinking back non-existent tears. "That's what I came to tell you yesterday."

"Oh?"

"My date with Peter was an unmitigated flop. I took him to Il Cielo on Beverly Boulevard. The place with the strolling violinist and gorgeous moonlit patio. It was the perfect setting for a love connection. But I could sense Peter wasn't interested in me romantically."

"How can you be so sure?"

"I sort of got the hint when he said, 'Lance, you're a very nice guy but I'm not interested in you romantically.'" Another pained sigh. "I was so upset, I could hardly finish my penne with arugula."

Penne with arugula? What sort of nut goes to an Italian restaurant and orders pasta with lettuce???

But I digress. Back to our stirring adventure . . .

"I guess I liked him so much," Lance was saying, "I talked myself into thinking he liked me, too."

This time there actually was a tear glistening in his eye.

And in spite of what a rat he'd been, I felt sorry for him.

"Oh, who cares about Peter?" I said.

If truth be told, I did. Especially now that I knew things were kaput between him and Lance.

"Anyhow," Lance said, "I'm sorry for all the dirty tricks I played on you—renting that ape suit and barging in on your dinner and sending you on that wildgoose chase out to Malibu."

"That's okay, Lance. I forgive you."

"I fought the valiant fight," he said with a brave smile. "But it's all over now. You win, Jaine. I get the strong feeling that Peter might be interested in you."

"Me?" I asked, trying to act as if I hadn't been praying for that very turn of events. "What makes you say that?"

"I just looked out the window and saw him walking up to your front door. I bet he's going to knock any second."

And indeed, at that very moment, there was a knock on my door.

I tried not to look too jubilant as I raced to get it.

There was Peter standing on my doorstep, in chinos and an blue oxford shirt.

"Hi," he smiled, looking every bit as adorable as the day I'd first seen him when I'd come back from burying Van Helsing. "Mrs. Hurlbutt told me what happened to you at the cemetery yesterday, and I stopped by to see how you were doing."

"Great. Just great."

*Now that you're here.*

"I guess I'll be running along." I turned to see

Lance standing behind me. In the excitement of finding Peter on my doorstep, I'd forgotten all about him.

"See you later, guys," he said.

He and Peter gave each other an awkward nod as Lance headed out the door.

"Wait!" I followed Lance outside and mouthed, "How do I look?"

"Fine," he mouthed back, "except for this."

With that, he plucked a chow mein noodle from the collar of my robe.

Honestly, one of these days I'm going to have to buy myself a bib.

Back in the living room, Prozac, the little hussy, was hurling herself at Peter's ankles like a vixen in *Cats Gone Wild*.

"What a doll," he said, picking her up.

She gazed up at him with sultry green eyes.

*Aren't I, though?*

Then he turned to me. "I suppose Lance told you about our dinner the other night?"

I nodded.

"For some crazy reason, he thought I was gay. Kept talking about his infallible gaydar."

"So you're not gay?" I asked, determined to clear things up once and for all.

"No, I most definitely am not."

Hallelujah. Somewhere out there angels were singing.

"In fact, that's really why I stopped by. I wanted

to invite you over for dinner tonight. Hopefully," he added, taking a step closer, "a romantic dinner."

Gulp. I felt my knees turn to Jello.

Now he leaned in even closer. I thought for sure he was going to kiss me. But no, he just plucked another noodle from my lapel.

"So how about it?" Peter asked. "Are we on?"

"For all eternity."

Okay, so what I really said was, "Yes."

"My place at seven?"

I nodded mutely.

The minute he left, I broke into a happy dance, skipping around the room like a crazed go-go dancer.

"He's interested! He's interested! He's interested!"

Prozac looked up lazily from where she'd stretched out on the sofa.

*I know. I had him at "meow."*

I continued to whirl around in a blissful glow, overjoyed at the prospect of my First Official Date with Peter. But then suddenly I remembered a tiny obstacle standing in the way of my happy ending.

That damn Buddha.

If Peter and I were going to be lifelong soul mates, he could never know that I was the kind of woman who went around decapitating valuable Limoges figurines with her Tummy Tamer.

That had to be my sacred secret forever.

Some time during our dinner, I absolutely,

304

positively had to replace the beheaded Buddha with the one I'd bought from Ms. Jaguar.

Only then could Peter and I live happily ever after.

Or at least until Official Date Number Two.

# Chapter 29

I showed up at Peter's that night, coiffed and spritzed for the occasion, the replacement Buddha tucked away in my purse.

It had taken me at least twenty minutes to blow out the curls in my unruly mop, secretly hoping that they might spring to life again in the steam of Peter's embrace.

"Hello, there!" He grinned when he saw me, the cleft in his chin looking more kissable than ever. "Come on in."

I took one sniff and swore I'd died and gone to culinary heaven.

"Is that roast lamb I smell?" I asked, my salivary glands doing the cha-cha.

"Studded with garlic slivers," he nodded. "And cheddar cheese mashed potatoes."

Note to self: Marry this man.

He ushered me over to one of the twin sofas that flanked his fireplace. Logs were blazing cozily in the hearth, and a glorious hunk of Brie, surrounded by a circle of crackers, awaited me on the coffee table.

This was my kind of love nest.

"Can I get you some wine?" Peter's brown eyes shone in the glow of the flames.

"Yes, please," I managed to gulp.

"Red or white?"

"White."

No way was I going to risk spilling red wine on his white flokati rug. Not after my flying brownie debacle.

"Be back in a sec," he said, heading off to the kitchen.

I sank back into his luxurious leather sofa, and—eager to pass myself off as a dainty eater—resolved not to touch a morsel of the cheese and crackers until Peter returned.

A resolve that lasted all of about seven seconds.

Alas, I couldn't resist the lure of the Brie and spread a glorious glob of the stuff on a cracker.

Bliss. Sheer bliss.

"Comfy?" Peter asked, returning with two glasses of white wine.

"Very, thanks."

That's what I meant to say, but due to the cheese and crackers in my mouth, it came out sounding like, "Ferry, wanks."

*Way to go, Jaine.*

He handed me my wine and joined me on the sofa, thighs just inches from mine, sending my heart rate soaring.

"A toast," he said, holding his glass aloft. "To Jaine Austen, Neighborhood Crimefighter."

We clinked glasses and sipped.

Dee-lush! What a step up from my usual Chateau Costco.

"And another toast," he added. "To the fabulous Marissa Rothman."

"Marissa Rothman?"

Who the hell was she? And what was she doing barging in on our romantic dinner à deux?

"Marissa's my agent at ICM," he explained. "And I've got fabulous news! After years of editing other writers' novels, I've finally sold one of my own. Marissa just closed the deal today. A six-figure advance!"

"Wow! That's wonderful, Peter!"

Indeed it was. Now we could afford that honeymoon in Tahiti I'd been fantasizing about.

"I couldn't think of a nicer person to share my good news with than you," he said, clinking my glass again.

Aw, what a sweetie. I just hoped he had more than news he wanted to share.

And it looked like he did, because just then he began moving closer to me.

I checked my chest for cracker crumbs, wondering if he was about to flick some away. But—hallelujah!—he was not on crumb patrol. No, he was zeroing in for a long-awaited kiss!

Then, just as his lips met mine, I realized something had come between us.

Namely, my purse. With my replacement Buddha inside. I'd plopped it on the sofa next to me when I sat down. Oh, hell. What if Peter locked me in a passionate embrace and the

Buddha shattered from the crush of our bodies?

In a panic, I managed to wrest the purse out from between us, but I was so busy worrying about that darn Buddha, I missed all the fun of the kiss. Before I knew it, it was over.

Damn!

Off in the kitchen, a timer dinged.

"Oops," Peter said, jumping up. "Gotta go mash my potatoes. Wanna watch?"

Under normal circumstances, I would be happy to watch this guy mash anything his little heart desired, but not then. Not when I had a Buddha to replace.

"Actually, I think I'll just freshen up in your bathroom, okay?"

"Fine. It's down the hall to your left."

I knew only too well where it was, still cringing at the memory of my wrestling match with the Tummy Tamer.

Naturally, I did not go to the bathroom. Instead I waited until I saw Peter disappear into the kitchen, and then, purse in hand, I tiptoed down the hall to his office.

Dashing to the bookshelf, I checked behind the thesaurus where I'd hidden the beheaded Buddha, happy to see it hadn't been moved.

With trembling hands, I unwrapped the replacement Buddha.

At last the Fates were with me.

It was an exact match.

I slid it on the shelf with a sigh of relief. Mission accomplished. The Tahiti honeymoon could proceed as planned.

Then, just as I was stashing the broken Buddha into my purse, I happened to glance down at Peter's desk. There, next to his computer, was a freshly printed manuscript.

Omigosh. This must be his novel. The one he sold for six figures.

I'd been yakking about writing a novel for years, but somehow there was always another toilet bowl ad or mattress commercial to distract me. But Peter had actually gone ahead and done it.

I admired him more than ever.

It was when I took a closer look and saw the title page, however, that everything fell apart.

There they were, six little words that would turn my world upside down:

## THE DEVIL'S POODLE
### by Peter Connor

*The Devil's Poodle*? Wait a minute. Wasn't that the title of Cryptessa's novel? The one she'd shown me the day I came to pay my condolence call for Van Helsing?

I remembered how Cryptessa had stormed into Peter's housewarming party, demanding that he read her book. He'd turned her away, telling her he never read unsolicited manuscripts. Was it possible he'd read it after all, and liked it? Liked it so much he wanted to be its author?

Had Peter Connor killed Cryptessa to get his name on the best-seller list?

No, it couldn't be. Not Peter. Not Mr. Right.

Besides, the Moores were the killers, weren't they?

Or were they? Maybe all they were guilty of was plotting to defraud Warren of his rightful inheritance. Maybe they pushed me into that open grave to stop my snooping, afraid I'd discovered their plans. And maybe the only reason Matt's fingerprints were on Cryptessa's DO NOT TRESPASS sign was because he'd helped her nail the stake into the ground.

As much as it pained me, I feared Peter was the killer.

But how could I prove it? Right now it was my word against his. For all anyone knew, he'd thought up the idea for *The Devil's Poodle* on his own.

In a desperate attempt to uncover some actual evidence, I began searching through his desk. I cringed to discover a cache of hard-core porn magazines in the top drawer, the kind of stuff that made me want to disinfect my eyeballs. I continued rifling through stacks of old bills, many stamped "second notice," entertaining a faint hope that I wouldn't find anything more damning. But then I found it, crammed in the back of the bottom drawer: Cryptessa's battered manuscript, *The Devil's Poodle* in ragged typeface on the title page.

"So you know my little secret."

I whirled around to see Peter in the doorway, a butcher's knife gleaming in his hand. I'd been so engrossed in my search, I hadn't even heard him coming.

"Who would have thought Cryptessa's book would be any good?" he said, strolling into the room. "Certainly not me. But she left it on my doorstep and I took a peek out of curiosity. Thought I'd die when I realized what a blockbuster it was. I knew it would sell for at least six figures. And that's when I came up with my little plan. I was sick of seeing my authors get all the big bucks. Why couldn't I get a piece of the action? So I paid Cryptessa a visit. Turned on the old charm. You know how good I can be at that."

He flashed me that grin I once found so attractive. Now it made the bile rise in the back of my throat.

"When Cryptessa swore to me that no one had read her book, that she'd kept it under lock and key while she was writing it, the paranoid old crone signed her own death warrant."

By now he was standing in front of me, the tip of his butcher knife just inches from my heart.

"And then you—sweet, silly Jaine—you gave me the perfect opportunity to kill her, the night of my Halloween party when I saw you taking off your ape suit. How easy it was to slip it on and blame the whole thing on you."

And to think I'd wanted to marry this maniac.

"Anyhow, after I whacked Cryptessa, I ran down the street and then up the alley behind my house. I popped in my back door and hid the ape suit in a safe under the floorboards in my service porch—a memento of my very first murder."

He giggled with pride.

"Then I hurried outside to join the crowd in front of Cryptessa's house. No one any wiser. Until now, that is. Too bad you had to be such a nosy parker. I figured you'd be fun in between girlfriends."

"In between girlfriends?"

He shot me an insolent smile. "I saw how crazy you were about me, figured I'd kill some time with you until somebody in my league came along."

With that, something in me snapped. Suddenly I was flooded with rage. Rage for the way Peter tried to frame me, and use me, and most of all, for the way he killed a perfectly innocent albeit highly aggravating woman just to make it on the best-seller list. I wasn't about to die at the hands of a bum like Peter. No way.

But what could I do with that damn knife only inches from my chest?

Then I had an idea. It was the oldest trick in the book, but maybe he'd fall for it.

"Mrs. Hurlbutt!" I cried out, looking over his shoulder. "Thank heavens you're here!"

Luckily he took the bait.

He whirled around to see if the Town Crier was really at the door, and when he did, I grabbed his laptop and whacked him on the head as hard as I could.

Then I ran for my life.

Unfortunately, I did not get very far. I did not take two steps before I tripped over my own purse and went sprawling onto the floor.

And clearly I had not whacked Peter hard enough, because two seconds later he was on top of me, straddling my chest.

"Time to write 'The End,' Jaine," he said, his hands inching up toward my neck. "Too bad you never got a chance to try my lamb. It's really yummy."

"Lance knows I'm here!" I cried out in desperation.

Which was a lie, of course. I hadn't told Lance about my date with Peter. I didn't want to make him feel bad. What a fool I'd been. If only I'd raced into his apartment and crowed in victory.

"When I'm missing," I said, "you'll be the first person they suspect."

Peter looked down at me with that smile I'd come to loathe.

"But you never showed up for dinner. That's what I intend to tell the cops, right after I dump your body in the nearest ravine."

Before I knew it, his hands were around my neck.

"I thought about killing you with the butcher's knife," he said, still smiling that awful smile, "but on second thought, why get my carpet all bloody? Strangling's so much tidier."

Oh, God, I had to do something. I couldn't let my life end at the hands of this miserable dirtbag.

And then I saw it. My salvation, peeking out from my purse:

The beheaded Buddha.

I reached out to grab it, but it lay maddeningly just beyond my grasp. Cursing myself for never taking a yoga stretch class, I reached out again, straining my arm till I thought it would come out of its socket. This time, I managed to grab hold of it.

And then, with every ounce of strength in my body, I pulled back my arm and plunged the Buddha's jagged edge in Peter's eye.

Bingo.

Yowling like a banshee, Peter released his hold on me to clutch his eye in agony.

Somehow I managed to shove him off me, and went hurtling through his house and out his front door, coughing and wheezing and hollering for help.

As I staggered down the street, I saw Lance rushing out from his apartment.

"Jaine, what's wrong?" he asked, hurrying to my side.

"Quick! Call the police!"

But he didn't have to bother. Amy Chang, who'd heard the ruckus in Peter's house from her apartment, had interrupted a session of dipsy doodle with a tenured UCLA professor and called 911.

Within minutes, the squad cars were roaring up the street.

The police found Peter trying to burn Cryptessa's manuscript. And a quick search under the floorboards in his service porch unearthed the ape suit he was foolish enough to have kept as a memento of his very first murder.

Lance and I were sitting on the curb in front of our duplex as the cops hauled him off to the criminal ward at the USC medical center.

"I always knew he was no good," Lance clucked as they drove away. "Honestly, Jaine. I can't believe you were silly enough to fall for him."

# Epilogue

If you ever need your fortune told, you absolutely must go to Madame Vruska, aka Gidget the Surfer Psychic. The woman is amazing. Remember how she spoke with Cryptessa on her Soul Phone and told me to take care of Bela the bat?

Well, not three weeks after Peter was indicted for Cryptessa's murder, I came home one day to discover Prozac clawing the stuffing out of poor Bela.

And you'll never guess what was inside. An emerald necklace, a diamond bracelet, and a Count Chocula decoder ring.

I was sorely tempted to keep the loot for myself, but I listened to my conscience and handed it over to Warren, the person I knew it was intended for.

Overcome with gratitude, Warren let me keep the decoder ring.

Remind me never again to listen to my buttinsky conscience.

It turns out the oil on Cryptessa's property was coming from an abandoned well—abandoned because it contained only enough oil to fill a small Volkswagen. So the Moores' efforts to buy Cryptessa's house were all in vain.

The authorities soon discovered that Matt and

Kevin were up to their eyeballs in shady real estate deals, and the larcenous couple were quickly stripped of their licenses. Last I heard, they were working for Warren at Falafel Land.

Much to my irritation, Mrs. Hurlbutt is still bragging about how she "solved" Cryptessa's murder. She and Mr. Hurlbutt recently celebrated their thirtieth wedding anniversary with a cruise to Alaska, where I'm told she scared off quite a few grizzlies.

Kandi's still dating the podiatrist dude she met in the museum parking lot. No diamond ring yet, but he did give her a pair of custom-fitted orthotics.

It took Lance exactly thirteen and a half seconds to get over Peter, and he's now head over heels in love with a guy he met at a "German for Beginners" class.

Thank heavens word never got back to Emmeline about her husband's affair with Cryptessa. She and Lana Turner are happy as can be with their new neighbor, a reference librarian with an arthritic cocker spaniel.

And guess what? It turns out I wasn't the only one who knew about Lila's fling with Ralph Mancuso. Apparently Mrs. Mancuso had been having Ralph tailed. (By that old coot who tried to pick me up at Belle Reve!) Armed with several incriminating photos, Mrs. M. was only too happy to bust her husband's love nest wide open.

Needless to say, Lila lost the race for neighborhood council president. Unable to face her neighbors after her fall from grace, she moved to a tiny retirement village in the Dominican Republic, where last I heard she was running for mayor.

Finally, you'll be happy to know that Amy Chang graduated with honors from UCLA and is now working as a congressional intern for one of her former clients.

As for Prozac, she's as impossible as ever. Now that Halloween is over and the world is safe from painted pumpkins, she is girding her loins for the Invasion of the Diabolical Christmas Tree Ornaments.

What with Cryptessa, Peter, Lila, and the Moores gone, several young couples with children have moved onto the block. It's nice to have children around after all these years.

In fact, I'm off to the market right now to stock up on Halloween candy.

(Okay, so I'm eleven months early. But who's counting?)

PS. Almost forgot. According to the latest from Gidget's soul phone, Cryptessa finally made it to heaven! Where, after only three days, several of her cloud-mates have already requested transfers to hell.

**Center Point Large Print**
600 Brooks Road / PO Box 1
Thorndike ME 04986-0001 USA

(207) 568-3717

US & Canada:
1 800 929-9108
www.centerpointlargeprint.com